# DOWN BY THE WATER

## JO-ANNE BERTHELSEN

**Down by the Water**
Published by JMB Books, Sydney NSW
© Jo-Anne Berthelsen 2020
www.jo-anneberthelsen.com

Cover and internal design by Impressum www.impressum.com.au

National Library of Australia Cataloguing-in-Publication entry

Author:    Berthelsen, Jo-Anne

Title:    Down by the Water / Jo-Anne Berthelsen

ISBN:    978-0-9946443-2-9 (print)
         978-0-9946443-3-6 (ebook)



All Scripture quotations are from The Authorised (King James) Version. Public domain.

# DOWN
## BY THE
# WATER

JO-ANNE BERTHELSEN

# Also by Jo-Anne Berthelsen

**Fiction**

*Heléna*

*All the Days of My Life*

*Laura*

*Jenna*

*Heléna's Legacy*

*The Inheritance*

**Non-Fiction**

*Soul Friend: The story of a shared spiritual journey*

*Becoming Me: Finding my true self in God*

*In memory of*
*my maternal grandparents*
*William Graham Scanlan Blackmore*
*and*
*May Josephine Blackmore (née Wright)*

# Richard and Meg's Family

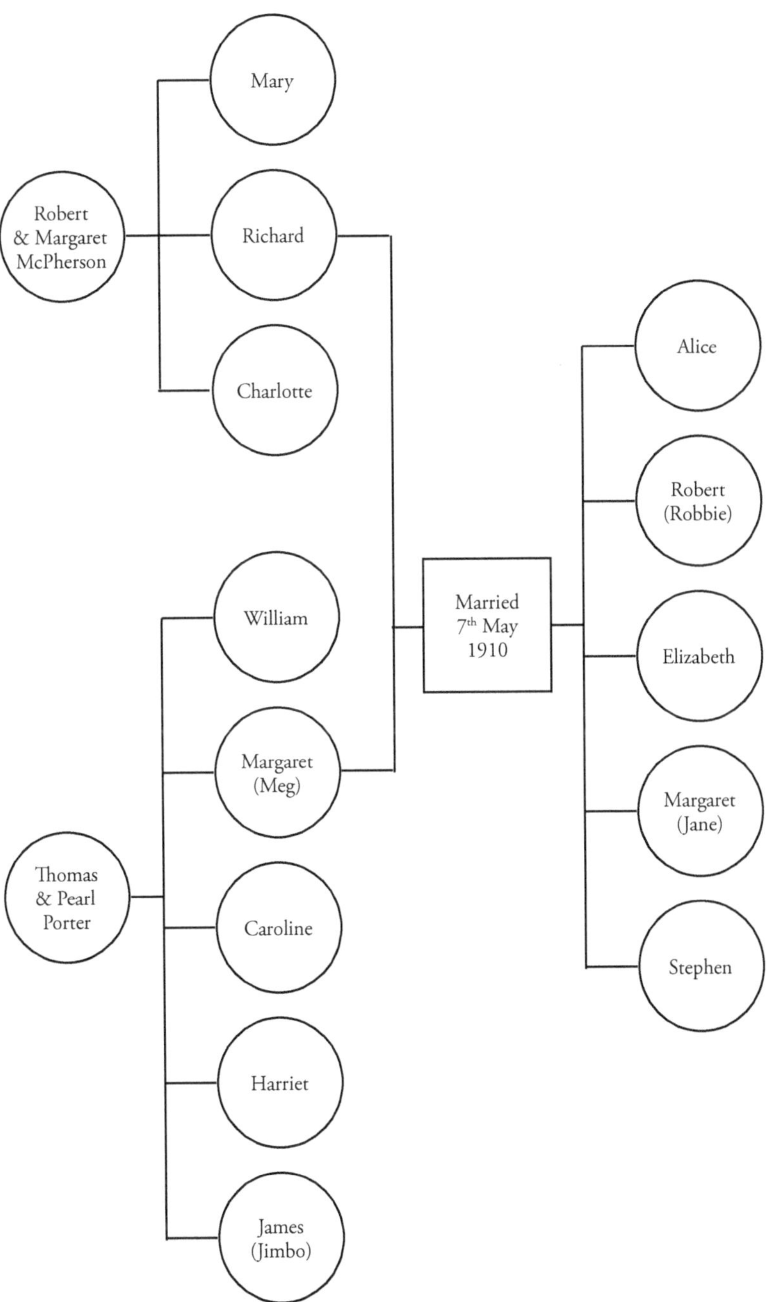

# Chapter One

'Meggie—me come too!'`

'Not this time, Jimbo. Besides, I think Mummy's going to visit Aunty June today. Then you can play with Bobbie. You'd like that, wouldn't you?'

'No, me want Meggie.'

Margaret Porter listened to her little brother's anguished pleas with a sinking feeling. It was the way he used his pet name for her that so often melted her heart. But today she wanted to disappear down to the creek and paint uninterrupted for a few hours. Today, she wanted to think about so many things all by herself. Today she wanted to dream big dreams. Today, 10th August 1909, she wanted to reach for the sky.

She stood hesitant in the doorway for a moment longer, her easel tucked under her arm. Then Isobel appeared as if from nowhere, picked Jimbo up, hugged him close and tickled him.

'Aw, come on, Jimbo—you love me too, don't you?'

His cries turned to delicious giggles, as Isobel's face burrowed into his neck.

'It's okay, Meg. You go—I'll look after him,' she told her with a smile and a quick tilt of her head in the direction of the door. 'We'll have such fun together, won't we, Jimbo?'

She was so grateful for Isobel's understanding. She mouthed her thanks, picked up her art equipment, together with some food she had grabbed from the kitchen, and hurried along the hall. Then, adjusting her easel under her arm, she bounded down the front steps as fast as she could.

Feeling a little guilty, she set out for her favourite spot along the creek. There were precious few places to explore around Helidon, on foot at least. But she loved Lockyer Creek and the way it kept changing in so many infinitesimal ways, widening almost to a river as it meandered through their area, before flowing on towards Gatton and, after much twisting and turning, into the Brisbane River and Moreton Bay. She could always find some different aspect to paint along its banks.

She had forgotten her hat, so was grateful when she reached the shade of the huge, old gumtrees, weeping willows and she-oaks that grew along the water's edge. Yes, there was the perfect, grassy spot to stand her easel and set out her paints and brushes. With a sigh of ecstasy, she raised her arms to the sky and stretched, before getting down to work.

Yet how could painting ever be work for her? It always brought her such joy and freedom ... and something more she could not quite put into words. It had to do with that creative force that welled up from somewhere deep within whenever she painted. Was this God's Spirit, as Sister Mary Margaret used to tell her? She did not know—and anyway, she could not envisage God knowing or caring about an insignificant, eighteen-year-old country girl like her. Perhaps when she was older, she would work it all out.

Right now, as she looked around, she knew what she wanted to paint. The bright light filtering through the leaves and shimmering on the surface of the water seemed to beg her to try a new technique she had wanted to explore for ages. After sketching her scene oh so lightly, she began choosing the smoky greens, soft tans and deep golden tones she needed and mixing them with care. Then she painted until her arms ached and her stomach rumbled.

She laid down her brush, wiped her hands on her skirt and took stock of her work. Sister Mary Margaret would have found something encouraging to say about her efforts. Then, in her gentle way, she would have shown her some little trick that added so much more depth to her painting. But Sister was no longer at the convent—and neither was she. It was almost two years since she had finished her schooling and said goodbye to Sister Mary Margaret. Two years during which so much had happened, yet so little too.

'Such a gifted artist!' the little nun would often tell her in her soft, Irish voice. 'One day, you'll make us all proud. But … perhaps some more colour here, do you think? Just a tiny bit. We don't want to spoil it. Perfect—well done, Meg.'

She chose a spot nearer the creek to sit and eat the biscuits and fruit she had grabbed as she escaped—that would have to do until dinnertime. Soon, snippets from her conversations the previous evening with her brother and then Isobel popped into her mind. William was so sure where he was heading, while Isobel seemed quite content to leave the future in God's hands. Yet what did she, Margaret May Porter, want out of life?  After two years of helping her mother at home, painting and keeping up her piano practice, she was still no clearer about her future.

She took off her boots, stretched out on her back and stared entranced at the leaves above her, as they formed ever-changing patterns against the clear, blue sky. Maybe she could talk her parents into letting her stay with Aunty Betty next year and take art lessons in Brisbane. Maybe …

Her mind wandered as she watched a few wispy clouds wending their way towards the horizon. Her mother was always telling her she had her head in the clouds too much. But the future her family envisaged for her seemed so boring. … Oh, her eyelids felt so heavy. Perhaps she could close them for a little while …

It was the screeching of the cockatoos that woke her in the end. She had been dreaming—a disturbing dream in which she had seen a beautiful rainbow lorikeet in a cage, flapping its wings and struggling desperately to escape. Then the bird had turned into Sister Mary Margaret—but even Sister Mary Margaret could not open the cage. She had rushed to help her old teacher, but could not reach her, however hard she tried.

She scrambled to her feet, her heart thumping. It must be well after three. She was angry with herself for falling asleep—she had stayed up far too late, talking with Will and Isobel. Then she had lain awake for ages, thinking over so many things. Well, no point in wasting time chastising herself now—she needed to focus on her painting. Yet as she did, something Isobel had mentioned the previous night kept coming to mind.

'God will sort it out, I know,' her friend had said, when they had tried to imagine where they might be in a few years.

Some of Will's comments had made her think too. It was different for boys, of course. One day, Will would be the breadwinner for his own family, whereas, according to her parents, she would soon have a husband and children to care for. She wanted that too—but not for a while yet. There were so many other exciting things to do before saying yes to anyone.

She needed to head home, but as the sun began to sink behind the mountain range to the north and bathe the sky in a beautiful, pale pink and orange glow, she stood still, entranced. What wonderful, subtle colours—but how hard it was to do them justice in her paintings!

With reluctance, she made her way along the creek and up the hill towards home. Now she could see her mother standing on their wide front veranda and gazing in her direction. And there was Isobel too, wiping her hands on her apron as she ran down to open the gate.

'Here, let me take your easel. Oh, look at those marks on your dress! You get yourself in more of a mess than I do, Meggie.'

Apart from Jimbo, Isobel Davidson was the only person allowed to call her that. She had valued Isobel's friendship ever since the day she had come to work for them, even though they were so different. Isobel was calm and capable, whereas she herself was always being told how dreamy and impractical she was.

'You don't have to help me, Isobel. You've got enough to do, looking after Jimbo and getting dinner,' she objected now, as Isobel wrestled the easel from her. 'But thanks—you're a good friend.'

They reached the front steps where her mother stood frowning down at her.

'I'm sorry, Mum. I lost track of the time. Then the sunset was so wonderful. Did you see it? Look over there—the colours are still beautiful.'

'Margaret, I have far more important things to do than stand here gazing at the sky. And look at you—you'd better tidy yourself up before your father gets home. You've had your own way for far too long. We'll talk about it all again tonight.'

Feeling a little chastened, she headed for her room and glanced in the mirror. Yes, she did look rather dishevelled. Her long, wavy, auburn hair was windswept, having escaped in places from the bright ribbon she had hastily tied around it. And on one cheek, there was a smudge of orange paint. She rubbed it off and set about brushing her hair in long, smooth strokes, just as her mother had taught her. Large, grey eyes stared back at her from the mirror—eyes she was grateful to have inherited from her mother, along with her dark eyebrows. She ran her hand over her smooth skin where the smudge of paint had been and smiled at her reflection, touching the dimple that emerged in the exact same spot. But even as she did, she could hear her old school principal primly warning her class about the perils of vanity.

'It's most unbecoming for a young lady to check her face in a mirror, girls, as I see many of you doing so often. You need to concentrate on more important things such as your studies. Remember, God's much more concerned with the inside than the outside.'

As she gave her hair a final tweak and headed for the kitchen, she wondered what her father's response to the impending discussion about her future would be. At least he seemed in a jovial mood as he joined them at the dinner table. She knew the quarry business was doing well, especially since they had won the contract for the new cathedral in Brisbane. He often talked about it all with pride and it seemed tonight would be no exception.

'Looks like this cathedral order's going to be an even better deal than those government contracts we won soon after we were married, Pearl. Not that we've done too badly in between either—in more ways than one,' he chuckled, as he glanced around at them all with obvious pride.

For once, all seven of them were together, with Will home from Sydney for the August holidays. Tonight, Jimbo—her mother was the only one who insisted on calling him James—was perched on a cushion on a normal chair, having at last become too big for his highchair at almost three. He looked such a dear little man tonight, with his blond curls and rosy cheeks. As for Caroline and Harriet whispering together next to him, they were pretty enough, she supposed, with their brown hair drawn back in plaits. She hated it when Caroline treated her younger sister with disdain and fought with her, but tonight, they seemed on friendly enough terms, as they kept glancing at Will and giggling.

'What are you two finding so funny?' her mother asked in a stern voice. 'This isn't the time or place for silly games.'

'We're not playing games, Mum. We just know something about Will,' Caroline announced with triumph.

'What would you girls know?' Will scoffed.

'We found this outside your bedroom and ... we read it,' Caroline told him, as she produced a crumpled piece of notepaper.

'It's a love letter,' Harriet giggled.

Will's face turned bright red.

'What? That's a private note to me—how dare you read it! Why didn't you give it back straight away?'

'You weren't here—you'd gone riding,' they chorussed.

'That's enough, girls,' their father broke in. 'Give it back to Will now. And Will's right. If that letter's his property, you shouldn't have read it. Both of you apologise this instant—and not another word until you've finished your dinner.'

It was hard to tell whose face was the reddest then—Will's or Caroline's or Harriet's. Later, when the younger ones were in bed, she would ask Will about it all. He would tell her—they had always been great friends. But she knew her father would be curious too and want to tease Will himself. Perhaps with luck, Will's letter might even deflect any impending discussion about her own future.

Her sisters mumbled their apologies, with sulky looks that did not bode well for Will in the coming days. But at that point, her mother steered the conversation in the very direction she had been dreading.

'I think we need to talk about Margaret's future this evening and not William's,' she announced with steely determination. 'We've let her do as she pleases for far too long now, Tom. She needs more discipline in her life—she's forever wandering off painting somewhere and forgetting the time.'

She knew what her father would say even before he opened his mouth.

'I told you we should have bundled her off to secondary school in Toowoomba, Pearl, rather than let her stay on at the convent. You got your way about sending her there rather than to the state school with Will, but I'm sure boarding school would have been good for her once she was older, just as it was for Will. Maybe then she would've headed to university like Will too.'

'Or perhaps she could have tried out for that teachers' college in Sydney at least,' her mother sighed. 'She was really a pupil-teacher by the time she finished at the convent anyway, from what Sister Mary Margaret told me. And I have to admit she's good with young children—James follows her everywhere. But all she wants to do is paint or draw or play the piano. I know these are worthwhile accomplishments, but she needs to take more interest in practical things too, Tom, and be more disciplined in general. If you could have seen how she looked when she came home this evening ...'

Meg hated it when her parents talked about her as if she were not there—it was time she interrupted them.

'I wouldn't have been happy at boarding school, away from you all,' she said as calmly as she could. 'And I've never wanted to go to university—or teacher's college. Besides, if I hadn't have stayed on at the convent, I would have missed out on everything Sister Mary Margaret taught me.'

'I'm sure the teachers in Toowoomba would have helped you as much as any nun could,' her father responded.

'Maybe. But Sister Mary Margaret understood how I feel about painting—and we were the best of friends.'

'Well, I doubt she has time to paint now at that orphanage in Brisbane where she was sent. Anyway, your mother's right, Meg. I like your pictures—and I enjoy hearing you play the piano. But you do need to learn more about cooking and sewing and the like. Soon there'll be a whole line of young lads asking me for your hand in marriage. And once that happens, you won't have time to run around the countryside painting or play the piano whenever you like. Look how busy your mother is, even with Isobel's help. That'll be you one day soon, Meg, mark my words.'

She laughed, despite herself.

'Oh Dad, I don't plan to get married for ages. Besides, there's no one around here I'd want as a husband. Certainly not Roy Davies or Leo Marshall—or even Harry Scott from Rosewood. And they wouldn't want to marry me either. I know they think I'm a bit too ... well, just a bit much somehow. But I don't care—they're all so boring. All they ever talk about is horses and cows and ...'

But her father was having none of it.

'You wait and see, my girl. You're a beautiful young woman—you could have anyone you like. And that's all the more reason I should have insisted we send you off to boarding school. At least then you might have mixed with girls from some of the better families, perhaps even from the big properties out west. I'm sure quite a few of them would have had eligible older brothers. But what do you say, Will? What about your university friends? Would any of them suit your sister?'

But before Will could answer, her mother interrupted.

'Let's leave this discussion until later, Tom, when we can perhaps be a little more serious. It's way past James's bedtime—and Caroline and Harriet have had a big day too. Please take the dishes to the kitchen, Margaret, while Isobel helps me with James and the girls.'

As Meg began piling up the plates with a sigh, her father gave her a sly wink. He was a man's man who worked with men day in and day out at his quarry business, yet he could also be gentle and sensitive. She was well aware how much he loved them all. But she also knew he would always bow to her mother's wishes in family matters—which meant that, right now, she did not want to talk about her future even with him.

It would be so much easier if she knew what she wanted to do with her life. For the hundredth time, she wished she could still talk with Sister Margaret Mary at the convent. Will would always listen, but in a few days, he needed to head back to Sydney for another term. Besides, he was a man, with so many more choices open to him. How could she expect him to understand? Of course, there was Isobel, who always seemed so content, despite what her family had been through. She could always talk to Isobel.

At that point, her father interrupted her reverie.

'Come on, Meg, hurry up and take these things to the kitchen, like your mother asked, instead of daydreaming. Then you and Will and I can have a little chat on the veranda.'

To her relief, Will ended up first in the firing line.

'So, been holding out on us, have you? What's this about a girl in Sydney?' her father said, as he reached across to where Will was sprawled and poked him in the ribs.

The colour rushed to Will's cheeks, but he managed to sound casual enough.

'Oh, she's just a girl I met last term, Dad. She's actually Harry Scott's sister—she was down visiting him at one stage. We aren't keeping company or anything like that though.'

'Well, just remember what you're in Sydney for, son. I need you to get that engineering degree so you can come alongside me in the business. Now if you were a boy, Meg, I could probably find ways for you to help me right now, since your mother thinks you need to do a few more practical things.'

She knew he was teasing but, for once, his words hurt.

'Look, I didn't mean that—I take it all back,' he said more gently when she stayed silent. 'What would I do without my beautiful, accomplished, eldest daughter? … Truth is, I envy the way you're able to paint and play the piano to your heart's content right now. I used to wish I could do such things myself, believe it or not, although I'd never have been half as good as you. I'm proud of you, Meg—but I agree with your mother. It's time to settle down, dear, and learn a few more practical, homemaking skills. As I said, before you know it, some young man will sweep you off your feet and whisk you away. Then you'll wish you'd listened to us.'

Just then, her mother joined them. It was clear she had overheard his words but was eager to add more of her own.

'I hope you've been listening to your father, Margaret. From next week, I expect to see much more attention paid to other things besides your painting and your music—and much more self-discipline too.'

'But I have to keep painting. And I need to practise the piano too. Mrs Watson's on the social committee now and she's asked me to play at the next dance. Anyway, Mum, you don't seem to have time to teach me things like sewing or knitting or ...'

At that point, Will almost fell out of his chair laughing.

'*You* knitting, Meg? I can't imagine it. I'd hate to be the one trying to teach you, that's for sure.'

'It's no laughing matter, William,' her mother cut in. 'But you're right, Margaret—I don't have time to be forever fixing up all the mistakes you make because you don't listen to my instructions in the first place. Maybe Isobel would have more patience with you, seeing you're such bosom friends.'

She decided to give in—or at least pretend to. Nothing would be gained by arguing with her mother anyway. She had learnt that only too well in the last few months in particular.

'I know I can be annoying, Mum, when I'm not interested in learning something. Even Sister Mary Margaret used to tell me that. "You want to run before you can walk, Margaret", she often said, when I'd get tired of practising the same thing over and over. But I promise I'll ask Isobel to teach me—maybe I can mind Jimbo for her in exchange.'

To her relief, her parents let it rest there and the conversation turned to how Will's studies could help their quarry business. She stifled a yawn—she found such talk boring, so decided to excuse herself and go to her room.

She curled up on her bed and tried to read, but could not seem to concentrate. Her eyes strayed to her easel standing in the corner and, in the end, she could not resist placing her half-finished painting on it and moving the nearby lamp closer. Something was still not quite right with it. Well, she would have to wait until daylight to try to fix it. She could never do justice to the subtle interplay of light and shade she had wanted to incorporate into the scene if she tried now.

With a sigh, she flopped on the bed again and stared at the ceiling. What was the matter with her? She hated to admit it, but her mother was right—she had little interest in anything much except art and music. One day often seemed to merge into the next as she floated along, doing whatever she felt like doing.

Soon she heard footsteps in the hallway and poked her head out of her room.

'Isobel, is Jimbo asleep? Can we chat for a while?'

'Let me check on the girls, but I'll be there as soon as I can,' Isobel whispered back.

She sighed with relief. However weary Isobel was, she always listened and tried to understand.

'I'm so glad you're here—sometimes I wonder what I'd do without you around,' she burst out when Isobel returned. 'You save me from so many scrapes with Mum. And you're always doing nice things for me, like setting my easel up here ready.'

'I don't mind—I like to help you. You're my friend, Meggie, after all.'

Isobel sank into the comfortable, old armchair nearby, while she herself sat cross-legged on the bed. At first, she continued brushing her hair the way her mother insisted she do every night. But soon she threw her brush down and stretched out full-length again.

'Isobel, I know I should learn more about housekeeping and how to manage a family, like Mum says. But I want to do so many other things before I settle down. I love painting and I love my music. And it'd be fun to see a bit of the world too, although I imagine I'd get homesick. One day I'll get married and have a family, I suppose— but not yet. Besides, all the boys around here are so boring.'

Isobel leaned forward, her big, brown eyes sparkling with mischief.

'So … does that mean you won't bother going to the dance this weekend?'

'No, of course not, silly. Besides, I'm playing the piano for some of the dances in a couple of weeks to give Mrs Watson a break, so I need to see how she manages everything. Anyway, you never know who'll turn up. Even Will said he might go—he reckons he's too busy for parties and dances in Sydney.'

They sat in silence then for a few moments.

'It must be nice for you to have Will home again. He seems so much more grown up,' Isobel said at last, as she glanced down and toyed with the end of her long, dark plait, her heart-shaped face half hidden in shadow.

Isobel's manner spoke volumes. At once, she was alert, but she decided to keep her thoughts to herself.

'Could you come to the dance too, Isobel?'

'No, I don't think so. I'm sure your parents will want to go, so I'll stay and mind Jimbo and the girls. Anyway, I can't dance very well.'

'I'll teach you—and you could teach me sewing and knitting, Isobel. Mum doesn't want to and you're so clever with your hands. Anyway, I'd rather learn from you—you're much more patient. I could take care of Jimbo for you in exchange. What do you think?'

'I think you could do anything you put your mind to, Meggie. You're so clever and creative. But you need to *want* to learn things, otherwise you'll give up. Still, you never know—perhaps you'll meet some dashing, new beau at this next dance who'll inspire you to learn all you can quick smart about being a model housewife.'

'Huh, I don't think that's likely. … You know, maybe I should become a teacher or, better still, a nurse—even though I hate the sight of blood. That way, I might meet a handsome, young doctor around the General Hospital somewhere. But Isobel, don't you ever feel restless and wish you had a more exciting life? Wouldn't you like to be a famous artist or actress—or somebody rich and important, with hundreds of dresses to choose from?'

'Oh, you and your dreaming, Meggie. Even if I did, I know that's not going to happen in real life. But one day, I do want to help others—perhaps look after sick children or work with poor families and teach them about God or...'

'Well, all I can say is you're much more noble than I am. Don't you ever think of yourself and what *you* want to do?'

'But that *is* what I want to do. Of course, I'd like to get married and have children one day, but I know God will work out something just right for me when the time comes.'

'That's the sort of thing Sister Mary Margaret used to say. Maybe you could become a nun.'

'Not if I want to get married and have children, silly.'

They fell silent again then, each lost in thought. Several times, she noticed Isobel open her mouth as if to say something, then shut it again. She wanted to ask her about it, but thought better of it in the end. There were things about Isobel she would never understand, including her strong faith in God, which had survived even her minister father's death when she was only twelve. If her own father died, she was sure she would never get over it—and she would certainly question God about it. Yet there was a serenity about Isobel she could not help but admire and she was hard-working and loyal and patient too. Oh, why couldn't she be more like that herself?

Eventually, Isobel broke the silence.

'Meggie, have you ever asked God what you should do with your life?'

The question was so gentle and tentative that she bit her tongue to curb the strong response she had been about to give. She was not religious, but she did not want to hurt Isobel, especially when she saw her friend's earnest expression. Yet she had to be honest—and she was sure Isobel knew what she would say anyway.

'That'd be a last resort for me,' she said in the end, trying to keep her tone light. 'After all, God might ask me to give up my painting and forget about having any fun in life. But that reminds me, Isobel ... I think you *should* come to the dance on Saturday night. You work so hard—you deserve to have some fun. I'll ask Mum if you can. And I've got a great idea. Why don't I ask Will to practise some of the dances with you tomorrow? I could play for you both—I want to run through some of the music anyway. Then you wouldn't be able to use that old excuse about being no good at dancing.'

Isobel blushed rosy-red and scrambled out of her chair.

'No, please don't bother Will. I'm sure we'll all have enough to do tomorrow, without wasting time teaching me how to dance. ... Anyway, I'd better go and let you get some sleep—we can talk more another time. And I need to get to bed too. But I'd be happy to help you with your sewing and knitting whenever you're ready.'

Yet the next day, there was no time for Isobel's dancing lesson—or for sewing or knitting either. At far too early an hour, she discovered her parents had other plans in mind when Caroline and Harriet raced in and ripped the covers off her.

'I got here first—I won!' Caroline yelled. 'Meg, wake up.'

'No, *I* did!' an indignant Harriet yelled back. 'That's not fair—you started before Mum even finished saying we could leave the table.'

'Go away,' she groaned. 'I'm not getting up yet.'

'But you have to,' the girls chorussed. 'Mum wants to talk to you right now.'

'Oh, go *away*!' she shouted.

'You'll be in big trouble, Meg,' Caroline gloated, as she headed for the door to be the first to tell their mother, with Harriet hot on her heels.

She knew sleep would elude her, even if she had been able to ignore her mother's footsteps in the hallway and the sharp rap on her door that followed.

'As if I don't have enough to do without running after you, Margaret. Your father and I talked more last night after you took yourself off so rudely and we want to sort things out with you before he leaves. I'll give you five minutes to get dressed and be at the breakfast table. And make sure you look at least a little respectable.'

It was unwise to argue with her mother when she used that tone of voice and her father would be impatient to get to work too. She scrambled out of bed, put on the first dress she could find and hastily brushed her hair. Then, with only seconds to spare, she made it to the table and flopped down.

'Please take that mutinous look off your face, Meg,' her father began. 'Your mother and I have discussed your future and you'll need to start moving, if you're going to head to your aunt and uncle's next week. That way, Will can make sure you get to Brisbane safely and save me a trip.'

She rubbed her eyes and wondered what on earth he was talking about. She loved her aunt and uncle, although she always found it hard to believe Aunty Betty was her father's sister. While he was tall and large and never worried about what he wore, Aunty Betty was small and dainty and loved all the latest fashions. If she could stay with Uncle Harold and her for a while, she might learn more about fashion herself—and she might meet some interesting people at the social events Aunty Betty often went to as well.

In the midst of all her tumbled thoughts, she realised her mother was talking to her.

'I'm not sure I'm entirely happy with the idea, but we've decided to ask your aunt and uncle if they'll have you stay with them for the coming term. However, this is not so you can waste your time flitting from one social event to the next, Margaret. Your father thinks you should have some professional art lessons, but I'd like you to learn all you can from your aunt about sewing and housekeeping in general. Of course, she can afford to employ others to do such things, but she knows a lot herself too—and I'd expect you to grasp this opportunity with both hands. If your father's prepared to pay for art lessons, then you need to do your part and learn everything Betty can teach you. And, needless to say, she's more up-to-date with the latest fashions than I am too.'

'This is your chance, Meg,' her father interrupted, as if fearful her mother would say too much. 'You remember how I told you I always wished I could learn to paint and play the piano? Instead, I had to work—and work hard. We've sent Will to university and we would've done the same for you or paid for you to train as a teacher or a nurse, but you didn't want that. Still, I think it's only fair you're given the chance to have good art lessons, before some lucky fellow marries you and carries you off. When I get to the office, I'll phone Betty and ask her and also find out about art courses. Betty may be able to arrange some piano lessons for you with her girls' old teacher too, which would be good.'

His face was red and his eyes seemed suspiciously bright. Her heart went out to him—she knew by the way he refused to look in her mother's direction that he must have argued her case long into the night.

'Thanks, Dad,' she whispered, holding back her own tears and giving him a hug. 'I'll try my best—at everything.'

'That's my beautiful, big daughter,' he murmured, then joked to hide his embarrassment. 'I hope all those lessons won't be a waste of money though. Chances are, as well as the local boys, I'll soon have a line-up of handsome, young Brisbane suitors knocking at my door.'

After he left, she tried to pull herself together and listen to her mother.

'I don't want to sound begrudging, Margaret, but I have to say you're very fortunate to be given this opportunity. I hope you value it as you ought to and help your aunt however you can. We used to be great friends when I was around your age and go to lots of social events together—we loved dressing in the latest fashion. But all that ended, of course, when I married your father and moved here. Then I had little time for such things, in between learning to manage a household and looking after William and you and the others. Anyway, there's no time to sit here talking about all that. William wants to catch up with a friend in Brisbane next Tuesday, so that leaves only a few days for you to decide what to take with you to Betty's.'

'But ... but I promised to play at the dance here in a couple of weeks to help Mrs Watson out. And I'll miss Jimbo's birthday as well.'

'That can't be helped. Mrs Watson will have to find someone else. And James isn't old enough yet to care whether you're here or not on his birthday. Now go and start sorting your things and packing— and try to be sensible about it all, Margaret.'

Over the next few days, her emotions soared and plummeted. She was grateful when Aunty Betty agreed to have her stay—she loved their beautiful, big home in Hamilton, not far from the river. But she was even more grateful when her father managed to enrol her in an art course at the Technical College in the city. She found it hard to believe that the world-renowned London artist, Godfrey Rivers, would be her main tutor. Yet she hated the thought of leaving home too. She would miss Jimbo and Isobel so much—and her parents and sisters as well. And she would miss her favourite haunts down by the creek where she loved to paint. Still, she could always come home for a visit—and there would be beautiful spots along the Brisbane River near college where she could sit and paint.

It was hard to decide what to take, but Isobel was good at packing and so calm and methodical about it all. The days flew by, yet she was still determined to make it to the Saturday night dance and say goodbye to everyone face to face.

'You look beautiful, Meggie,' Isobel told her when she was ready at last. 'All the boys will want to dance with you tonight, for sure.'

'I wish you were coming too. I feel guilty leaving you here, but I'll tell you all about it on Monday. I hope you have a good day tomorrow—and thanks for everything.'

She gave her hair one final brush and swished her skirts around in front of the mirror, just as Will poked his head in to tell her to hurry up. Despite being a little distracted, she did not miss seeing Isobel blush and turn away. More than ever, she wished Isobel could have come with them. On top of that, she knew Isobel would spend most of her day off helping out at Sunday School and church, then entertaining her brothers and sisters while her mother had a rest. With a sigh, she picked up her evening bag and gave her a quick hug, before hurrying after Will.

They soon reached the School of Arts in the centre of town. Judging by the number of buggies already lined up outside, she was sure she would have plenty of partners—and she was right. In fact, she barely had time to greet her friends before someone claimed her for the first dance. After that, she whirled her way through several more in quick succession, including the Boston Two-Step and a lively barn dance, before being asked to stand up for the Jolly Miller. To her relief, the initial waltz was soon over and it was time to move onto a new partner—she had only agreed to dance with Leo Mullens because she knew she would not have to put up with him for long. But as the next waltz began, she found herself gazing up into the face of a tall stranger. He smiled down at her and clasped her hand firmly in his.

'Hello—I don't think we've met. I'm Richard McPherson, the new teacher at Rosewood.'

# Chapter Two

She tried to sound calm as she responded but ended up stumbling over her own name.

'Oh, I ... I wondered why I didn't recognise you. My name's Meg—I mean, Margaret Porter. But most people call me Meg.'

'I happen to like the name Margaret. It was my mother's name—she passed away when I was in my teens. But perhaps if I want to be accepted around here, I'd better call you Meg.'

It felt so effortless to dance with someone who took control and guided her around with such confidence. But soon the music quickened again and it was time to move on. As he released her, she smiled up at him.

'I enjoyed dancing with you, Richard. I hope you'll be happy in Rosewood.'

She glanced across at him once or twice, as he twirled his next partner around. She liked his wavy, dark brown hair—and the way he smiled back at her for a brief moment too. But then she had to focus on her own partner, who seemed to have two left feet. And the one after him was so shy she could feel his arms shaking. She tried to help him, but in the end, took the lead herself. And all the while, she kept thinking how good it had felt dancing with Richard McPherson.

When suppertime came, she soon found him right there beside her.

'You *have* to try Mrs Benson's delicious passionfruit sponge,' she blurted out. 'She's a fantastic cook. I'm going to eat my sandwiches fast so I have room on my plate for some.'

As they ate, the conversation flowed, although Richard did most of the talking.

'I've had a few different occupations, including working for a newspaper reporter, but then I decided I wanted to be a teacher like my sister,' he told her. 'I've taught in a couple of provisional schools in the Darling Downs area, but I'm looking forward to starting at Rosewood.'

She wanted to know how old he was, but while she was wondering how to find out, he started talking again.

'So … what's a beautiful young lady like you do here in Helidon?'

His rather superior tone rankled, so she decided to give him a slight set-down.

'Oh, there's always something to do. I paint and I play the piano—and I help look after my little brother. Then there's often a dance on somewhere in the district. But next week, I'm heading to Brisbane to study art at the Technical College—Godfrey Rivers will be my main tutor. I'm so looking forward to it all. I'm hoping to have piano lessons too. And my aunt has to attend lots of social events, so no doubt I'll go along to some of those with her.'

He was laughing at her now, she was sure. She had hoped to come across as poised and assured, but had sounded more like an excited little girl looking forward to her first real birthday party.

'Well, Margaret or Meg, you seem to lead quite a hectic life here in Helidon. … I don't know much about art, but I *have* heard of Godfrey Rivers—I believe he's a graduate of the Slade School in London. I don't play the piano either, but I was part of the

Blackstone Ipswich Cambrian Choir when I lived close enough to get to the practices. And I also learnt singing from our conductor, Leonard Francis, for a while. Have you heard of him?'

She hadn't—and she was sure he knew that would be the case. She could feel her colour rising, but she wanted to show him she knew something at least about music.

'Oh, I'm so bad at remembering names, but I *have* heard of the Blackstone Ipswich Cambrian Choir. And I think my parents went to a concert put on by your conductor not long ago. Now I wonder if you're a tenor or a baritone. Or maybe a bass? No, I think you're a tenor. Am I right?'

She caught a momentary look of surprise in his eyes and felt quite pleased with herself. She had wanted to impress him but also put him in his place. She was not a silly schoolgirl anymore.

'Madam, your guess is correct,' he responded, after a slight pause. 'Now I can see Mrs Watson signalling, so it must be time to sing for my supper—of which I've eaten far too much. I hope we can catch up again later.'

She remembered then how Mrs Watson had said there would be guest artists after supper and quickly found a seat near the piano. First, a somewhat ancient soprano from Grandchester managed to make it through two solos, all the while glaring at anyone who dared talk. Then Richard stood up—and soon had everyone listening as he proceeded to sing a jaunty, Irish ballad. He had a pleasant voice, but she sensed it was as much his good looks as his singing that caused most of the females present to stop chatting. During his second item—a Gilbert and Sullivan favourite, *Take A Pair of Sparkling Eyes*—he seemed to glance straight at her. And as an encore, he sang an old Scottish song, *My Ain Folk*, which she found touching. Yes, Richard McPherson was quite impressive—but she had so much else to think about right now.

At that point, her parents indicated it was time to leave. As she picked up her purse, she noticed a crowd of people congratulating Richard. Well, she was not planning to join them and she was thankful her parents did not seem to want to either.

'That new Rosewood schoolteacher has a good voice,' her father commented on their way home. 'I'm glad he's coming for lunch tomorrow with the Davies.'

Her ears pricked up, but she did not say anything. Will would be sure to tease her if she showed any slight interest in Richard McPherson. Yet … imagine seeing him again so soon.

'I thought it was rude not to include him, seeing he's staying with the Davies,' her mother said. 'His sister's been friends with Lillian Davies since their schooldays, I understand.'

She slept in the next morning, then took her time deciding what to wear for the visitors. The Davies never missed a Sunday service at the Methodist church, according to Isobel, so she needed to show some respect for the Lord's Day, as they called it. Besides, she did not want Richard McPherson to think she knew nothing about fashion. Perhaps he was sitting in church right now with the Davies, bored to tears. Or was he a committed churchgoer too? Well, she would wait and see what unfolded over lunch.

But there would be no more idle waiting around for her that morning. Long before lunch, she heard her mother calling her from the kitchen.

'Margaret, please come and make yourself useful. Isobel might have prepared the soup and dessert yesterday, but there's still lots to do. I don't have ten pairs of hands.'

With a sigh, she reached for an old apron, took one final glance in the mirror and headed for the kitchen. Perhaps being away from her mother would be a good thing, even if it meant not seeing Jimbo and Isobel for ages.

By the time their guests were due, she felt tired and cross. She had peeled the vegetables to go with the roast lamb and put them in the oven, without too many arguments with her mother along the way. But when she was left to shell the peas while her mother set the table, she almost lost her temper. She would much rather have made everything look nice and also decided who would sit where. She was even irritable with Jimbo when he came and wanted to be picked up, at which point he burst into indignant howls. Still, at least that gave her a means of escape.

'Heavens, Margaret, I can't *think* with all this noise,' her mother complained. 'Please take James away and tidy him up before the visitors arrive.'

She scooped Jimbo up, quickly combed his hair and deposited him with her sisters. Then, once back in her room, she ripped off her apron and checked in the mirror again, just as Will walked past her door.

'Making a special effort to impress Mr Richard McPherson, are we?' he said with a grin.

She pushed past him, pretending not to hear, and headed for the front veranda, just as the guests arrived. Yes, Richard McPherson certainly cut quite a distinguished figure, in her opinion, as he chatted with her parents. At one stage, he went to move towards her, but just then, her father ushered everyone into the dining room and the moment was lost.

At first, she was kept busy helping her mother serve Isobel's vegetable soup, which required her full attention—she would hear about it later if things were not done properly. But once or twice when she stole a glance at Richard, he seemed to be looking her way, even as he chatted with her father. She tried to catch snippets of their conversation, but knew she needed to concentrate on not spilling anything. Soon it was time to help with the main course, but once Isobel's delicious apple dessert was served, she was able to relax—and it was then that she heard Richard telling her father about his plans.

'I'm catching the train to Brisbane on Tuesday. I'll stay with my sister for a few days and then head back to Rosewood to get ready for my new class.'

'That's a happy coincidence—Will and Meg are catching the train to Brisbane on Tuesday,' her father responded. 'Will's visiting a friend and Meg's been invited to stay with my sister and her husband while she takes some art classes. Anyway, she can tell you about that during the trip, I guess.'

She cringed, wondering if Richard would welcome their company all the way to Brisbane. But when they met up at the station on Tuesday morning, he seemed happy enough with the arrangement.

Once on the train, Will and Richard soon found plenty to talk about, but from time to time, Richard was kind enough to glance her way and try to include her in the conversation. At one stage, he told her about his two sisters, while at another, he asked her what music she liked. On the whole, she found him charming and attentive—although he had been rather condescending about her musical tastes, which had made her feel a little ignorant. Anyway, she was happy to let them talk—she had so much to think about. Already, her stomach fluttered with excitement at what lay ahead for her in Brisbane. Besides, she enjoyed looking out the window and noticing the different shades of green everywhere, as the train passed through Grandchester and Rosewood and on to Ipswich, and how the terrain changed as they drew closer to Brisbane.

During the final stages of their journey through Darra and Corinda and on over the Brisbane River, Will dozed off—or pretended to. She had not missed the sly wink he gave her before he leant back and closed his eyes. Richard was quiet at first, as if lost in thought. And when he spoke, she jumped. She had been miles away, dreaming about her upcoming art lessons.

'Meg, I hope I'm not being too premature, but may I call on you at your aunt and uncle's? I'd like to see you again while I'm in Brisbane. I'm looking forward to meeting your aunt too. I've heard a lot about her from my older sister Mary—they were at school together.'

At first, she was unsure what to say. There would be so many new and exciting things to occupy her in the days ahead, yet she did not want to discourage him completely. Besides, he would be going back to Rosewood soon.

'Well, Aunty Betty's bound to have lots of plans, but I'm sure she'd like to meet you and hear about your sister,' she told him, hoping her voice sounded non-committal enough.

'I'm only in Brisbane for a week, but perhaps we can have dinner one night and take in a show. I'll see what's on and get some tickets for it.'

He did not seem to expect her to respond, so she left it at that. She was excited at the thought of going out with him, but his manner had unsettled her a little again. She would have liked some say in what they did, yet it was clear Richard McPherson preferred to organise things himself.

He chatted on and she quite enjoyed his company, but was still glad when they arrived at Roma Street Station. At one stage, Will had given her another wink that had made her want to kick him. She thought of accusing him of pretending to be asleep, but suspected Richard might think they were squabbling like children. He must be at least nine or ten years older than her, judging by all the jobs he had had.

Soon she caught sight of Aunty Betty hurrying towards them. She chuckled as Will endured their aunt's hugs and kisses with a grimace, but at last he managed to extricate himself and introduce Richard.

'Aunty Betty, this is Richard McPherson from Rosewood. Richard, this is our aunt, Mrs Elizabeth Whitmore. Aunty Betty, it seems you already know Richard's sister, Mary.'

'I'm pleased to meet you,' their aunt gushed. 'I remember hearing about you from Mary—and I saw your other sister last week at a party. She told me you were coming to Brisbane for her birthday. You're a schoolteacher like Mary, aren't you?'

She stifled a giggle—Aunty Betty could be overwhelming at times. Richard's response was courteous, but she soon caught him casting an anguished glance in Will's direction. Rising to the occasion, Will picked up their bags.

'So … which way, Aunty Betty?'

'Oh, our neighbour's son brought me today. Harold's busy at the surgery and then has to head straight to the hospital. But George should be waiting out the front. Mr McPherson, I'd offer you a lift, except I think the buggy will be overflowing with all this luggage Meg's brought. But please come and visit us sometime.'

She was sure Richard would seize the moment—and she was right.

'Please don't worry about me, Mrs Whitmore. I have some business to attend to in town first anyway. But … would it be convenient for me to visit you tomorrow afternoon? I'd like to see Meg again—and you and Will, of course.'

She could feel herself blushing, as Aunty Betty looked at her with raised eyebrows.

'Well, perhaps not tomorrow—or the next day either, come to think of it. I have so much to sort out with Meg. But you're welcome to come on Friday afternoon. Otherwise, I imagine I'll see you at your sister's party on Saturday evening.'

Richard seemed a little crestfallen but responded politely enough.

'Yes, of course. I don't know who Charlotte's invited, but I'm delighted you'll be there. Did the invitation include Meg … and Will? I'm sure they'd both be welcome—I'll talk to Charlotte about it.'

She was glad her aunt was too busy waving to various acquaintances to comment about Richard's upcoming visit. She felt flattered, but was also determined not to let Mr Richard McPherson think his visit was all she had to look forward to. The days ahead were bound to be full of so many exciting things—this was not the time to commit to any serious relationship.

Yet neither Richard nor her aunt seemed to share that opinion. After Richard arrived on Friday, she did not appreciate it when her aunt took herself off elsewhere for some time.

'I'm so sorry—I had to sort something out with our cook,' she told them when she returned, with a conspiratorial glance in her direction.

'I need to get back to my sister's now, Mrs Whitmore,' Richard said, as he stood up, 'but would it be all right with you if Meg and

I took a picnic lunch to Newstead tomorrow? I'll look after her well—we'll stay where others can see us at all times.'

She felt almost embarrassed at Aunty Betty's obvious delight at how things had unfolded and her immediate offer of a picnic hamper. Later, she tried to explain how she felt.

'Aunty Betty, I admire Richard and enjoy his company, but I'm also looking forward to meeting other men my age here in Brisbane.'

Yet it was clear her aunt had already decided Richard was the one for her.

'You'll see, my dear. One day, I'll be saying to you, "I told you so",' she said, with a knowing look. 'All the more reason to put time aside for that sewing and knitting and whatever else your mother wanted me to teach you. They're just as important as your art or your music right now.'

'I only agreed to go with Richard tomorrow because I felt sorry for him. After all, he has to head back to Rosewood soon.'

'So that was the *only* reason, was it?' Aunty Betty said, rolling her eyes. 'Well, I think it was lovely that he walked all the way here from his sister's today, just to see you. I'd say he's quite smitten, Meg.'

'He told me he's borrowing his brother-in-law's bicycle tomorrow, so that'll be easier. … Well, I'd better go and sort out those new clothes we bought—unless you need help with anything.'

It felt good to escape upstairs to her large, comfortable bedroom. She had had quite enough of being teased about Richard McPherson.

Richard arrived right on eleven the following morning and, soon after, the two of them walked up the road and caught a tram crowded with other picnickers most of the way to their destination. Once they had reached the river, Richard slowed down to match her more dawdling pace, although she sensed it irked him. But she was determined to take time to stop and admire the river as it swirled along.

'I love rivers and creeks, don't you? Look at the sun dancing on those little waves—I wish I could paint it all.'

Richard seemed bemused. She had been babbling, she knew, but she could not help herself. Did he not see the beauty around them? He seemed to think she was acting like a child, as she revelled in it all. Maybe she should curb her excitement, but right now she wanted to dance with joy.

Now he had gone on ahead and made for an unoccupied bench under a tree, where he put their picnic hamper down and beckoned her to join him. But on an impulse, she called out to him.

'Race you to the bridge!'

She took off laughing towards nearby Breakfast Creek, discarding her hat and allowing the wind to whip through her long hair. Life held so much excitement and promise and she wanted to celebrate it all.

She was halfway there before she turned to see where Richard was. He had not even begun to follow her and his entire stance shouted disapproval. Well, he could object all he liked—life was meant to be lived on beautiful days like this. Nevertheless, she checked her headlong rush, put her hat on again and began trudging back towards him.

'Oh Richard, that would have been such fun, but never mind. Are you hungry already?'

'Not particularly,' he said, his irritation obvious. 'Meg, you aren't in Helidon now. You'll have to behave in a more ladylike way here or you'll embarrass your aunt at her social events.'

She wanted to blurt out an angry retort. How *dare* he criticise her? He had no right, after all. … Yet as he stood there, tall and forbidding, she could not help thinking how handsome he looked. Even if she did not want things to be too serious between them, she could not deny what an asset he would be at any dance she was invited to. With a small sigh, she straightened her dress, sat down beside him and smiled what she hoped was her most winning smile.

'I'm sorry, Richard—it's just that I'm so excited about everything. My mother's always telling me I need to be much more sensible. I don't want to disgrace either her or Aunty Betty—and I won't disgrace you at your sister's party tonight either. But I'm hungry now. Can we eat?'

Once or twice, Richard glanced at her with a quizzical lift of his eyebrows as she munched the delicious egg sandwiches Aunty Betty's cook had made and chattered on. She wanted to ask him what the matter was, but decided not to. If her behaviour was too childish for him, so be it.

In the end, she quite enjoyed sitting by the river with him, with the cool breeze fanning her face and sending a stray curl across her forehead. He was well-read, had a broad range of interests and seemed to take pleasure in explaining things in a way she could understand. How little she seemed to know, in comparison. The nuns had done their best, but she had not been the most dedicated of students, except in her art and music lessons. Yes, she would not be averse to spending more time in Richard's company. And as they strolled back to the tram stop and made their way home again, she sensed Richard felt the same about her.

She enjoyed the party for his younger sister that night too, despite his older sister Mary's cool manner. Charlotte laughed and chatted warmly enough with her, as Richard busied himself entertaining her three rowdy boys. But Mary seemed much less impressed and was quick to assign Richard the task of ensuring no young lady lacked a partner when the dancing began.

'I felt like a silly schoolgirl,' she fumed on the way home. 'Mary McPherson looked down her nose at me just like Sister Mary Catherine used to when she thought I was misbehaving.'

'I suspect she experienced some big disappointment a few years after we left school—I think she was engaged once,' Aunty Betty told her, stifling a yawn. 'Oh dear, how are we ever going to get up in time for church tomorrow?'

She caught only a brief glimpse of Richard after the service at their local Church of England the next morning, but on Tuesday evening, they attended an orchestral concert together, along with Mary. Then, just before he returned to Rosewood, they met again for lunch in the city, while Aunty Betty obligingly went off to shop with a friend.

'Don't fall for any of those young men in your art classes, will you?' Richard said, as he reached for her hand. 'They're bound to be a disreputable lot—I don't like leaving you in Brisbane where I can't keep an eye on you. I'll be back again in a month, so don't forget me, my Meg.'

She stiffened. What made him think he could call her 'his' Meg? And since when did he have the right to keep an eye on her? Yes, she had enjoyed his company—and the admiring glances directed their way at the concert in particular, where he had indeed cut a distinguished figure. But her art classes awaited, along with so many other exciting things. She did not belong to Mr Richard McPherson at all, but she did not want to be too rude either. He had been kind to her and treated her well. No doubt she would enjoy his company again in a month.

'I'll try my best not to,' was all she said then, as they parted.

Richard wrote often—and, to her surprise, she began to look forward to his letters. She was impressed too with his beautiful copperplate handwriting and took extra care with her own as a result when she found time to reply. He had re-joined the Cambrian Choir in Ipswich, he told her, and been given a lead role in the Gilbert and Sullivan operetta *The Gondoliers*. Also, he hoped to see her again before long—he was having some eye trouble, so needed to see his doctor in Brisbane anyway.

She was glad he was looking forward to seeing her, but she had little time to sit dreaming about him. Her art classes took up two days each week, but she spent many extra hours practising what she was learning. Godfrey Rivers turned out to be a patient teacher and his gentle but firm manner often reminded her of Sister Mary Margaret. She particularly enjoyed the days when he shepherded their class down to the banks of the nearby Brisbane River or along to the Botanic Gardens to paint. The beautiful, purple jacarandas that had inspired his own most famous work were not yet in bloom or the huge, old poincianas either, but at least they could practise painting their overall shape and delicate foliage.

Early on, Godfrey Rivers also challenged them to paint a self-portrait in oils. She much preferred her landscape painting—and her watercolours. But when she discovered her teacher was also a talented portrait artist, she was determined to learn as much as she could from him.

She also spent some hours at least each week practising the piano, after discovering how Miss Sabina Lang, who had taught Aunty Betty's two daughters, did not tolerate laziness.

'She's just like crotchety old Sister Bridget,' she burst out one evening, after a disastrous lesson when Miss Lang's patience with her had run out.

'Well, your father wanted you to keep learning and Miss Lang did her best to fit you in, my dear. She's a highly sought-after teacher,' her aunt said, with a hint of tartness. 'I suspect your Mrs Watson in Helidon was far too easy-going with you.'

If only there was time for all the things she wanted to do. Each weekend, she had to choose between outings with her college friends and various social events with Aunty Betty, while on Sunday mornings, Aunty Betty and Uncle Harold expected her to attend church. At least there was time in the afternoon to paint, unless Edward or Percy or Victor from college invited her out somewhere. She enjoyed spending time with each of them, especially Percy. She loved their lazy Sunday afternoons sailing on the river in his father's boat, along with two or three other college friends. And Aunty Betty liked him best too.

'I'm sure your parents wouldn't mind your going out with Percy Smithers,' she told her. 'After all, his father's a solicitor. And at least Edward's well-mannered, even though he doesn't have much money. But my dear, don't you think Victor's just that little bit too … well … bohemian? So untidy-looking. I don't think your parents would approve at all.'

At first, she had resented such comments. At almost nineteen, she was not a child any longer. Yet she knew her aunt was right— it was indeed unwise to go out with Victor, especially by oneself.

Edward was a dear and always a true gentleman. Besides, she felt sorry for him. He worked hard to pay for his art classes, so was not about to fritter his time away at college, as Percy seemed to. All the same, Percy was fun—much more fun than Richard McPherson, in her opinion.

She decided not to tell Richard that, however. In fact, she decided not to tell him anything about Percy. Or Victor. Or even Edward.

But when Richard made it to Brisbane again a few weeks later, her heart skipped a beat. He was just as handsome as she remembered and so mature, compared to her college friends. Then and there, she decided to invite him to a special exhibition at the National Art Gallery that weekend. She did not care so much about the exhibition itself, but she wanted her girlfriends to meet him, especially Sybil and Molly. They would be so jealous—but she would not tell Richard that either.

After a delicious dinner at her aunt's, they sat chatting together on the veranda, as the last rays of the sun painted the sky in beautiful shades of gold and pink.

'There's a special exhibition on this weekend at the Art Gallery I thought you might enjoy,' she told him after a while. 'Some of my friends are going—perhaps we could meet up with them.'

But to her disappointment, Richard's response was less than enthusiastic.

'I suppose we could go if you really want to, Meg, but … well, I think our weekend might be full enough already without that. Tomorrow morning, I have another doctor's appointment, but I thought we could meet for lunch in the city at Rowe's Café. Then perhaps we could come back here and have a game of tennis on the grass court right here, if that suits everyone. You do like tennis, don't you?'

She opened her mouth to reply, but he went on.

'In the evening, there's a concert on at the Theatre Royal featuring the Irish tenor Michael O'Rourke. I managed to get two cheaper tickets because I'm in the Cambrian Choir and some of the other choir members will be there too. Then on Sunday afternoon, perhaps we could take a tram to the city and walk down to the river. And afterwards, I'm sure my sister would be happy for you to have dinner with us.'

She hesitated—again, he seemed to have everything organised. She thought of insisting on seeing the art exhibition, but, after a brief struggle with herself, she decided to fall in with his plans.

In the end, she had to admit everything worked out well. The concert was excellent and she enjoyed meeting Richard's friends from the choir. Once or twice, she noticed two of the girls glancing her way and whispering together, so she moved closer to Richard on purpose, tilting her head up and smiling at him. That would show them she was not too young to have captured his attention. And Richard was warm and accommodating towards her all through their Sunday afternoon together and at dinnertime too. She was sure his manner would not escape his sister's notice—and she was right.

'Rosewood must agree with you, Richard,' Charlotte commented with a mischievous smile, as they sat chatting after dinner. 'You seem very content with life right now. Your class must be behaving well—I guess having Mary on staff at the same school is a help.'

'Well, let's say *most* of my class are behaving. But I'm also enjoying our choir rehearsals for the upcoming operetta. And it's good to be able to see you again—and Meg too, of course.'

Later, when Richard took her home in his brother-in-law's buggy, he walked her to the door and held her hand. Even in the half dark, she could see he was smiling down at her.

'It's been a wonderful weekend, Meg. I wish I could see you more often, but I'll come down again soon. Work hard—and don't go out too often with those young men at college, will you? Remember, I met you first.'

He kissed her on the cheek, hesitated for a moment longer, then left. She could not help feeling disappointed but tried not to show it, as she fended off her aunt's questions. Later, however, she lay on her bed and thought about it all. Had he wanted to hold her close, just as she had wanted him to? Had he perhaps wanted to kiss her on the lips, as Percy had done several times already, unbeknown to her aunt or anyone else? Oh, why did she have such mixed feelings about him? She was flattered by his attentions—after all, he was handsome and knowledgeable and gifted in so many ways. Yet ... well, sometimes he was far too dictatorial and sure of himself for her liking. Oh, *why* was it all so complicated?

Halfway through term, her father decided to come to Brisbane and pay her a visit.

'I have a few business matters to attend to for the cathedral project—their deadline's looming,' he explained. 'I can't spare much time away from the quarries, but I'll be with you from Wednesday to Friday.'

At first, she thought of heading back home with him for the weekend. But she had so much college work to do and she had also promised to help her aunt cater for a special church event. On top of that, Richard had written to say he planned to head down to Brisbane the following weekend. *It will only be a brief visit*, he told her, *but I'm looking forward to seeing you again, Meg, and I hope you feel the same.* That meant she would have to leave going home until another time—she could not ignore her college work two weekends in a row.

Her father was delighted to see her, but seemed quieter than usual and a little nervous, as they sat down to chat.

'How's Jimbo? Is he missing me?' she asked, after a lengthy silence.

'Eh? Oh yes ... yes, I'm sure he is.'

He sat forward then and cleared his throat.

'Listen, Meg ... I've got something serious to talk to you about. It's to do with Richard McPherson. He met with me in Ipswich recently and ... well, he asked for my permission to marry you. I was a bit shocked—I didn't expect to hear a request like that for some time yet, even though I joked a while back about that line-up of young men at my door. To me, you're still my little Meg. ... Besides, you met Richard only a few days before you came down here. I understand you've been corresponding since then, but it's a bit sudden, don't you think?'

She was stunned. Richard had given her no inkling of what he was planning. Her mind whirled. … It must be true, but it felt so surreal.

Her father seemed to understand her confusion.

'Take your time, Meg. Looks like this is news to you too. … It's a big step, my dear, isn't it? I understand Richard's coming down next weekend to see you and he'll no doubt propose while he's here, but I wanted to get in first. He's a determined fellow—he knows what he wants.'

As they sat there together, all sorts of emotions welled up inside her. She liked Richard and was flattered he wanted to marry her. In fact, in some ways, her heart leapt at the idea. After all, he was handsome and personable, with good prospects as a teacher. Yet since his last visit, she had decided she was not ready to marry anyone. There was so much more to learn and experience in Brisbane—and the very thought of giving up her art course sent shudders through her. Besides, it was true she did not know him well enough to marry him—part of her felt angry he would even think of proposing to her at this early stage. Was he perhaps taking her 'yes' for granted?

Eventually, she stumbled through some sort of response.

'Thanks for warning me, Dad. I … I don't know how I feel, to be honest. Richard's a wonderful person, but I think it's far too soon to be talking of marriage. I love my art classes and I love being here in Brisbane—I'd hate to have to give it all up. … Oh dear—what will I say to him?'

'Perhaps what you've just said to me—and I admit I agree with you. I'd like to see you do at least another term at college before you think of marrying anyone. As for your mother … well, I know she likes Richard and thinks he'd provide the stability you need. But we'd never push you into anything you might regret later. Whatever you decide, we'll always be there for you. Remember that, Meg.'

Her father rose then, but she had seen the tears in his eyes and heard the tremor in his voice.

'I know,' she said, as she hugged him. 'Thanks, Dad. I miss you all, but I love being here too. And if I do well enough this term, I'd like to stay on next year.'

'I'll see what your aunt says. But for now, you'd better do your best to impress Godfrey Rivers—and Miss Lang too, for that matter.'

That week, she had great trouble concentrating on anything apart from the fact that Richard was coming to propose. Her answer would be no—but would that mean the end of their relationship? After all, Richard was ten years older than her. No doubt he wanted to settle down and start a family of his own. But he had had many opportunities to do different things in his life, while she had done nothing much until now. And, although she loved children, she was not ready for motherhood yet. … Still, she liked him and would be disappointed to lose his friendship.

Richard arrived soon after breakfast on Saturday. Once again, she could not help thinking how handsome he was, with his thick, wavy hair and stylish moustache. He seemed less formal than usual too, kissing her on the cheek and keeping his arm around her shoulders as he went to greet her aunt.

'Good to see you again, Mrs Whitmore. I hope it's all right if I spirit Meg away for the day. I thought we might take a tram down towards the river again. We can pick up a bite to eat along the way.'

'Oh, I can organise a picnic lunch for you,' her aunt responded at once. 'No, don't bother coming to help, Meg. Just make yourselves comfortable and I'll be with you soon.'

They chatted together on the veranda as they waited.

'I had a good trip down,' Richard told her. 'I had the carriage to myself most of the way. Oh, I've brought you a gift too—I hope you like it.'

She unwrapped the small package he held out to her and gasped. In it was a beautiful, tiny, wooden bird.

'I thought of you often as I carved it, Meg. I like whittling— it helps me relax in the evenings after I've finished my school preparation. This one's made from a piece of gidgee wood I saved from my time on a cattle station,' he told her with pride.

'It's beautiful, Richard. Thank you for such a special gift,' she managed to get out, hardly daring to look at him.

Her hand was shaking, as she gently cradled the little bird. Richard put his hand beneath hers, then reached for her other hand.

'I have something else for you too, Meg, that I hope you'll like, but let's wait until later for that.'

All sorts of unsettling emotions welled up inside her. She hated to hurt him, but she did not want to give him false hope either. Part of her very much liked the idea of becoming his wife and of being with him—yet she felt cornered too. Oh, why was it all so hard? Well, whatever lay ahead, she had agreed to spend the day together and would do her best to make it enjoyable for him.

At that point, Aunty Betty appeared and handed them a picnic basket with a sly smile and a wave of her hand.

'Have a good time, you two. And you're most welcome to join us for dinner tonight, Richard.'

As they headed down to the river, Richard regaled her with tales of his young pupils' escapades and his operetta rehearsals. She would have liked him to ask her about college too, but whenever she tried to steer the conversation in that direction, he somehow managed to regain control. Was he feeling unsure of himself? Was that why he wanted to take charge? She felt sorry for him then—she liked him too well to take any pleasure in disappointing him, if and when he proposed.

They enjoyed a stroll along the river together, during which she relaxed a little, until it was time for lunch. Richard was still carrying the picnic basket and they managed to find a spot away from other picnickers, for which she was grateful. But as they finished eating, she sensed the moment she had been dreading was not far away— and she was right. She had just packed up their picnic basket when he reached for her hand.

'Meg, I hope this isn't too much of a surprise, but I arranged to talk with your father the other day and … well … I asked him for your hand in marriage. He seemed happy with the idea, but what do you think, my dear? … I know we haven't known each other long, but I hope you'll say yes. … Of course, if you do, you'd have to give up your art classes, because you'd need to go home and prepare for the wedding. I'd like us to be married in the school holidays, perhaps in mid-January. And that's only a little over three months away.'

Despite her father's warning about the proposal, she was still taken aback. Everything seemed so cut and dried in Richard's mind. She still hated to disappoint him, but his definite, even self-centred manner strengthened her resolve to turn him down. She liked him a lot—perhaps she even loved him—but she did not want to make a life commitment at this stage. If she had stayed home in Helidon, things might have been different. As it was … well, all she could do was tell him the truth.

'Richard, I'm … I'm flattered you want to marry me, especially since we've known each other for only a short while. I feel honoured and I hate to disappoint you, but … well, my answer's no. I … I don't feel ready to settle down yet. And I certainly don't want to give up my art classes right now.'

Richard interrupted her then, his face red.

'But Meg, *I'm* ready to settle down—*more* than ready. I'm twenty-nine—it's time I had a family of my own. Besides, it's lonely in Rosewood. I know my sister's there and I also have good friends in the choir. But it'd be wonderful to come home to you each day, my dear. I know it'd work out, even though you're so young. And you could still use your artistic gifts to create nice things for our home. Why waste more time in these art classes of yours? At least you've had the chance to have some fun here these past few weeks, courtesy of your parents—and your aunt and uncle. But *I'd* like to take responsibility for you now, Meg. Please say yes.'

More than anything else, his comment about her art classes decided her.

'Yes, I've had fun, Richard—and yes, my parents and aunt and uncle have been good to me. But I don't for one moment feel my art classes have been a waste of time. I hope we can still be friends, but I don't want to commit myself to anyone yet. I'm so sorry.'

His face was set now, as he sat staring into the distance. At one stage, he opened his mouth as if to argue, but seemed to think better of it. Then he stood up and gathered their things together.

'Well, there's nothing more to be said, I suppose—at least for now. I won't come to see you again in Brisbane, Meg, but I hope we can remain friends too. When you get time, write and let me know how you're going. I'll try to do the same, but I'll be busy with the musical for the rest of term, as well as with everything else.'

She could tell from his stiff tone how disappointed he was and how much his pride had been dented. Perhaps if he had waited another six months, her answer might have been different. But he wanted a wife now—and she was sure one of those young women from the choir would be more than willing to accommodate him.

With a sigh, she stood up too and they headed back to the tram stop. During their silent ride home, she remembered with relief that Aunty Betty was out for the afternoon. At least she would not need to explain why they were back so soon. She felt wretched—she would have to say something more to him before they parted.

When they arrived at Aunty Betty's, Richard opened the gate and carried their picnic basket to the door. As he turned, she put her hand on his arm and tried to meet his gaze.

'Richard, I'm sorry to have hurt you. I wish I could have said yes—I admire you so much and I'm sure you'd make an excellent husband. But the timing just isn't right for me. Please try to understand how I feel.'

He looked down at her, his eyes bleak.

'Goodbye, Meg—for now at least,' was all he said, as he bent and kissed her lightly on the cheek.

Then he was gone, pedalling off without a backward glance.

# Chapter Three

It was a few days before she managed to write to her parents to let them know the outcome of Richard's visit. But that task was easy, compared to enduring Aunty Betty's constant reproaches.

'But he'd make such a *good* husband, Meg,' she said more than once. 'He's so handsome and distinguished and gifted. What more could you want?'

'The chance to stay here a while longer,' she responded. 'I know my art isn't important to Richard, but it is to me. I've learnt so much at college, especially from Godfrey Rivers. And some of my friends plan to go to Sydney or even Melbourne next year to see paintings by artists like Roberts and McCubbin and Streeton. I'm still young—I'd like to have a little more fun before I settle down. Richard and I plan to stay in touch, but I'm sure he'll find someone else before long.'

She hoped she sounded nonchalant enough, yet it was hard to quell the turmoil inside her. Did she love Richard, after all? Was what she felt for him strong enough to last a lifetime? Had she made a big mistake, wanting to stay on in Brisbane? Round and round the questions went in her mind, making her feel tired and miserable.

She was glad she had so many college projects to work on—even the self-portrait for Godfrey Rivers, which provided her with a good excuse to escape to her room and paint. And she also started going out with her friends again, including Percy, who knew how to have a good time. She was not the only girl he invited out, but that did not concern her too much. Plenty of time to be serious later.

Yet despite these distractions, she began to feel even more tired and homesick. She worked and played hard—she was determined to make the most of each day. Or was she also trying to forget a certain handsome, distinguished-looking man who kept coming to mind at unexpected times? Whatever the reason, she often longed to be back home, painting at her favourite spot down by the creek. It would soon be Harriet's birthday—and her own not long after. She had already missed Jimbo's earlier in the term.

She tried to tell Aunty Betty how she was feeling but received little sympathy.

'You can't have it both ways, Meg,' her aunt told her with spirit. 'You chose to come to Brisbane, after all—and to turn down a perfectly good marriage proposal. Now instead of feeling sorry for yourself, I'd appreciate it if you focussed on cutting out this dress pattern. Your mother wanted me to teach you sewing and knitting and the like and we've had almost no time for such things.'

Soon after, however, she received a rather more sympathetic response from her father.

*I have to come to Brisbane again and, seeing it's your birthday soon, as well as your sister's, we thought you might like to come home with me for the weekend. Everyone would love to see you—especially Jimbo.*

She did not hesitate this time. And, to her surprise, the prospect of a visit home spurred her on to complete her self-portrait at last, as well as some smaller projects. She was sorry to miss a special birthday outing with Percy and hoped he would not be too ready to find a replacement partner, but that was a risk she was willing to take. She was so looking forward to seeing everyone again, including

Isobel, who had written faithfully each week, despite receiving only one or two letters in return.

The train seemed to take forever, especially after they changed at Ipswich, but they made it home just in time for Friday evening dinner. Everyone had lined up to greet them and, even before they reached the gate, she could see Jimbo bouncing up and down on her mother's hip. Soon he was in her arms, clutching her around the neck as if he would never let go.

'Welcome home, Margaret—even if only for a couple of days,' her mother said warmly enough.

'Oh, Meg, you look so grown up,' Caroline told her with a sigh. 'I wish my hair looked like yours.'

'Hi, Meg—it's my birthday tomorrow,' Harriet informed her, clapping her hands with excitement.

She tried to wiggle Jimbo onto her hip then to give Isobel a warm hug.

'He's missed you so much—and so have I, Meg,' Isobel whispered.

The weekend flew by. On Saturday morning, she spent time talking with her mother. She tried her best to avoid the topic of male friends, but her mother was not to be put off.

'I was very sorry you turned Richard McPherson down, Margaret. He would have been good for you, being older and more mature. I think you need someone like him to pull you into line, but ... well, I suppose it's your decision.'

'I hated disappointing him, Mum, but it wasn't the right time for me to marry anyone. I still like him, even though he often told me what to do and how to act. Right now, I'm enjoying going out with different college friends, but there's nothing serious with any of them, so don't worry.'

She told Isobel more when they chatted while Jimbo had his afternoon nap, including how Richard had proposed to her. Isobel was sympathetic, yet her response also surprised her.

'I've never even seen him—I wasn't here when he came for lunch and I wasn't at the dance where you met. I think your mother was hoping things would work out between you, but he has to be right for you, Meg. And … well … the most important thing I'd want to know, if someone asked me to marry him, would be whether he loves God.'

'*Loves God?* What's that got to do with getting married? … I'm pretty sure Richard would though. At least, I know he goes to church sometimes, but we never talked about anything like that.'

Isobel stood up and straightened her dress.

'Well, it doesn't matter now anyway, since you've turned him down. But even if I loved someone, I don't think I could marry him if he didn't have a strong faith in God, because that's so important to me. … Oh Meggie, I wish we could chat more, but I need to help your mother with the birthday dinner. And I think Jimbo's awake too.'

'I'll look after him, Isobel,' she offered. 'I can take him down the creek with me. He can play around while I paint.'

Jimbo jumped at the chance to go with her, as she knew he would. At first, he wanted to carry her brushes and paints, but it was not long before he gave up and dropped them.

'Pick me up, Meggie,' he pleaded, arms held high.

With a sigh, she heaved him onto her back, where he clung like a limpet. Then she retrieved her brushes and paints, along with her hat that had fallen off, and trudged on.

'You're a big boy now, Jimbo. You could walk,' she scolded him.

His only response was to cling on tighter. At last they reached the creek and she was able to put him down.

'Phew! Now, would you like some paper for your own painting? We could put it on the grass over there. Or would you rather look for some special stones for me?'

'Um … stones for Meggie,' he decided, then headed for a nearby rocky spot.

She set up her easel and paints and gazed at the creek below. It was all so beautiful and tranquil. She hoped she could manage to replicate the dappled reflections of the gumtrees on the surface of the water before the sun sank too low. Perhaps if she did it well enough, her painting would earn her extra praise from Godfrey Rivers.

She sighed with ecstasy, as she took in the familiar sights and smells of the surrounding countryside. Oh, it was so good to be home—she could hear cockatoos squawking in the distance and the chattering of lorikeets in the nearby grevilleas, as they ate their fill of nectar. Things went well at first, as Jimbo trotted back and forth, showing her his precious finds. But then he decided he had found enough stones and wandered away towards the creek bank.

'Jimbo, come back! Here, you can have some paper and a brush all to yourself. You could paint a special birthday picture for Harriet.'

This idea worked for a while, with Jimbo splattering paint all over himself as well as the paper. But when he headed for the creek again, she decided to give up.

'I told you to stay away from the water, Jimbo,' she scolded, as she ran after him. 'You can't swim yet. Besides, I don't want to take you home with your clothes all wet.'

'But Meggie, I need to wash my hands,' he said, then promptly fell on his bottom in a muddy pool at the water's edge.

She dried him off with an old rag, packed up her things and heaved him onto her back again.

'Let's go or we won't have time to clean you up before our birthday dinner. But you mustn't go near the water unless you're with a grown-up. I know I wasn't far away, but I might not have been quick enough to help you if you had fallen in.'

They made it back just in time. It was wonderful to be together again around the dinner table—yet, in an odd way, she felt a little removed from everything too. Had she changed so much during her few weeks away in Brisbane?

'You're just the same, but different too,' Isobel said, as she hugged her goodbye before heading home for her usual Sunday off. 'Don't change too much, will you, Meggie? Don't let your Aunty Betty or Percy or Victor or Edward—or even Richard—make you into anyone different. Just be yourself, the way God meant you to be, so creative and full of life.'

'Oh Isobel, you sound like a wise old woman. You're so much more grown-up than I'll ever be. I wish you could come back to Brisbane with me and have a bit more fun in your life. I'll try to write more—and I'll be back at the end of term again. Then we'll have lots of chats, I promise.'

The next day, as the train clattered along on its way to Brisbane, she let her mind wander. It had been wonderful to be home again, but it would be good to be back with Aunty Betty too. And once she arrived at Roma Street Station and listened to her aunt bubbling over with plans for the weeks ahead, she was soon caught up in the excitement of it all.

'Welcome back, Meg. Goodness, I have so many things to tell you. There are lots of garden parties and picnics on at the moment—they're always more pleasant before the weather gets much warmer. But I know you'll want to make the most of the rest of your college term, as well as your lessons with Miss Lang. And we must do some sewing too—we can't let your mother down. You never know when one of your beaus will pop the question, after all.'

'I doubt that will happen, Aunty Betty,' she managed to respond. 'But I want to do well at college—and for Miss Lang. I'll try my best at any sewing and knitting you can teach me too, but I can't promise I'll ever excel at it.'

'It wouldn't surprise me if you did, Meg, but you'd have to put your mind to it. Your mother was an excellent dressmaker when she was young. We both used to make our own outfits—even our hats at times. It's a shame she hasn't been able to teach you more herself really. She always looked elegant wherever she went—and it wasn't only because her family were well off.'

'Mum doesn't talk much about when she was young, but I remember how she used to make my dresses when I was little and also my dolls' clothes. My dolls had so many outfits. But as I grew up, I think I became too picky about what I wore and, in the end, Mum refused to make anything more for me. I know I wasn't the easiest person for her to teach either—I'm still not, according to her. I'm not sure why we clash like we do.'

Her aunt hesitated for a moment, then plunged on.

'You know, Meg, you're very like her when she was young. You both have beautiful, big, grey eyes and all that lovely, auburn hair … And she was quite stunning, just as you are, my dear. So maybe … well, maybe you remind her too much of those days when she herself was free to do what she liked and very much part of the social whirl. Who knows? … Oh dear, that wasn't what I wanted to talk about at all with you, Meg. I wonder … well, I don't suppose you happened to run into Richard McPherson when you were home, did you? I thought he might have been visiting his friends in Helidon again.'

She sighed. She had known her aunt would be curious about Richard, but she was determined not to be drawn into any discussion about him, so merely smiled and shook her head. She still thought of him often herself—but she was not going to tell Aunty Betty that.

As the weeks passed, she began to enjoy her art classes even more, as she developed her own style and technique. She was delighted too that Godfrey Rivers loved the scene she had begun to paint down by the creek and had taken the time to suggest small ways to improve it. But it was she herself who thought of incorporating Jimbo into the painting. She remembered his expression as he had laughed up at her from the water's edge, his messy hands held high. She had painted him in the same outfit he had worn that day—a red shirt, blue overalls and a little straw hat—which added interest to the whole scene. But it was his tiny face that seemed to capture everyone's attention.

'Well done, Margaret—I can sense his personality through those clever, little touches you've used around his lips and eyes. See how practising your portrait painting has paid off?' Godfrey Rivers commented, which was praise indeed from him.

'He looks like me when I was young,' Percy laughed. 'I was mischievous even back then.'

Aunty Betty was impressed too.

'You've captured him well, Meg—and the whole scene, in fact. Now let's see if you can do as well for Miss Lang at her end-of-year recital. And let's see if we can finish sewing this dress too. We have to have *something* reasonable to show your mother.'

She practised her two pieces for the recital as often as she could and, to her relief, managed to get through them both on the night itself without stopping, if not mistake-free. No one except Miss Lang seemed to notice her few wrong notes. But what everyone did notice, according to Aunty Betty, was the dress her aunt had helped her make.

'My dear, you looked wonderful on the platform. That beautiful, green material goes so well with your auburn hair. You have such a good eye for colour, even if some of your stitches leave a lot to be desired.'

But nothing could surpass the joy she felt when Godfrey Rivers told her he wanted to include one of her paintings in a special exhibition at the Queensland National Art Gallery the following month.

'The trustees and I viewed all the students' submissions and we selected three to display, together with some of my own recent works. Your painting of the scene by the creek was the first one chosen, Margaret, along with Edward Green's 'Botanic Gardens Afternoon' and also 'Sailboat on the Brisbane River' by Percy Smithers. Congratulations! I do hope you come back next term. You're a promising young artist, so don't waste your talent.'

A few weeks later, both her father and Will managed to make it to Brisbane in time to catch the final night of the exhibition. She had known her father was coming for dinner with Aunty Betty and Uncle Harold first, before they all headed into the Art Gallery, but gasped when Will walked in with him.

'I wanted to surprise you,' he told her, grinning from ear to ear. 'Mum and Dad told me about the exhibition, so I decided to come and see it for myself. I was held up at Wallangarra yesterday for ages though and only just made it to Toowoomba in time to catch the

Helidon train.'

He was the same old Will, ready to tease her at the slightest opportunity. But once they arrived at the Art Gallery, there was no more teasing from him. He stood staring at her painting for some time, then turned and gave her a huge hug.

'I *knew* you could do it, Meg. I don't know much about art, but I've always thought you have loads of talent. Congrats!'

Then she noticed tears in her father's eyes and almost burst into tears herself.

'It's … why, it's wonderful,' he managed to say, after a long pause. 'I recognised that spot down by the creek at once. As for that little rascal James, you've captured his cheeky expression to a tee. Well done, Meg—I'm so proud of you. And … well, your mother would be too, if she could have come.'

It was hard to sleep that night. She was so thankful for her art course and looked forward to returning in the new year.

The following day as they travelled home together, Will regaled her with colourful accounts of his adventures in Sydney with his university friends. In turn, she told him about Percy and Edward and Victor and tried to explain too how much Godfrey Rivers had helped her.

'I hope you love studying engineering as much as I love my art classes, Will. I think being an artist is what God truly has created me to be, just like Isobel told me once.'

'That sounds like something Isobel would say,' Will smiled, 'and I think she might be right. … But I envy you, Meg, because I'm not sure yet what I've been created to be, as Isobel would put it. I plan to finish my engineering degree, but I can't see myself being an engineer forever.'

She glanced in their father's direction as the train jolted along and was relieved to see he was asleep.

'Dad wouldn't want to hear that,' she whispered.

'No … and I'm not saying anything to him yet either. Right now, I just have a feeling there might be something different ahead for me to do. You know, some of my friends in Sydney believe in God like Isobel does and reckon God can direct our path in life. I'm not convinced about that—but I suspect there must be a God out there somewhere. I'm sure this world couldn't have come into being by chance. My friends and I have lots of discussions about that.'

'Isobel never rams her religious views down my throat, but I admire her for the way she's kept on trusting God. She'd love me to have the sort of faith in God that she has—I know she even prays I will one day. Yet whatever I believe, she still rescues me when I mess things up or forget to do something for Mum.'

They arrived home to a warm welcome, but she could see how flustered her mother was. There had been delays on the rail line and they were quite late.

'Your dinner's been ready for ages—I hope it's not spoilt. And I've already put James to bed, I'm afraid.'

But Isobel soon rescued their meals and served them all with her usual warm smile. Then, just as they began eating, Jimbo started bellowing at the top of his lungs.

'I'll try to settle him down,' Isobel said. 'He must have heard your voices.'

But Jimbo would not be put off. 'Meggie … Meggie,' he wailed. 'Want to see Meggie!'

'Let him come and sit with us for a while, Pearl,' her father suggested.

She could see her mother did not approve, but decided to back her father up.

'It's okay, Mum—I'll look after him. He won't be any trouble.'

As soon as Jimbo saw her, he wriggled out of Isobel's arms, raced across to her and climbed onto her lap. She let him stay there, even though it was hard to eat her dinner. And as the conversation flowed around him, he snuggled down and soon drifted off to sleep.

When the meal was over, Isobel offered to carry him back to bed.

'I'll take him, Meg—you must be tired. Maybe we can catch up tomorrow.'

From the outset, she was determined to make the most of her holidays. They had been invited to several Christmas celebrations, as well as a New Year's Eve party, and she was looking forward to them all. There was a dance on that weekend too and, for once, Isobel had decided to come.

'I'm only helping out with supper, Meggie—I don't plan on dancing, so don't worry,' Isobel told her. 'The committee's a bit shorthanded, with Christmas so close. Your mother doesn't want to go in all this heat and my brother said he'd pick me up on Sunday morning in time for church. Oh, I almost forgot—Mrs Watson said she might have to get you to play for some of the dances too.'

'Thanks for warning me, Isobel—that gives me time to think up a good excuse for saying no. There's too much else to do right now.'

But Mrs Watson dropped in before she had time to think of any excuse at all.

'If you could take over from me after supper, Meg, that'd be wonderful. And perhaps you could give us a solo earlier in the evening too. Your mother told me you played at a recital in Brisbane—you can't have forgotten those pieces yet. Then Richard McPherson can sing straight after supper.'

In the end, she did not have the heart to say no. And what did it matter if Richard McPherson would be there? Still, she would need to practise as much as possible, instead of playing with Jimbo or skipping off to paint. She did not want to make any mistakes— especially with Richard there.

The days leading up to the dance were frantic. And on the night, she was thankful Isobel was with her to calm her down. She could not see Richard anywhere, but just as she stood up to play, she noticed him near the door. In an instant, she remembered his comment about her art classes. They had not been a waste at all— and she wished she could tell him about having her painting on display at the Art Gallery. At least she had the chance now to show him her lessons with Miss Lang had not been wasted. She took a deep breath, lifted her chin and proceeded to put her heart and soul into her performance.

'Well done, Meggie,' Isobel whispered afterwards. 'That's the best I've heard you play ever.'

Will was not far behind either.

'Wow, Meg—you're a bundle of surprises these days. Hey, everyone—this is my talented little sister. Can you beat that?'

She relaxed then and Roy Davies soon whisked her away for the next waltz. When suppertime came, she found herself the centre of a rowdy group of fresh-faced young farmers, all vying for her attention. But soon she had to excuse herself to prepare to play for the next few dances.

She found a spot near the piano—that way, she would be behind Richard while he sang. And she was glad she had when, after singing a pleasant Irish ballad, he explained that his second item, '*Don't Be Cross*', was about a girl who refuses to marry her beau. Had he chosen the song on purpose? She suspected he had—especially when he turned and looked straight at her as he finished singing. She tried not to blush and was glad she had to play for the next dance.

But at the end of the night, just as she was leaving with Will and Isobel, their paths crossed. It would have been the briefest of meetings, except that Will decided he needed to tell Richard about her painting.

'You and Meg both performed well tonight—congratulations.'

'Thanks, Will. I hope you did well in your studies this term—and you too, Meg.'

Before she could open her mouth, Will was talking again.

'I did okay, but Meg had a great triumph. One of her paintings was included in the recent Godfrey Rivers exhibition at the Art Gallery. I'm quite proud of my kid sister right now.'

'Oh … well … congratulations, Meg,' Richard managed to say, his astonishment obvious.

Before she could stop herself, the words came tumbling out.

'Thanks, Richard. It was such an honour—and it showed me my art classes weren't wasted, after all. I'm looking forward to going back to college even more now.'

They made it home just before the skies opened with one of the heaviest downpours any of them could remember. She lay awake for a long time, listening to the rain drumming on the roof. In her mind, the sound seemed to merge with the rhythm of the songs Richard had sung. He had performed well—and he had also congratulated her on hearing about her painting. Had her response been too pointed and rude then? Yet he deserved it, after all. So … why did she feel so upset? And why was she crying, after her playing had gone so well? Perhaps she was just tired. Oh, *bother* Richard McPherson for turning up in Helidon, just when she had put him out of her mind.

It was still raining hard when she woke the next morning, but she knew there would be no more sleep when she heard Jimbo calling her. Then she remembered it was Isobel's day off and her mother had asked her to mind him. She crawled out of bed and opened her door—and there was Jimbo, crouched down on all fours and clutching his blanket.

'I sawed you, Meggie, under the door,' he said, laughing up at her.

She took him back to bed so as not to wake everyone else.

'Shh—Mummy and Daddy are asleep. Let's play under the covers for a bit.'

At first, they pretended they were hiding in a cave and that the wicked witch was looking everywhere for them. But when she felt Jimbo's little heart pounding, she decided to try a different game.

'Don't worry, Jimbo, she couldn't find us—we were far too clever for her. Now let's see. I think I'd like to be Snow White and I'm sure you're quite handsome enough to be her special prince. Then you can kiss me awake.'

After a while, they decided they felt like some pancakes. They tiptoed to the kitchen, where she set about making them as quietly as possible. But soon Jimbo climbed onto the bench and insisted on helping.

'I like cooking,' he announced through a cloud of white, as the flour he was trying to sift went everywhere except in the bowl.

She heaved a sigh and held the sifter steady for him. Then she only just managed to save the egg and milk mixture from crashing to the floor. She finished off the batter as fast as she could and began cooking the pancakes. And as soon as the first two were cool enough, she handed them to Jimbo.

'Here you are. Would you like butter on them? And some jam?'

But Jimbo had already stuffed a pancake into his mouth and was busy squishing the second one in his hand.

'I love you, Meggie. More, please,' he said with a huge smile, pancake and all.

She could not resist giving him a hug.

'Oh Jimbo, I love you too. You've been such a help.'

She occupied him most of the day without too much effort, but was glad when Isobel returned the next morning. She loved Jimbo, but she had so much to do before Christmas. First and foremost, she wanted to finish a painting for her parents and another one for Isobel.

It continued to rain hard all week, so she had no choice but to paint in her room, which made things difficult. It was hard enough having Jimbo interrupt her so often, wanting to play. But she also did not want Isobel to see her Christmas present ahead of time. She had decided to paint a small portrait of her friend—she remembered how pretty Isobel had looked at the dance in her soft pink dress, with her long plait coiled around her head, and was pleased with her efforts so far. As for her parents' gift, she had decided to paint a portrait of Jimbo for them in a natural pose, with his hands cupped under his chin and his big, brown eyes brimful of mischief. She had almost finished theirs, but had just placed Isobel's portrait on her easel to work on it further when Will burst in.

'Is Jimbo with you? Mum wants him ...'

His voice died away as he stared at Isobel's portrait.

'Whoa—that's amazing, Meg. Even I can see how good that is. Isobel looked so pretty in that pink dress ...'

His face reddened and he stopped dead, but already her mind was spinning at what he had said. … Isobel and *Will*? Could that ever happen? … What about the girl from Rosewood he had met in Sydney? Besides, Isobel and he were so different. Isobel had such a strong faith in God, whereas Will … well, from what he had said on the train, he was not quite sure yet what he believed.

'I can see Jimbo isn't here,' Will mumbled eventually, his face still red. 'I'll check in his room.'

But as he turned to go, she had an idea.

'I'm glad you like Isobel's portrait, Will. Tell you what—how about I paint a special landscape for you? I couldn't do it before Christmas, but we'll still be here on your birthday. You could take it back to Sydney with you and make me famous there.'

He grinned at her.

'That'd be great, Meg—thanks. Then I can brag to my friends about my artist sister. And if you paint me a scene down by the creek somewhere, it'll remind me of home too.'

Soon the business of Christmas engulfed the whole household. What with helping her mother with cooking and minding Jimbo, especially after Isobel began her Christmas break, she had little time to paint anything. But at least she had managed to finish the two portraits and find just the right frames for them among some of her mother's old ones.

It was good to see Aunty Betty and Uncle Harold again too when they arrived to spend Christmas with them.

'It's a shame we can't be here longer than two days, but Harold needs to get back to the practice—he couldn't find a locum at this time of year,' Aunty Betty told them over a cup of tea. 'But I also promised our family and friends that we'd have a bang-up New Year's Eve party at our place and I still have loads to organise for that. Too bad you won't be there to help me, Meg.'

Her mother jumped in then before she herself could respond.

'Well, it looks like she'll be with you again soon enough anyway. Thank you for having her stay with you, Betty and Harold. We're very grateful, aren't we, Margaret?'

Her mother sounded quite tense and abrupt—she never found it easy having guests and always worried so much about other people's opinions, especially Aunty Betty's. Then the constant rain leading up to Christmas had not helped her cope well either. Time and time again, she had complained about all the noise, as Caroline and Harriet and Jimbo tried to occupy themselves indoors. And there was no Isobel to come to the rescue either. Well, she herself could never measure up to Isobel, but she had tried her best to help her mother rather than dream about what she would paint next.

One thing she knew for sure—she was not going to end up like her mother, with little life of her own outside the home, except for the occasional local dance. Yet, according to Aunty Betty, her mother had been so different before she married and moved to Helidon to raise their family. Well, that was not what she planned to do with her own life—at least, not for a long time anyway.

She said goodbye to her aunt and uncle with mixed feelings two days later, as they caught what turned out to be the last train that made it through to Brisbane. Not long after, the overflowing creeks eroded the tracks in various spots, making them unsafe to use. The rain eased a little as New Year's Day approached, but the runoff from the range ensured the creeks would stay swollen for some time. She was grateful Will was still happy to brave the weather and drive them to the New Year's Eve party over at Iredale, although, in the end, they had to stay the night, with Will bunking down in the barn with his mates, while she shared a room with Nancy Waters and her cousin. It had been fun, but she wanted more from life than most of the girls at the party seemed to. Some were already going steady with local boys they had known for years who were destined to be farmers like their fathers. But there was a big world out there—and she was determined to explore more of it while she had the chance.

She was glad her parents seemed to like the portrait of Jimbo she had given them for Christmas. Her father had already hung it in the hallway near the front door and her mother had not objected.

'Everyone will see it here,' he commented, as he stood back to check if it was straight. 'I love it, Meg. And I'm so glad you signed it, just in case anyone doubts you painted it.'

Her heart swelled at the pride in his voice. She was sure Godfrey Rivers would not have considered the portrait her best work, but at least her father liked it. And Isobel seemed to like hers too, despite maintaining it was far too flattering.

'What a special gift—fancy taking the time to paint me, with everything else you've had to do. And you hid it from me too, you sly thing. I'll treasure it forever, Meg … thank you for making me look so good. Now when you're a famous artist, I can tell everyone I own one of your paintings.'

She had managed to do some work on Will's painting but was longing to get back down to the creek to finish it. She wanted to capture the scene in the best possible light, but each day, the rain kept falling as if it would never stop. Even Jimbo began to annoy her, with his constant demands for her attention. He loved playing with Will, but she was always his first choice. And, as heart-warming as that was, she wished at times he would let her get on with other things.

At last one morning, she woke to a few streaks of pale sunlight, although the sky was still overcast. She could hear the rest of the family having breakfast—she had slept in again.

In an instant, she had made her decision. There was an apple beside her bed from the previous night and a few lollies left over from Christmas—she could skip breakfast and take them with her down to the creek, along with everything she needed to work on her painting. If she hurried, no one would know she was gone, including Jimbo.

She scribbled a note to say where she had gone and left it on top of her half-made bed. Isobel was back and would keep Jimbo occupied, if her mother was busy. She wrapped her painting in a cloth and then in her raincoat, picked up her small easel and the other equipment she needed, then tiptoed down the hall and across the veranda. She hurried down the steps and almost ran to the gate, juggling everything in one hand while she reached for the latch. The gate creaked as she opened it and she held her breath. Surely no one would hear it above the noise at the breakfast table. She eased her way through, turned to secure the latch and heaved a sigh of relief. She had made it. And she knew Jimbo could not undo the latch, even if he had seen or heard her go.

She half jogged along the lane leading down to the creek, being careful to avoid the worst of the puddles. Her boots were already caked in mud—it would take hours for the soggy ground to dry out, even in full sunlight. Still, she was sure she would find somewhere dry enough to set up her easel.

She chose a higher spot than usual—it looked far too muddy around the rock where she often sat. The sun was still struggling to come out and she thought she heard thunder in the distance, but at least there was no rain. How wonderful it was to be alone again! She lightly sketched in a few more details on Will's painting—she wanted to capture the exact shape of the creek bend for him and the trees that overhung the water. They had played there many times as children, laughing and screaming as they climbed up high, then jumped into the creek. The scene did not look as inviting today, with all the moisture-laden branches drooping low and the brooding grey skies above, but later she could add more colour and light, just as she remembered it from sunnier days.

Her spirits rose as she worked on. She imagined the look on Will's face as she gave him the painting—it was his twenty-first birthday and her parents had planned a special celebration. Perhaps Richard would even be there—her parents had talked about inviting him to sing. As she painted, snippets from the song he had sung at the dance popped into her mind again. She could still hear his clear, tenor voice and see his stern face, as he had looked straight at her. But then she heard a different voice—a child's voice—calling her name.

'Meggie, Meggie—I find you!'

She turned and stared in disbelief. There was Jimbo, covered in mud and laughing as he ran towards her.

'Jimbo, how on *earth* did you get here? Did you follow me? But … how did you open the gate? I'm sure I closed the latch.'

'I look for you, Meggie—I look in your room and everywhere. Then I seed you a looooong way away down the lane. I got under the gate in the mud, Meggie—I digged a big hole and then I wiggled and wiggled like a big, wiggly worm.'

He held up his muddy arms, then touched the mud that caked his clothes. He was so proud of what he had done that she almost did not have the heart to scold him. But she was relieved to hear she had not left the gate open—she would be in even more trouble with her mother if she had. Instead, Jimbo must have burrowed into the soft mud beneath it and squirmed his way to freedom.

She stood with her hands on her hips, wondering what to do. To make matters worse, it had begun to drizzle and the sky was becoming blacker by the minute. Hoping her painting was dry enough, she wrapped it in the cloth again and stowed it in her bag, along with all her equipment. Then she looked for somewhere to shelter. Perhaps the old gumtree nearer the creek was the best place, although she knew the danger of sheltering under trees in a storm. Still, it was all she could think to do, apart from turning Jimbo around and marching him straight back home in the rain.

They crouched under the tree for some time, their backs to its trunk, but soon the rain began to lash down at an angle, penetrating the one dry spot there and drenching them both. She pulled Jimbo onto her lap and held him close, as she tried to keep him as dry as possible under her raincoat. Surely the storm could not last much longer?

After a while, she could not feel her legs where they rested on the wet ground with Jimbo's weight on them. She was worried about the creek too—it had broken its banks and was creeping towards them. They needed to head for higher ground, but her legs were so cold and stiff. If she tried to move, would she be able to carry Jimbo? Then, in the distance, she heard what sounded like a peal of thunder that kept rolling on and on.

'It's only thunder,' she told Jimbo, as he clung to her. 'You've heard thunder lots of times before.'

But the sound grew louder, until it was almost a dull roar. It seemed to come from behind them somewhere, so she peered around the tree, trying to make out what was happening.

At that exact moment, a foaming mass of brown water surged towards them, uprooting trees and consuming everything in its path.

She screamed and tried to hold Jimbo close, as the floodwaters wrenched them from their spot and tossed them this way and that. Locked together, they tumbled along, powerless against such a formidable force. At one stage, she managed to grab onto a thick branch with one hand, but it was soon wrenched from her grasp as she slammed against something hard and unyielding. She cried out in shock and pain. Then, before her body could recover from the jolt, Jimbo had slipped from her arms and disappeared into the swirling, murky waters.

# Chapter Four

Terror gripped her. She heard him call her name once, then once again. She tried to move towards the sound of his voice, but the torrent was too much for her.

'I'm coming—I'm coming, Jimbo. Hold on! Where are you?' she cried out, willing him to hear.

But there was no response.

'Jimbo, I'm here—I'm here, darling. … Jimbo!'

Over and over she called out, in between gasping for air and thrashing around for anything to hold onto. Then she felt something firmer beneath her feet and realised she must be on the flooded creek bank, although she had no idea where. She tried to steady herself, as she inched her way towards a fence post she could see half-submerged nearby. Once she reached it, she lay there for a few moments, her arms circling the post just as they had encircled Jimbo.

But Jimbo was gone—and it was all her fault.

She could not tell how long she held onto the post—it seemed like an eternity. But at one stage when the rain eased a little, she thought she heard voices somewhere in the distance.

'Meg … Meg! Are you here anywhere? *Meg!*'

She was sure it was Will calling her name—or was she imagining it? She listened again. Now the voices were closer.

'Meg, can you hear us? *Meg!*'

At last she managed to answer him, her voice shaking and croaky.

'I'm … I'm over here—I'm at the fence.'

They were almost there. First Will appeared, followed by Mr Davies and his two sons, with her father some distance further back.

'Meg, are you all right? Here, let me lift you up a bit—just relax now. We thought we'd never find you.'

Will's voice cracked, as he held her close. Then her father was there as well and helped carry her further back from the water.

'Oh Meg, you gave us all such a fright. And did James come down to the creek with you? We can't find him anywhere at home.'

She looked up into his anguished face and her heart failed her. She had to tell him—there was no time to waste.

'He followed me, Dad—I didn't know he would,' she gabbled, her teeth chattering. 'We were sheltering under a tree, but the flood came out of nowhere and swept us away. I tried to hold onto him, but I lost my grip. Please … just leave me here and go and look for him. We *have* to find him.'

Without another word to her, her father turned and went with the others to search further down the creek.

'Take care of her, Will,' he muttered, as he left.

She could tell by Will's face how torn he was.

'Go with them, Will—I'll be fine here,' she sobbed. 'We can't lose Jimbo.'

'Well … look, we brought a couple of blankets with us, Meg. Let me wrap this one around you at least and then lie down here where it's a bit drier. We'll be back as soon as we can. And we'll find Jimbo too, don't worry.'

She lay there shivering for what seemed like hours, but then must have dozed off, because she came to with a start when Will spoke her name and turned her over. She was so thankful to hear his voice again and to see the Davies boys with him too, but her father did not seem to be there—or Mr Davies.

'Did you find Jimbo, Will? And where's Dad?'

But Will seemed focussed on helping the others place a homemade stretcher on the ground nearby and did not answer her straight away. Her stomach tightened as he stayed silent and she could feel panic rising up inside her.

'I'm sure I could walk—you don't need to carry me. But … did you find Jimbo? Is he all right?'

'Don't worry, Meg—we'll carry you. You've had a bit of a battering and we need to get you home as soon as we can,' Will told her. 'And yes, we found Jimbo. But let's not talk now.'

She did her best to help them as they placed her on the stretcher and covered her with a blanket. A dreadful foreboding came over her as she looked up at Will. And then she knew. Even in the half light, she could see the despair on his face—and he could not seem to look at her directly either.

'Is Jimbo … did he drown, Will? Please tell me.'

'I'm so sorry, Meg. I … I know you would've done your very best to hold onto him. He was just a little bit further down the creek. Dad found him.'

'No … oh no, Will. Not our Jimbo!'

Huge, gulping sobs overwhelmed her. Try as she might, she could not stop them, as the men carried her home. Ahead, at the foot of their front steps, she saw another group of men gathered, with her father in the centre. He was holding a small bundle close to his chest and, as she watched, he began to climb the stairs like an old, old man. She saw her mother emerge from the hallway and run to meet him.

'Oh, thank God you found him, Tom. Oh, my poor James— where did you get to? You gave us all such a fright. James? What …? Oh no … not my baby—not my precious baby!'

She knew she would never, ever forget her mother's anguished cries as she cradled Jimbo's body. Hauling herself up, she went to comfort her, but Will held her back, then half carried her up the stairs and along to her bedroom.

'It wasn't your fault, Meg,' he told her, as he sat beside her on the bed and held her close. 'Even if you left the gate open, it was an accident.'

'I *didn't* leave it open,' she sobbed. 'Jimbo told me he burrowed underneath it—the ground was so soft and wet there. But I know I'm still to blame because I tried to sneak away without anyone knowing. If I'd have told Mum or Isobel I didn't want to take Jimbo with me, they would have kept him occupied.'

Will continued to hold her close, smoothing her wet hair away from her face and trying to comfort her, until Isobel arrived.

'I'll leave you to it,' she heard him whisper. 'I need to go and help Dad. And I'll tell them how Jimbo got out too, Meg.'

Somehow, she made it to Jimbo's funeral at the local Church of England. She could not remember much of it, except for the sight of Jimbo's little, white coffin at the front and the sound of her mother's sobbing. But she would never forget Isobel's loving support through it all—how she helped her dress on the day and gently brushed her hair, then walked with her into the church and later to the cemetery. She was grateful Aunty Betty had been able to put all her commitments aside too and come back to take charge of the meals, help look after Caroline and Harriet and run the household. Her mother sat staring into space most of the time, barely communicating with anyone—least of all her. The day after the funeral, when she had tried to sit with her and comfort her, she had been rebuffed in no uncertain terms.

'I don't need you here, Margaret. I'm glad you survived the whole ordeal, but my baby didn't. Nothing can change that. And nothing can change the fact that he got out of the yard and followed you that day. You *must* have left that gate open, Margaret, whether you think you did or not.'

At first, she could not believe her ears. Surely Will had told their parents what had happened?

'Perhaps Will didn't tell you, Mum, or you didn't hear what he said, but I did shut that gate. I was so shocked when Jimbo turned up. I asked him how he managed to open the gate and he told me he'd dug a big hole and wriggled under it instead. The ground was so soft there from the rain—and all his clothes were covered in mud, so I know he was telling the truth.'

'But are *you*, Margaret?' her mother responded, her voice cold. 'And the fact still remains that, had you acted in a responsible, adult way, you would have told us you wanted to go and paint by yourself and asked us to keep an eye on James, rather than sneak off like you did. Whatever you say, you're still to blame.'

She wanted to justify her actions. She wanted to explain how she had tried to avoid a scene with Jimbo and how she knew he would not give up until she had let him come with her. She wanted to say it was all a huge, tragic accident. And she wanted her mother to hold her close too, despite her own terrible grief—to comfort her and forgive her for whatever foolish or selfish decisions she had made. But she could see it was too soon for her mother to do anything like that or even to listen to what she said.

Instead, she retreated to her room, where Isobel found her and tried to comfort her.

'Oh Meggie, you poor thing. I wish I could take all your pain away, but I know I can't. Shush, dear—you'll make yourself ill crying this hard. Would you like a hot cup of tea? I'm here for you, Meggie. You're my best friend and I want to help you.'

She calmed a little, as Isobel continued to speak softly to her and bathe her face with a warm cloth, but it was as if a dam had burst inside her.

'Oh Isobel, I can't bear it. Our Jimbo—gone. Everyone thinks I left the gate open and that's how he managed to follow me to the creek. Isobel, I *didn't*. I was so careful not to because I wanted above all things to be by myself and finish painting Will's birthday present.'

'Meggie, don't take to heart anything your mum says right now. I know she doesn't mean it. When she can think straight again, she'll realise that herself. I know in my heart you didn't leave that gate open—and I know your father and Will believe that too. And if anyone thinks it was your fault, they'll soon find out it wasn't—we'll make sure of that. … You know, Meggie, when Dad died, my mother felt she was to blame. She thought she should have looked after him better or helped him more so he didn't end up so worn out, but it wasn't true. I think we all want to work out how and why things happen and who's to blame, but none of us can see the whole picture. Just give your mum some time and space. She'll come around.'

She heard the wisdom of Isobel's words but could not shake the guilt that weighed her down, almost crushing her.

'I hear what you're saying, Isobel, but it's still true what Mum said—that I'm to blame. I shouldn't have just left that note. I should have come and told Mum or you where I was going, even though Jimbo would have been so upset.'

'Hush, Meggie. I'm glad you did leave that note, dear—I found it when your mother sent me to wake you up for breakfast, so at least we knew where you were. But I didn't notice Jimbo leave the kitchen before everyone else—I was busy stacking up the dishes. I just assumed he was with your mother. And she assumed he was with me. So perhaps we're all a little to blame, if we want to blame anyone. Right now, we're so sad—but, while it might take a long time, we all have to learn to forgive, instead of looking for someone to blame. My father used to preach about that often and I believe he was right.'

'I'd like to think I could forgive others after a while at least, Isobel, but I'll never forgive myself—never. When we were sheltering under the tree near the creek, I felt at one stage we should head home, even in all the rain. But I decided to stay. Then the water came roaring down and it was too late to do anything. And I should have been able to hold onto him in all that water too, but I couldn't. Oh Isobel …'

She was overwhelmed with grief again, as she remembered those brown, swirling waters roaring towards them. She could hear Isobel speaking to her and feel her soothing touch on her forehead, but the words kept tumbling out.

'Oh, Isobel, I shouldn't have been down by the creek at all. It was just that I'd been cooped up here so long and I wanted some space to myself. I know Will wouldn't have minded if my painting wasn't ready in time for his birthday. But I'll never go down there again. And right now, I never want to paint again either. It would remind me too much of what happened to Jimbo—I'd feel so guilty.'

She was glad Isobel merely sat and listened and let her talk. Nothing anyone said seemed to make sense to her at the moment. But when her father came to check on her, at least one thing he told her penetrated her tired brain. She suspected Isobel had asked him to come, but, whether that was true or not, his words were balm to her spirit.

'Meg, please listen to me. I want you to know that what happened wasn't your fault. I thought it might have been at first, but I know you would never do anything to hurt our James. And all the men who found you down at the creek could tell you had done your best to save him. Whatever your mother might say right now, dear, *it wasn't your fault.*'

He held her close for a long time and she could feel his tears on her cheek as they mingled with her own.

'Thanks, Dad,' she whispered. 'But I'm still so very, very sorry it happened.'

'I know, dear. We all are. And it's good to cry, even though I'm no expert at it. We'll never forget our baby—it's going to take a very long time to get over losing James. But this will make us stronger, Meg. This will make us all stronger.'

She had never heard her father sound so sad. She knew he meant well, yet right now, she had trouble believing she could ever be strong enough to go on or that life would ever be meaningful for her again.

A few days later, she tried to talk about it all with Isobel, who always seemed to be hovering nearby like a shadow, ready to meet her every need.

'I don't know what to do, Isobel. Will's heading back to Sydney this week for his final year, but I feel as if time's somehow standing still for me right now. Aunty Betty wants me to come and live with them again so I can go back to my art classes and my piano lessons, but I know I couldn't do that—I just couldn't. Besides, I need to help Mum with Caroline and Harriet. After all, it's the least I can do to try to make up for what happened.'

Isobel's response was immediate and heartfelt.

'Please don't worry about Caroline and Harriet if you feel you'd like to go to Brisbane. I'll still be here. And I'll do my best to care for your mother and help out more with your sisters. Caroline's at an awkward age, but she'll settle down soon. And I'm sure your mother will get stronger as time goes by. … Meggie, I hope you don't mind my asking you again, but … well … have you thought about what God wants you to do with your life? You have so much to offer, with your art and everything.'

She knew she could be honest with Isobel, but as always, she did not want to hurt her.

'Oh Isobel, you know I love you and respect your faith in God. Sometimes I've even wished I *could* believe like you do. But I know God doesn't care about me—not after what happened to Jimbo. So why should I care about what God wants me to do? Jimbo was only three—he had his whole life ahead of him. Why did he have to die? It's all so unfair—don't tell me it's not.'

As soon as her outburst was over, she felt ashamed—and even more so when she noticed the tears in Isobel's eyes. She reached out to her to apologise but realised as soon as Isobel placed her other hand on top of hers that she was not offended.

'Meggie, I pray each day you'll come to see how kind and loving God is, even though life can seem so cruel and unfair. I can't explain it well—I wish I could—but I believe with all my heart that God *is* good, despite all the bad things that happen in this world. Jimbo's death was the most awful thing, but I'm praying God will give you the peace you need, even in the middle of all your pain. I know God can comfort us and bring good out of even the worst situation. And I pray you'll see that one day soon too, dear.'

She thought about Isobel's words late into the night, as she tossed and turned, unable to get to sleep. Whenever she closed her eyes, she could see the huge, brown torrent of water coming towards her again and feel herself gasping for air, as she struggled to hold onto Jimbo. But worse still, she kept reliving the moment when Jimbo's hand was jerked from her grasp and he disappeared. Yes, she desperately needed that peace Isobel talked about. Yet how could she believe that a God who would take away her baby brother could ease her pain and bring her any sort of comfort?

She thought about her future too and Isobel's comment about having so much to offer. But what if she could no longer bring herself to paint? She had no idea what else she could do, apart from helping her mother, and no energy even to think about it all. If she believed in God like Isobel did, maybe God would pull her out of the deep, dark pit she was in and show her what to do next. But that was impossible. She was on her own. And she could not seem to save herself in any way.

The following Monday, she decided to get out of the house for a while and walk to Mrs Watson's place to return some music. She did not feel up to playing anything, let alone the dance music Mrs Watson had lent her. Surely her old teacher would be sensitive enough not to ask too many questions. But just as she reached Mrs Watson's gate, the front door opened and Richard McPherson came down the steps towards her.

For a moment, she stood stunned. In the end, Richard was the first to speak.

'Well … good morning, Meg. I'm glad I've run into you like this. I've been meaning to come and see your family while I'm here with the Davies again for a few days. Er … did you walk here? Would you mind if I came along with you after you've seen Mrs Watson? I'm happy to wait—take your time. Or I can come back.'

Mrs Watson joined him then.

'Oh hello, my dear, it's good to see you. Please come in. Can you stay for a cup of tea? Perhaps you'll change your mind and have one too, Richard?'

She was unsure what to say—she did not feel like talking to anyone for long, least of all Richard. Still, it might seem rude not to accept Mrs Watson's invitation. She opened her mouth to respond, but Richard beat her to it again.

'I'm sure we'd have time for that, thank you. At least … does that suit you, Meg?'

She had felt herself withdraw and even flinch a little when he spoke on her behalf. Was that why he had checked with her after all? She hesitated again, but at that point, Mrs Watson took matters into her own hands.

'The kettle won't take long to boil—and we deserve a nice cuppa after all that playing and singing. We've been practising Richard's solos for the next dance in a few weeks. It's a good opportunity while he's with the Davies. But how are you, dear? And how is your mother? … Oh, I see you've brought back that dance music of mine. I'd forgotten about it. Thank you, Meg.'

She murmured some sort of response, grateful that, between Mrs Watson and Richard, there was little need to contribute much to the conversation. She sipped her tea and listened, as she tried to pull herself together. It seemed so long since she had last seen Richard— she felt she had aged years since that dance just before Christmas. Now, as she glanced at him across the table, she thought again how handsome and self-assured he was.

A moment later, he smiled at her and finished the last of his tea.

'Well, we'd better be off, Mrs Watson. Thanks for everything.'

'My pleasure. And Meg, when you feel you can play for any of the dances again, just let me know.'

Richard had already set off at a good pace, so she merely nodded and waved goodbye. But soon he slowed and matched his steps to hers, before stopping altogether and reaching for her hand.

'Meg, I heard about your little brother from the Davies, although I was in Brisbane when it happened. I'm so sorry. Roy and Tom Davies both told me how they helped with the search—and how you tried so hard to save James. It must have been such a terrible experience for you. I wanted to come and see you straight away, but thought it might be best to wait. Then the Davies invited me to stay until school starts next week, so I decided I'd call in on you all while I'm here.'

'That's kind of you,' she managed to say. 'My father had to return to work, but my mother isn't doing so well. That's partly why I'm still here, trying to help her with my sisters. Will's back in Sydney, getting ready for another year of study.'

She removed her hand and began to walk on. She hoped Richard would not ask her any questions about her own plans—she had no answers anyway. But her hope was in vain.

'And where does that leave you, Meg? Are you going back to Brisbane as you planned? I imagine you're keen to start your art classes again.'

'Oh *no*,' she responded with more vehemence than she had intended. 'Aunty Betty wants me to, but … well, I … I find I don't have the energy to paint at the moment—or play the piano. And I don't feel like going to parties or balls or anything like that right now either.'

'But … but you were so keen to continue your art course. Godfrey Rivers will be disappointed. I remember how one of your paintings was included alongside his at the Art Gallery.'

'I don't want to think about all that yet, Richard, to be honest. And I'm sure Godfrey Rivers would understand. My situation has changed a lot—I feel like a different person from the girl who had such fun in Brisbane.'

After a short pause, he changed the subject.

'Do you think your mother would like to see me? If not, I can come back another time. In fact, perhaps I should wait until your father's home. But would it help … would you like to go for a walk with me now and then while I'm here? That way you wouldn't be by yourself—and it'd get you out of the house too.'

It was good of him to offer, especially after how they had parted. At least with Richard she would not have to say much—he was never at a loss for things to talk about. Besides, it would be something different to do. And he would soon be heading back to Rosewood anyway.

'I … I think I'd like that, but I'm not much company right now,' she warned him.

'I won't expect you to entertain me, Meg. I'll meet you at your gate tomorrow morning around ten. Would that suit?'

The next few days, they wandered in any direction other than towards the creek. Sometimes, she had to hurry to catch up when Richard took his usual long strides. But on the whole, she found him kind and considerate and somehow a little more mellow than he had been. He told her about all sorts of things and, most days, she was happy to listen rather than talk. Then on Saturday, he asked again if he could see her parents.

'I'll make it brief, but I'd like to offer my personal condolences,' he told her.

It was true, as Isobel had predicted, that her mother was becoming a little stronger as the days passed, but she was still surprised to hear her inviting Richard for lunch, after chatting with him for a while.

'We're not entertaining yet, of course, but you're welcome to join us. Isobel's made some delicious-smelling soup and there's fresh bread as well. Perhaps then you'll have time to tell us what's happening in Brisbane these days.'

After lunch, while Richard talked with her parents on the veranda, she helped Isobel clear the dishes and organised Caroline and Harriet to wash and wipe them.

'Why can't *you* do it, Meg?' Harriet complained. 'Why do *we* always have to?'

'She wants to be with her old beau, silly,' Caroline sniggered.

'Didn't you notice how he kept looking at her at the table? I heard Mum and Dad talking about him ages ago when he wanted to marry her. Remember I told you about it?'

She felt her face redden, but before she could think what to say, Isobel cut in, her tone sharper than usual.

'That's enough, you two. Stop talking and get on with it all or your mother won't be happy when she finds you haven't done your jobs.'

She felt self-conscious after what Caroline had said about Richard, so took her time returning to the veranda. Richard smiled at her, but seemed a little distracted. And soon after, he announced it was time to leave.

'I meant to make a brief call and here I still am,' he joked. 'It's been good to chat, but I have to get back to the Davies. Would you like to walk part of the way with me, Meg?'

She decided not to look in her parents' direction as they set off—not after what Caroline had said. At first, Richard was silent, but when they reached the corner, he turned and took her hands.

'Meg, I've been thinking a lot about your situation—things have changed so much for you since I asked you to marry me last October. Back then, you weren't ready to give up your art classes and settle down. But the other day, you told me you don't plan to go on at college and that you feel like a different person since your brother's death. I know it might be too soon to ask you again, especially after the terrible tragedy you've gone through, but I'd like you to reconsider my offer of marriage. I took the liberty of sounding your parents out when you were in the kitchen and it seems they'd be delighted if you changed your mind. Your mother in particular thought it might be just what you need, after what's happened.'

She stared at him, unsure how to respond.

'I … I don't know what to say, Richard …' she began, but he interrupted her.

'Don't say anything now, Meg. Your father was adamant I need to give you time, so that's what I plan to do. I know it's hard for you to think things through yet and I don't want to rush you. On the other hand, I'm still keen to be married as soon as I can. I'm scheduled to sing at the next dance here in two weeks—would that give you time enough to decide? If you say yes, we could get engaged straight away and be married in the May school holidays. … Anyway, I hope you'll give it some thought. In the circumstances, my dear, it might be the best way forward for you—and for your family.'

Her mind was whirling. How convincing he sounded—and how easy it would be to fall in with his plans straight away. It would all be settled then. But something stopped her. Perhaps it would be better to think it over—she would need to be sure to give him the right answer this time around.

At last she managed to stumble through some sort of response.

'Thanks for giving me time to think about it, Richard. I never expected you to propose to me again, but … well … as you say, everything's changed. I hope I can say yes, but …'

'I hope you can too, Meg. I'd like that very much,' was all he said, as he pressed her hands and kissed her on the cheek.

That evening, she went to her room as soon as she could, her mind still in a whirl. There was so much to weigh up. Was marrying Richard indeed the best way forward for her, as he seemed to think? After all, when she had turned him down, she felt she had done the right thing. Should she stick to that decision, despite what had happened since? Oh, it was all so confusing.

She was glad when Isobel knocked and poked her head in.

'Just wanted to make sure you're all right before I head home, Meggie. Please don't let those sisters of yours upset you. They've been through a hard time too—and Caroline's at that age when nothing's right, whatever we do or say.'

'I know, but thanks for checking on me. Isobel … remember how I told you I felt time was standing still for me? You asked me then if I ever thought about what God wants me to do with my life—and I said I didn't care about that. But this week, ever since running into Richard again, I've begun to wonder if … well …

if it was somehow meant to be. Then this afternoon, he proposed to me again—he's given me two weeks to decide. I'm thinking of saying yes, but I feel so confused about it all. I said no to him last year partly because I wasn't ready to settle down, but things are so different now. I'm still not sure I love him, but I do like and admire him. Besides, I can't stay here forever. I know Mum resents me for what happened to Jimbo. I can feel it, even when she doesn't say anything, and I can see it in her eyes. I hope one day she'll forgive me for going down to the creek that day, but maybe she'd get over everything better if I wasn't around.'

It had all poured out in a rush, but she felt relieved to have told Isobel.

After a brief silence, Isobel came and hugged her.

'I'm so sorry I have to go right now—my brother's waiting outside. I'll pray and ask God to help you think it all through, then we can talk again on Monday. But Meggie … don't rush into anything just because you can't see any other way out, will you? You have your whole life ahead of you, after all.'

She found it hard to sleep that night, with so many conflicting thoughts in her head. She could see the advantages of getting engaged to Richard at this point. It would give her a fresh start and force her to focus on new and different things. Perhaps then she would not keep thinking of Jimbo and everything that had happened down at the creek or dream about it all at night. It would give her mother space to recover too—then maybe she would stop blaming her for Jimbo's death and their relationship would improve. On the other hand, she was only nineteen. And, as Isobel had said, she had her whole life ahead of her. She did like Richard, but … oh, it was all so *hard*.

The next morning, she woke with a fright when Harriet banged on her door and yelled to her.

'Meg, wake up! Mum wants to see you straight away. And she's not in a good mood, so you'd better hurry.'

She dragged herself out of bed, all the tangled thoughts that had kept her awake during the night returning in a flood. She peered at herself in the mirror, not liking what she saw. Perhaps a cup of tea would help clear her mind. She shuffled to the kitchen and reached for the teapot, but her mother stopped her.

'Margaret, leave that for now. I need to talk to you. I know Richard McPherson planned to propose to you again yesterday—he talked about it with us while you were in the kitchen. I'm assuming he did when you walked to the corner with him, so … what have you decided?'

She was wide awake now, shocked by her mother's blunt question.

'Well … yes, he did ask me to marry him, but I haven't decided anything yet. He gave me two weeks to think about it. He told me Dad suggested he should, so …'

But her mother interrupted her, impatience written all over her face.

'Yes, I know what your father said, Margaret, thank you. But what more is there to think about? Of *course* you should marry Richard. After all, didn't you turn him down last time because you weren't ready to give up college and all your fun in Brisbane? But now you tell us you don't want to go back to your art classes—and you couldn't go to parties and balls like you did last term anyway. I've appreciated your help here in this difficult time, Margaret, but … well … while I'll never get over losing James, I'll have to learn to manage everything myself again soon.'

It was the coldness in her mother's voice rather than her words that pierced her to the core. At first, she was too stunned to speak, but her mother went on.

'You could do much worse than Richard McPherson, Margaret. He's handsome and talented and well-read. And, being ten years older than you, he has the maturity and common-sense you lack. He'd help you grow up faster than you would here—and perhaps you'd be more willing to listen to his advice too. Besides, after all the grief you've caused us, I feel you should be prepared to fall in with whatever we suggest for your future.'

At that point, the anger and grief rising up inside her almost overwhelmed her, choking off any response she might have made. How could she defend herself anyway? She stared at her mother, seeing her own grief mirrored there, but also a hardness, a need to blame someone, a need to find some explanation for Jimbo's death. Now was not the time to argue with her. Yet what should she do? There was no one else to talk to. Isobel was not due back until the next morning and she remembered her father had planned to spend the day helping a friend on his farm.

For once, she was relieved when Caroline burst into the room, with Harriet close behind.

'The little beast, Mum—Harriet took my best hairclip without asking and now she's broken it!'

She seized the moment to escape. She went straight to her room, curled up in a ball on the bed and let the tears flow. Oh, how she wished she could walk down to the creek again and somehow paint all her pain away. But that was impossible. In fact, everything seemed impossible right now. How could she hope to make the right decision about Richard, given the way she was feeling? Perhaps her mother was right. Perhaps Richard's maturity and common-sense would balance out her childish behaviour. Perhaps she needed a husband like him who would help her make good decisions—or even make them for her. Yet part of her was shocked to find herself thinking along these lines. Where had the Meg gone who had been so strong and independent and carefree, who revelled in her art and in life in general?

She knew the answer to her own question. That Meg was gone forever—just like Jimbo.

She must have fallen into an exhausted sleep in the end, because when she woke, it was late afternoon. In a rush, she remembered the conversation with her mother and how her sisters' argument had provided her with a golden opportunity to disappear. Now she could hear Caroline and Harriet laughing together down the hall, as if nothing had happened between them.

She had missed lunch altogether, but did not feel hungry. And she did not want to have to talk to her sisters. She tried to read, but the words made no sense. With a sigh, she put her book down and stared at the ceiling, willing her thoughts to become clearer. What should she decide? Was marriage to Richard her best option right now?

She roused herself enough to head to the kitchen in time to help her mother with dinner, a task they achieved with as few words as possible. Dinnertime itself turned out to be quiet too, since her father was tired from his day out. Soon after, she headed for her room again, determined to try to relax. She glanced at her paints and brushes in a jumbled heap in the corner—she needed to sort through them, then put them out of sight so they would not keep reminding of the last time she had painted. Mechanically, she started putting old brushes and empty paint tubes in a pile to one side. And as she did, the tears began pouring down her cheeks. Yet she worked on, sorting everything and packing any good paints and brushes in a box she had found under her bed.

When she had finished, she pushed the box back into the far corner under the bed. Then she headed for the bathroom and soaked every bit of paint and dust from her body. Feeling exhausted, she returned to her room with a heavy heart and lay on her bed again, willing sleep to come.

# Chapter Five

She woke late the next morning, her mind still filled with vivid images from her troubled dreams. She could hear Isobel singing while she polished the floor in the hallway and poked her head out.

'Hello, Isobel. Did you have a good day yesterday?'

'It was lovely, thanks. It was Sam's birthday, so after church, we all helped make him a cake. At least, Nancy and Esther helped me. Johnno just got in the way and ate lots of icing before we could even put it on the cake. … Anyway, Meggie, are you all right? I knocked earlier, but there was no answer.'

'I slept in—I kept waking up last night and had lots of dreams. Isobel, can we talk tonight? I need to see Dad sometime, but I want to catch up with you as well.'

She spent most of the day in her room again, sorting through old clothes, something her mother had asked her to do several times. It was hard to find the energy to tackle such a task, but at least it kept her out of her mother's way. Yet as she worked, she often found herself staring into space as she tried to make sense of her tangled thoughts. One moment, she was convinced she should accept

Richard's proposal, while the next, she was overwhelmed with doubt and determined to do the exact opposite.

She was glad when her father came home—perhaps a few words with him would help. She managed to catch him by himself as he sat on the veranda before dinner, enjoying a cold drink, and came straight to the point.

'Dad, Richard proposed to me again yesterday—I know he told you he planned to. But … well … I feel so confused about it all. I'm glad you suggested he give me time to think it over because I seem to have trouble making any decisions right now, let alone a major one like this.'

'I understand, Meg—I'm finding it hard to make good decisions myself, even with our smallest project at work. That's why I insisted Richard let you have a couple of weeks at least to mull things over. It seems so long since he proposed to you the first time but, as I said then, we'd never want to push you into doing anything you don't want to. Whatever you decide, Meg, we'll be here for you.'

She hesitated, unsure how much to say.

'I don't think that's how Mum sees it, Dad. She seems to think it's my duty to marry Richard because of my part in what happened to Jimbo. She doesn't want me around—that's the truth of it.'

She could see the pain in her father's face as he reached for her hand.

'Meg, please don't take to heart anything your mum says at the moment. She's trying to come to terms with everything in her own way and is grieving the same as we are. … Tell you what, I have to go to Brisbane on Thursday for a few days. How about coming with me? That might give you a clearer perspective on things. And while you're there, perhaps you could see Godfrey Rivers in person and explain why you won't be back at college this term. Besides, I'd like to have some company during the trip.'

'Oh Dad, I don't know. I'd be useless at any of Aunty Betty's dinners or parties right now—and Mum might need my help here too.'

'I'm sure Betty wouldn't expect you to be involved in anything. And Mum will be fine. I'll talk to her about it, so don't worry.'

Isobel said much the same when they chatted later.

'Go to Brisbane, Meg. I'll be here to help your mum. And even if your aunt has some special dinner on, you can always excuse yourself. She'd understand.'

'Oh Isobel, I don't mean to drag you into helping me solve all my problems, but I'm so glad you're here. You're such a good listener. When Mum gets stronger, I hope she doesn't decide she can do without you, now that you don't have to mind Jimbo.'

'We'll cross that bridge when we come to it, as my mum often says—no point in worrying. And Meggie, I know you wanted to talk about Richard's proposal, but it might be better to wait until you come back from Brisbane, don't you think? In the meantime, I'll be praying you make the right decision yourself and not let anyone else influence you. But I wish Richard could have given you a bit longer to think it over.'

'I know I have to decide for myself in the end, Isobel, but talking about it with you helps. As for your prayers … well, you believe in them at least and I guess that's what matters. Richard told me the other day he plans to become more involved in his church this year. So, if I marry him, I guess I'd have to as well. I hope the Rosewood minister's better than old Reverend Spence—although I'm sure he tried his best at Jimbo's funeral.'

'It sounds as if you've already made your mind up, Meggie, if you're thinking about what things will be like in Rosewood. But it's less than a month since we lost Jimbo—and I remember how hard it was to make big decisions after my father died when we were still grieving so much. Mum and I *had* to, so we could get by as a family. But do you need to make your mind up so soon? If Richard loves you, he'll wait.'

'I'm … I'm not sure about that, Isobel.'

Even as the words left her mouth, she realised their meaning was unclear. She had meant she was unsure whether Richard would wait—but did her uncertainty run deeper than that? Was she also unsure whether Richard truly loved her? He *seemed* to—he had reached out to her at Mrs Watson's and given up his holiday time to be with her. Besides, hadn't he asked her to marry him, not once but twice? Oh, it was hard enough to figure out her own feelings, let alone Richard's too.

As Isobel got up to leave, she could see the concern on her face.

'Well, just know I'll still be here for you, Meggie, whatever you decide.'

'Don't worry about me, Isobel. I'll go to Brisbane, since you and Dad both want me to. And I'll think about everything you've said while I'm there. I hope Aunty Betty gives me lots of time to myself though and doesn't fuss or want to talk too much.'

The trip to Brisbane turned out to be pleasant and even soothing—she was glad her father did not want to talk much. But for the first few hours after arriving at her aunt's, she wondered if she had made a huge mistake in coming. While she unpacked, her aunt sat chatting on the bed and seemed intent on suggesting all sorts of low-key activities for the days ahead.

'I know you're not up to parties, dear, but we do have a tennis tournament and fundraising high tea here on Saturday afternoon. You're most welcome to join in. And on Sunday, there's your cousin's birthday celebration, so of course you're invited. And …'

She decided to interrupt at that point.

'I should be able to help out at the high tea, Aunty Betty. And Dad might be happy to go with you to Dorothy's birthday party. But if you don't mind, I'd like to go for a long walk on Sunday afternoon by myself. I need some space to think things through.'

She hoped her parents had not mentioned anything about Richard's latest proposal. She remembered her aunt's firm conviction that he was the one for her and, right now, she felt incapable of dealing with any discussion along those lines. She needed to make up her own mind, like Isobel had said. She almost had—but she wanted to be sure.

The next day, she steeled herself to pay a visit to college. Classes were not due to begin until the following week, so she was spared the ordeal of seeing her friends at least. But she felt she owed it to Godfrey Rivers to explain why she would not be back. After knocking on his door, she was almost relieved when there was no answer, but then he appeared along the corridor.

'Margaret, I'm delighted to see you. Does this mean you're extra keen to get started for the term?'

Her heart sank—it was going to be even more difficult than she had expected. But once she was seated in his office, she managed to pull herself together enough to explain.

'I won't be coming back at all this term, I'm afraid. I wish I could, but … well … my little brother died a few weeks ago, so I don't feel up to focussing on my art again yet.'

'Oh … I'm so sorry, my dear—this must be a very sad time for you all. But Margaret, while you may not feel like painting right now, please don't wait too long before you take it up again. Doing something we love can be so healing—and you have a great gift. Perhaps we'll see you back here next term?'

'I … I doubt it. You see, I might be getting married soon, so that will change everything for me.'

'Oh, in that case, I wish you well—although I'll be very sorry if you can't come back at all. … You know, whatever we do in life, our art will always be an intrinsic part of us and needs to be expressed somehow, so please don't put it aside altogether. … By the way, who's the lucky man? Is he one of my students?'

'No, no … he's a schoolteacher in Rosewood.'

As they stood, he shook hands with her and patted her on the shoulder.

'Remember, Margaret—keep painting.'

After leaving the college, she headed down to the Botanic Gardens—she had always loved painting there. The massive poincianas, now resplendent in their bright orange flowers, took her breath away and, somewhere deep inside, she felt the stirrings of a desire to try to paint them. They had not been in bloom when her class had last been there—it all felt so, so long ago. Maybe she would start painting again one day, as Godfrey Rivers had urged her to—but not yet.

She wandered on towards the river and stood staring at the ever-changing patterns on its surface. For a moment, memories of Jimbo and the flood threatened to overwhelm her and she closed her eyes. But then she took a deep breath and, for some reason, thought of Isobel and how she had promised to pray for her. She opened her eyes again. No, these wide, fast-flowing waters looked nothing like the brown, raging torrent in the creek back home. And as she gazed into their depths, the turmoil inside her began to lessen. Then a psalm Sister Mary Margaret had often quoted came to mind. What were the words again?

*The Lord is my shepherd; I shall not want.*

*He maketh me to lie down in green pastures: he leadeth me beside the still waters.*

*He restoreth my soul …*

The waters before her were not so still, but as she listened to their gentle murmur and noticed how the sun danced and sparkled on each ripple, she felt a little stronger. It was all so beautiful. Perhaps one day she would be able to paint this and other equally beautiful scenes again. And perhaps one day—although she could not imagine how—her own soul that had shattered into a million pieces when Jimbo slipped from her arms might somehow be restored too.

As she turned to walk up towards the main part of town, she felt a stirring inside and a firm resolve rise up in her. She did not want to live at home with her parents any longer—and she need not. Just as the river kept moving and changing as it journeyed towards the ocean, she too needed to move on with her life and be open to change. And in that instant, her decision was made. She did not know what marriage to Richard would be like. She could not guess what course their life together would take. But she would do her best to make it work and, in the process, somehow try to recover from Jimbo's death.

She strolled down Queen Street, exploring several clothes shops and draperies along the way, until she arrived at the new Finney Isles store. She found the bridal section and examined some of the beautiful fabrics on display, although it seemed so strange to imagine herself as a bride. She had not progressed much with her sewing, but Aunty Betty would be in her element, helping her create a special wedding outfit.

She cringed at telling everyone her decision, but it turned out to be easier than she had imagined. Something in her face that evening must have alerted her father, because as they all headed to the veranda for a pre-dinner drink, he was soon there beside her.

'I think you've decided already, haven't you, Meg?' he whispered in her ear.

She nodded and he grasped her hand, holding it tight.

'Well done, dear—I'm proud of you.'

It was inevitable her sharp-eyed aunt would not miss such an exchange.

'What's happened, Meg? Tell us all about it.'

She was left with no option and was soon smothered in warm hugs and kisses.

'I'll refrain from saying "I told you so"—but I was right, wasn't I?' her aunt gloated, pleased beyond measure. 'Now while you're here, perhaps we could start planning your wedding outfit. Or do you think Pearl would be offended, Tom? She used to design such wonderful dresses herself—perhaps it'd take her mind off everything else if I left it to her.'

'I think she'd be relieved, to be honest, Betty. She's isn't her old self quite yet.'

She was glad her father did not elaborate any further and also glad she would not have to rely on her mother for her wedding outfit. Already, she dreaded the thought of having to consult her about the reception and so many other matters. But Aunty Betty was different—she would much prefer to arrange things with her.

Her aunt could not seem to contain her excitement after that.

'Then please tell her I'd be happy to take care of the wedding dress and the bridesmaids' outfits—and organise the reception as well, if she'd like. We could hold it here, just as we did for our Bessie. Perhaps we could even have the ceremony in St John's Cathedral. That would be fitting, when you think of all the sandstone they're using from your quarries, Tom.'

'Well, it *would*—except I can't see the first stage being finished until later in the year. And I expect Richard hopes to be married well before then. But Betty, Richard will no doubt want a say in the venue too. After all, it's his wedding as much as Meg's.'

She suspected not even that thought would deter Aunty Betty and she was right. Her aunt talked of nothing else throughout dinner until they pleaded with her to stop. Even then, the only way she could manage to silence her was to promise to look at some dress patterns after dinner and to spend Monday shopping for material.

In the end, they spent a pleasant evening together, poring over different designs, but she was glad when Aunty Betty began yawning at last.

'Better leave it there, dear. I have a big day ahead tomorrow, with the high tea and all. But I'm so pleased for you, Meg. This has come just at the right time when you need something good to look forward to that might help you get over James's death.'

She was sure she would never get over Jimbo's death, however wonderful her wedding was, but she kept that to herself. Aunty Betty was only trying to be helpful. Yet she hoped she could curb at least some of her aunt's enthusiasm in the coming days. She had tried to tell her she did not want a big, fancy wedding with all the trimmings—and she was sure Richard would not either.

The next day, she helped at the high tea, glad to have something practical to do while her mind skipped here and there, thinking about what lay ahead. But on Sunday, she stuck to her plan of going for a long walk rather than to her cousin's party. She took a tram to

Newstead again and strolled down to the river. It was good to be alone and relax, now that she had made her decision, yet she felt sad too. She remembered how carefree she had been the day she had first gone there with Richard and how her high spirits had shocked him. But she was no longer that same joyous, carefree person. Somehow in losing Jimbo, the old Meg who loved to paint and play and have fun had slipped away too and disappeared. Instead, she found herself hurtling towards a very different future about which she seemed to have little choice.

Yet that was not quite true—she had chosen to marry Richard of her own free will, after all. She had already written a brief note to him, telling him her decision, and planned to post it the following day. Then there would be no going back. *Dear Richard,* she had begun, *I thought I should write to you from here in Brisbane as soon as I could to let you know I've decided to say yes to your proposal. I feel honoured that you asked me not once but twice. And I've been touched by your kindness and thoughtfulness towards me in recent days in particular. I admire and respect you—and I'll do my best to make you a good wife, although I know I have a lot to learn. While I'm here, Aunty Betty will help me organise my wedding dress, but I'll of course wait until after I see you before arranging anything else. I look forward to seeing you again back in Helidon. Kind regards, Meg.*

The shopping trip on Monday turned out to be a pleasant and productive time all round. At first, she wondered if her father had cautioned her aunt about respecting her wishes, but, as they made their way into town together, she discovered Aunty Betty had made up her own mind on the matter.

'After thinking more about it, my dear, I tend to agree with you about keeping things simple. I can see it'd be quite inappropriate for you to have a big wedding with all the usual frills and finery. I'm sure your mother wouldn't want that either. I had planned to take you to Mrs Walker's rooms in Adelaide Street, upstairs from where her Ladies' Emporium used to be. Mrs Walker's made so many gorgeous wedding outfits over the years, including both our girls' dresses. But now I agree a simple, elegant design similar to the one you pointed out last night would be much better, given your circumstances. I'm sure I could manage something like that for you, if your mother doesn't mind.'

'I … I think Dad's right that she isn't up to any big task like that quite yet—and I doubt she'd want to anyway. Since Jimbo died, we seem to clash even more than we used to, so let's go ahead and buy what we need today.'

'I don't want to cause any trouble with your mother, that's all— and of course I don't want to make things harder for you either, dear. As I told you a while back, Pearl and I were great friends when we were young, but we were also something of rivals at times when it came to fashion—and to beaus! Then she met our Tom, your father, and that was that. Anyway, let's not talk about such things now, Meg. This is your day—and I hope you'll be happy with everything.'

To her surprise and relief, she was. She loved the beautiful, soft, cream silk voile they found for the wedding dress itself in the second shop they visited. And in the third shop, they bought some pretty lace trimming for the bodice and hemline and tiny pearl decorations as well.

'The material's so wonderful and soft, Meg—I'll make the skirt quite full and shape the back into a small train for you,' her aunt told her as they enjoyed lunch together, her cheeks pink with excitement. 'And I love the design you chose, with that high neck and long, full sleeves—very elegant. I can add those little pearls we bought to the neck and cuffs and also around the edge of the tulle we found for your veil, if you like. Now … what about your bridesmaids?'

Her aunt's enthusiasm and joy in helping her with everything warmed her heart, but she knew she could not go any further without consulting Richard—or her mother.

'Well, I'll need to get back to you about that, Aunty Betty, after Richard and I have talked—although I've already decided I want Isobel as my bridesmaid. She always looks lovely in pink, but I'll come back as soon as I can and we'll shop again.'

On the way home to Helidon later that week, her father was more silent than usual. She assumed he was thinking about some business matter, but after a while, he turned and took her hand.

'Meg … are you sure about this decision you've made? I trust Richard McPherson, otherwise I wouldn't let you marry him. You know that, don't you? And I guess you realise no marriage is ever perfect. Your mother and I have had our challenging times, but we survived. And you will too, whatever happens in the years ahead. I wish … well, I wish things hadn't turned out as they have for you, my dear. I wish you could have gone on with your art classes as planned and seen something of the world. But promise me this, Meg—please take up your painting again soon. You need to, you know, for your own sake as well as ours, because you have a wonderful gift.'

She was touched beyond measure at his words.

'Godfrey Rivers said something like that to me too, Dad,' she whispered through her tears. 'In the next little while, I know I'll be busy learning how to run a household, but maybe later I'll try. That's all I can promise right now.'

It was hard to keep her spirits up, after telling her mother her decision. She had not expected any warm hugs from her like the ones she had received from her aunt, but her abrupt response cut her to the heart.

'Oh, so you're going to marry Richard after all. Well, that's a relief. At least you've had the sense to make the right decision this time around, Margaret. But I hope you don't want a big wedding— I'm afraid I don't feel up to planning anything like that at all.'

'Don't worry, Mum. I'm going to tell Richard I'd prefer a small celebration—and Aunty Betty has offered to help organise everything, if you'd like her to. We've already bought the material for my dress. I've chosen a simple style and Aunty Betty's promised to make it for me.'

Her mother sniffed.

'Well, you both could have consulted me first. I'm sure Betty could have altered my own wedding dress to fit you, but it sounds as if it's too late for that now. I presume Caroline and Harriet will be flower-girls, so she'll need to sort out their dresses as well. Then there's the reception to organise—oh dear, I can't bear to think about it all. When's this wedding supposed to be?'

For a moment, she considered walking out of the room, but knew that would achieve nothing.

'Richard mentioned the May school holidays when he was here. I've written to him and I should hear from him soon. Then I'm sure he'll come up again quickly to sort everything out.'

Richard's letter arrived a few days later, brief and to the point. *Thank you for your note, Meg, telling me your decision. I'm delighted, my dear. I felt we suited from the beginning and I'm looking forward to becoming husband and wife soon. I plan to come up and stay with the Davies again next weekend, so we should have time to arrange everything then. I'll bring the engagement ring with me—I hope it's the right size and that you like it. Regards, Richard.*

She told Isobel about his letter as they sat on the front steps in the cool that evening.

'I … I guess I'd like to have been with him when he chose the ring, but he wants to have the wedding in May, so we don't have lots of time. … Oh, Isobel, I hope I've made the right decision. Everything's happening so fast.'

Isobel squeezed her hand.

'I think you were very brave to make such a big decision by yourself in Brisbane, Meggie, but I'm going to miss you so much.'

'I don't know who Richard has in mind for best man yet, but I want you to be my bridesmaid, Isobel—Aunty Betty's offered to make your dress. Caroline and Harriet will be flower-girls as well and I'm sure she'll make theirs too. I'd like to include Will somehow, but we'll see what Richard thinks.'

Richard exuded confidence when he bounded up their front steps on Friday evening. She greeted him with mixed feelings—it still seemed surreal that she had agreed to marry him. But when he took her hand, drawing her close and kissing her lightly as he turned to her parents, she felt a little more reassured.

'Thank you to both of you for allowing me to marry Meg—I'm a very lucky man. I'll look after her well. But perhaps you'd all like to see the engagement ring straight away?'

She watched with trepidation as Richard pulled a small box from his pocket and flipped the lid open. Inside was a gold ring with three diamonds in a simple but elegant setting. Her hand was shaking as he slipped it on her finger and she let out a sigh of relief when it fitted easily.

'It was my mother's ring,' he explained. 'Charlotte wanted something different for hers and Mary isn't one for much jewellery, so we thought it might suit you, Meg. I hope you like it.'

'It's beautiful—and it's special that it belonged to your mother. Thank you, Richard.'

He kissed her hand then and her father stepped forward to give her a hug.

'Now it seems a bit more real, doesn't it, Meg? Imagine having an almost married daughter!'

'We're eager to know all your plans, of course,' her mother added. 'I understand you want to be married in the school holidays, but what about the wedding and the reception?'

'Well … I'd like the wedding to be at St Luke's in Rosewood— unless you prefer your own church here. I know our minister, John Trimble, quite well now. As for the reception, we could have it in our church hall or even the grounds outside. I'm sure the Women's Guild would help cater for it—my sister Mary's involved in that. But you'd know a lot more about such things than I do, Mrs Porter. What do you think?'

Before her mother could respond, she decided to speak up herself.

'I don't want a big wedding, Richard—just immediate family members and a few close friends would be lovely. We're not … we're not up to big celebrations yet, as you would understand.'

'Yes, I appreciate that. But I do have several teaching colleagues and friends from the choir who would expect to be there, as well as family, of course. Perhaps if we had an afternoon tea, we could invite more people.'

At that point, her mother intervened.

'I think an afternoon tea would be excellent, Richard. Of course, I'm not up to organising anything at the moment, but Tom's sister, Betty, has already offered to help out. She's an expert at such things.'

'Sounds as if everything's going to sort out then,' her father added in a relieved tone. 'But perhaps we'd better leave you two alone now—you must have so much to talk about.'

She was glad Richard did not speak straight away—everything seemed to be moving so fast. She breathed in, trying to still the whirling in her brain, and gazed down at her engagement ring. It felt so foreign on her finger and was a little too big, but she was thankful it was the style of ring she herself would have chosen. Then she straightened her shoulders and took another deep breath. What did it matter how or where they celebrated their wedding, when all was said and done? The important thing was that they would be married and she could move on with her life—away from her mother and home, where so many memories of Jimbo surrounded her.

She tried to listen then, as Richard told her what he had planned.

'I've already found a small cottage for us not far from school—it belongs to someone at church and the rent's reasonable. I can move our things in during the last week of term, which will be convenient. I thought we could be married on the first Saturday of the school holidays, if that suits you, Meg, then honeymoon at Sandgate. We can get there by train without any trouble and I know a nice hotel where we can stay. Then afterwards, we could spend a couple of days with your aunt or my sister in Brisbane before heading back to Rosewood. What do you think?'

In some ways, she was glad he had already arranged so much, but it nettled her too. Still, at least he had asked her opinion about the wedding date and the honeymoon. She would have liked to go somewhere a little more exciting, perhaps even down to the Blue

Mountains, but the May holidays were only short and it was a long way to travel. And she would have liked some say in where they would live, but at least it was settled now. Besides, she had plenty other things on her mind, including the reception and dresses for Isobel and Caroline and Harriet. No, she would agree with his suggestions and not make a fuss. It was not worth it.

She saw then how Richard was looking at her quizzically, as he waited for an answer.

'I'm sorry, Richard—I was dreaming. Yes, that wedding date suits me—and Sandgate should work out fine for our honeymoon. And let's get married in your church, as you suggested. Our minister's quite old and we don't go to church here often. But … do you think I could come and stay with your sister sometime and meet your minister? We must need to sign papers soon for the wedding anyway. Perhaps I could see our cottage then too.'

'I'm sure that can be arranged, Meg. As for the wedding itself, I'd like to have my sister's husband Jim for my best man, as I was best man for him. Then I planned to ask a couple of other friends from the choir to be groomsmen …'

But she knew she had to stand her ground when it came to the wedding party at least.

'Let's not worry about groomsmen, Richard. I don't want a big wedding party—and I've already asked our house-help Isobel to be my bridesmaid. Caroline and Harriet will be flower-girls too, but they won't need any partners.'

'Oh … well, I suppose I don't *have* to have groomsmen. I would have thought … but never mind. Anyway, I plan to have some of the choir perform a beautiful Bach chorale while we sign the register, so I guess my friends can still be involved in the service that way. As for the actual wedding and the reception, I'll try to keep the numbers down, but as I said, I do have quite a few people who'll expect invitations.'

He seemed a little disgruntled, but she remained resolute. She was prepared to fall in with his other plans, but she wanted to have her way in some things at least.

The weeks slipped by at an almost frightening pace after that, with trips to Rosewood to meet with Richard's minister and several to Brisbane for dress fittings and more shopping. She was thankful the Women's Guild agreed to cater for their reception, although she had not appreciated Mary's comments when told of Aunty Betty's offer of help.

'Our women are quite capable of providing a wonderful afternoon tea, thank you,' she had said in clipped tones. 'Your aunt might think she knows what's required at social functions in Brisbane, but it's different here. However, I suppose she can help out with the table decorations.'

She was thankful too when Aunty Betty agreed to come to Helidon for a few days to add the final touches to their dresses and also to stay with her in Rosewood the night before the wedding, along with Isobel and Caroline and Harriet.

'You're such a lifesaver, Aunty Betty,' she told her. 'I hardly know if I'm coming or going. Mum's not much help right now—and she definitely wants to be somewhere quieter in Rosewood than with all of us girls. She and Dad are planning to stay at the Royal George, along with Uncle Harold and Will.'

'It's probably for the best, Meg—don't be too hard on her,' her aunt said, after a slight pause. 'She used to love all sorts of social events, but living in Helidon for so long and being busy with the family has changed that. Then of course losing James has been so hard for her …'

'I know, Aunty Betty. It's just that … well, I do feel a little let down, but it doesn't matter. Anyway, I'm grateful for everyone's help, especially yours.'

It was a squash in their cottage on the eve of her wedding, but her aunt's cheery chatter, combined with Isobel's warm support, helped calm her nerves. And when her father knocked on the door the following day to escort her the short distance to the church, she was touched to see tears in his eyes.

'Oh Meg, you look so beautiful—all I can say is, Richard's a very lucky man.'

She gripped his arm tight as they entered the church behind Isobel, who looked so lovely herself, in her soft pink dress and matching hat trimmed with tiny roses. Richard had turned to face them—how tall and distinguished and handsome he looked in his dark suit! Surely *she* was the lucky one? And surely she had made the right choice?

The church seemed crowded and she wavered, remembering the crowd at Jimbo's funeral in their church back home and his little white coffin at the end of the aisle. But then she felt her father's reassuring hand on hers and took a deep breath to steady herself. Isobel had now joined Caroline and Harriet at the front and had turned to smile at her, which gave her strength. And for a brief instant, she noticed the big, brass altar cross gleaming in the light of the nearby candles, which somehow comforted her too.

She lifted her chin then and stepped out. Yes, she would be strong—this day and throughout the days ahead. She would do her best to love and care for Richard. And she hoped with all her heart he would love and care for her too.

The reception passed in a blur. She smiled and nodded, as Richard held her hand and proudly introduced her to his various teaching colleagues and friends from the choir. And she did her best to thank the Women's Guild who had done a wonderful job with the afternoon tea, as Mary had asserted they would. But she was relieved when it was all over and the final goodbyes had been said. Aunty Betty had cried and her father had wiped his eyes as well. But her mother had given only the briefest of smiles and had said little.

Then at last they were in their own little home, just the two of them. They would head to Brisbane the following day, Richard had decided, and then travel on to Sandgate. As she curled up in his arms that night, a comforting warmth flooded over her. She was safe. Richard would look after her and care for her, just as her father had done. She was a married woman now—her new life had begun.

As it turned out, Richard had indeed made the right choice for their honeymoon. It was good to be able to go for walks along the beach together, despite the cooler winter weather, and to get to know each other in a more relaxed way. But soon it was all over. Back in Rosewood, Richard was busy most nights, reading or writing or preparing lessons for the following day. His weekends were full too, with choir practice in Ipswich each Saturday, often followed by a meeting in the evening. And of course on Sundays, there was church.

She did not mind—these were things Richard had been involved in long before they married, after all. And there was so much for her to do at home anyway. Now she wished she had spent more time helping her mother and Isobel cook, just as her father had predicted. But she tried her best and Richard assured her she was improving each week. She began some sewing projects as well, using an old treadle machine Richard's sister had given them.

'I trust you know how to use it, Meg,' Mary had commented in a patronising tone. 'I could show you, but I don't have a lot of time.'

She had wanted to make an angry retort but stayed silent, for Richard's sake. Still, at least this had spurred her on to produce several household items and even some outfits for herself, using different techniques Aunty Betty had shown her. Yet as the months passed, she began to feel a little restless. Richard tried to encourage her to join the choir, but with no success.

'They wouldn't want me, Richard. I can play the piano, but I'm hopeless at staying in tune. That's why you haven't heard me singing around the house. No, I think I'll leave that to you.'

'Well, I certainly can't draw or paint like you can, Meg—I'm sure you've noticed my efforts with my teaching materials. You could help me prepare them sometimes, if you like. My eyes get so strained with it all, so I think I'll need to go to Brisbane again soon to see my doctor.'

She cringed at the thought of helping him, however. She still could not bring herself to paint and, although she did not plan to point it out to him, she knew how definite he could be about what he wanted.

'I know your eyes have been troubling you more, but … well, it's just that I still can't quite bring myself to paint or even draw much yet. It makes me feel sad whenever I try to—and I can't seem to think of any creative ideas anyway. Sometimes I add a frill or a fancy stitch here and there when I'm sewing though. And I try to be a bit more artistic these days when I ice my cakes.'

She was glad when the August school holidays arrived so they could head to Brisbane. It was good to be with Aunty Betty again, but she found it tiring, shopping all day with her or helping her organise a social event. So when Richard went to see his doctor about his eyes, she decided to have a check-up at her uncle's practice.

She was asleep when Richard arrived home late that evening, after catching up with friends in town. As a result, his announcement at the breakfast table the next morning surprised her as much as it did her aunt and uncle.

'I've got some news for you all—I'm giving up teaching. I've been thinking about that anyway, but yesterday, the doctor told me all the lesson preparation I do at nights isn't helping my eyes. I plan to resign as soon as we get back and start looking for some other sort of work here in Brisbane. Then I'll be near my doctor and you'll have your aunt close by too, Meg. I've always wanted to run my own business—perhaps a grocery store or the like. I think I'll start looking around today to see what's available.'

She tried to hide her surprise and hurt, but was unsure if she had succeeded. Why had he not told her before this what he had been thinking? Did he not trust her? Well, better not to say anything, with her aunt and uncle present. Besides, he seemed so excited at the prospect of doing something new. Already in their marriage, she had seen how much he enjoyed tackling fresh, interesting challenges. And she wanted him to be happy, whatever work he decided to do.

But she also had news of her own that she hoped would make him even happier.

'Well, Richard, I have some news too—and I might as well share it with you all right now. We're going to have a baby!'

# Chapter Six

At first, Richard seemed unsure how to respond, but soon his delight was obvious.

'Oh Meg—oh my dear, that's the best news—that's wonderful!' he told her, as he held her close.

He seemed unable to focus on his plans for the day ahead for some time after that, but eventually he left her in her aunt's care while he went to discover what businesses were on the market. Her own spirits had lifted too, despite her tiredness, and she was happy to fall in with her aunt's plans for a morning of shopping for nursery items, followed by lunch at Rowe's Café.

'My only concern is that I've heard about the baby before your mother has,' her aunt commented, as she finished her breakfast. 'Should we wait until you tell her? She might even like to go with you herself, if she feels well enough.'

'I … I don't think so. I'm sure she wouldn't want to come to Brisbane at the moment. Anyway, she doesn't need to know I told you first. But if she does find out, I could always say I was so excited, it burst out of me. … Besides, this might be my only chance to shop for a while, if Richard gives up teaching.'

'I hope he's making the right decision. He'll have another mouth to feed soon—and businesses can be risky.'

She hoped he was too. But when she tried to discuss it with him that evening, she saw he was not about to change his mind.

'As far as I'm concerned, Meg, we don't have a choice. Teaching isn't good for my eyes and that's that. Besides, I need to do something different—it's not always much fun being cooped up in a classroom all day.'

'But I thought … oh, never mind. … Did you find any businesses you might be interested in today?'

'I saw a shop that looks promising. It's a corner store in Red Hill that stocks fruit and vegetables, as well as groceries—and it also offers light refreshments like tea and scones. It's done well, but the owners are getting too old. It's a bit above my price range though, so I'm wondering if your father might help us out. I'll ask him when we go to Helidon next week.'

She had been surprised Richard had enough savings even to contemplate buying a business. They rarely talked about financial matters, partly because she had discovered Richard wanted it that way and partly because she had little interest in such things. But she hated the idea of borrowing from her parents.

He seemed to have read her mind, because he reached for her hand then and tried to reassure her.

'Don't worry, Meg. Remember, I worked for quite a few years before I ever took up teaching. And I never liked wasting money, so I've saved up a tidy amount. But you don't need to know about such things, my dear. Leave it to me—your father and I will sort it out.'

She felt sure they would too, as Richard held her close. She knew she could trust him, just as she trusted her father.

Yet it was with mixed feelings that she climbed the front steps of her old home a few days later, along with Richard. She was sure her father would be delighted with the news of his first grandchild—but how would her mother react?

They had barely reached the top step when the front door was flung open and her two sisters raced out. Then she saw Isobel standing next to her mother—and somehow the sight of her friend enabled her to put her concerns aside and greet them all with a smile and a hug.

They told everyone about the baby over dinner that evening, including Will, home again for the holidays. Caroline and Harriet squealed and talked over each other in their excitement, until her mother put her hands over her ears. Will grinned broadly, then strode around the table to give her a huge bear hug and shake Richard's hand.

'Congratulations to you both. … "Uncle Will", eh? I like the sound of that.'

A moment later, she was surprised to see both her parents had tears in their eyes.

'That's the best news I've heard in a long time—I'm so delighted for you. Imagine being grandparents!' her father said, as he blew his nose and tried to regain his composure.

Her mother seemed beyond speaking, as she dabbed her eyes. Yet the rest of the family made up for her silence, all wanting to know when the baby was due and whether they had picked out any names. But after dinner, when Richard went to talk to her father, her mother seized the moment to make her feelings clear.

'I can't say your news was a surprise, as I was sure Richard would want a family as soon as possible. I suppose you can have James's old cot—I'll talk to your father about it. I still have some of his baby clothes too, but I don't think I could bring myself to part with them yet. Anyway, you might have a girl. You'll have to watch your dreamy ways when the baby arrives though, Margaret. I hope what happened with James has taught you something at least.'

It was as if she had been punched in the stomach. At first, she could not trust herself to speak, but then the words tumbled out.

'There's not a day goes past that I don't think of Jimbo and everything that happened. I should have told you where I was going—and I'm so sorry he followed me down to the creek. But I did close that gate, Mum. You *have* to believe me! And I tried my best to hold onto him in the water too. I know we'll never forget what happened, but I hope one day you'll forgive me, Mum. It must be so awful to lose a child—but I loved Jimbo so much too.'

Even through her tears, she could see there was no softening in her mother's face. A terrible heaviness descended on her—how could she ever make things right between them? She could feel the tension in her mother as she sat opposite and, despite her own anguish, she almost went to put her arm around her. But at that moment, Caroline and Harriet came back from cleaning up in the kitchen.

'Mum, Caroline reckons the baby's going to be a girl because both Dad and you only had sisters. But that doesn't make any difference, does it? It could be a boy, couldn't it?' Harriet blurted out, heedless of the atmosphere in the room.

'Of course it could be a boy, silly,' Caroline responded in her most contemptuous voice. 'I just meant it's more likely to be a girl. I know because we learnt about it at school. Sister Eileen said …'

But her mother cut in then.

'That's enough, both of you. Have you finished helping Isobel? If you have, you can get ready for bed, Harriet—and you can find William for me, Caroline. Tell him I'd like to see him straight away.'

She knew there would be no further serious conversation with her mother that evening—and perhaps throughout their stay. Will arrived soon after and winked at her, as their mother tried to talk to him about what clothes he needed before heading back to university.

'I'm not a child, Mum,' he responded gently enough. 'I can buy what I need in Sydney. Besides, I'm sure Meg will keep you busy, getting things together for the baby. I bet you wish you'd taken more notice of Mum and Aunty Betty now, Meg, with all that sewing and knitting stuff they tried to teach you.'

She was sure Will noticed her reddened eyes, but she tried to respond in the same light manner.

'As it happens, my dear brother, I don't mind sewing—and I love fancywork. I might even tackle some knitting soon too for the baby.'

He ruffled her hair then to tease her, just as he had when they were growing up.

'Well, don't forget your painting either, Meg. You haven't given me that picture you promised me for my twenty-first yet.'

She saw his stricken look as soon as the words left his mouth and her heart went out to him. How could she ever forget what had happened to his painting and why they had not celebrated his twenty-first birthday at all? Yet she could not bring herself to pick up a paintbrush, even to keep her promise to him. She sighed—she needed to give him some sort of explanation.

'I … well, the truth is, Will, I don't paint these days. It … it's just hard for me because of what happened. If I ever do though, the first picture I paint will be yours. But I still enjoy being creative in other ways around the house. I've even discovered icing a cake can be a bit like painting at times, if I use my imagination.'

She had tried to joke about it, but when her voice shook a little, Will gave her shoulder a quick squeeze.

'You've always been a fast learner, Meg. Richard's a lucky man, I reckon. And I'm sure you'll make a great mum too.'

She was glad when Richard joined them soon after, along with her father. They both seemed happy enough, but she wished she knew what had transpired between them. Will suggested a game of cards, but she decided to leave the four of them to it.

'You can play in pairs then. Anyway, I want to talk to Isobel. I'll see if she needs help in the kitchen.'

But Isobel would not hear of it and encouraged her to go and rest.

'I'll come and find you, Meg, as soon as Harriet's in bed. We have so much to catch up on.'

It was wonderful to be chatting again in her old room, but she soon realised that, while her life had changed so much since leaving home, Isobel's had not. Isobel still had a soft spot for Will, she was sure—she had intercepted several glances between them earlier in the evening and seen Isobel blush when Will smiled at her. Yet she knew nothing would come of it unless Will had a firm faith in God. And Isobel soon made it clear she was as adamant as ever about that.

'It's good Richard and you go to church together, Meggie. I can't imagine being married to anyone who didn't share my faith in God—although I suppose that's because of how I was brought up.'

'Well … Richard likes John Trimble, but I find his sermons a bit boring, to be honest. He uses too many big words and I'm sure he confuses others in the congregation as well. I'm … I'm still not sure what I think about God, Isobel, but Richard is. He wants to train as a lay reader when he gets time. Perhaps he will after we move, although we'll both be busy if he buys this corner shop.'

They talked on until they heard the card game end, at which point Isobel stood and gave her a warm hug.

'It's so good to have you back, Meggie. I wish you weren't thinking of moving even further away, but it sounds as if Richard's made up his mind. I still pray for you every day, you know—and now I'll also pray you find a good church in Brisbane where the minister isn't so boring,' she added, with a mischievous twinkle in her eye.

Before the final school term began, Richard decided to make another quick trip to Brisbane to check out a few more details about the Red Hill business. He did not want her to come with him, but for once, she insisted.

'There'll be no time for gallivanting around,' he told her, his annoyance clear. 'This is a business trip—and I've already asked your father to come with me.'

'I know, but I want to see where we'll be living—and the shop too. I think that's fair enough. It's going to take more than one of us to run it, after all. You can't be there all the time.'

She tried not to be in the way when Richard and her father inspected the property, but soon realised they were interested in quite different things from her. While they checked foundations and floorboards and gutters and plumbing, she took in the general layout of the small house at the rear of the shop. It had two bedrooms and a tiny, enclosed back veranda that could work as a sleepout, along with a kitchen, loungeroom and bathroom. As well, there was a small office in one corner of the shop. From the kitchen window, she could see into the backyard, which was mostly grass. But against the fence, she noticed a narrow garden filled with gerberas and zinnias just coming into bloom and edged with pansies and alyssum. Part of her itched to paint each colourful flower, but another part still cringed at the thought. Well, at least she could enjoy looking at them and caring for them.

From the side windows, there was little to see apart from fence palings. But from the front of the store, which was situated at the top of a hill, there was a wide view of the surrounding houses with their corrugated iron roofs and sloping yards. For a moment, she longed to paint everything she saw there too. Yet, even if she could, there would be no time for such things. She was bound to have more than enough to do, helping Richard in the shop, dealing with the housework and caring for their baby.

To her relief, her father liked the look of the business and agreed to lend them the necessary funds to complete the purchase. Richard seemed to take on a new lease of life, as he began packing their possessions and making arrangements for everything to be transported to Red Hill the moment a teacher was found to replace him.

'I hadn't realised how draining teaching here would be,' he told her one day, as she helped him sort his books. 'Of course, my eyes made things more difficult but, to be honest, being next door to Mary's class hasn't helped either. I know she's more experienced— and I know she was asked to check on me because I was new, but I can't say I've enjoyed having her tell me what to do.'

She would have liked to add a few more comments about his sister but had already discovered that was unwise. It was one thing for him to criticise his family, but another for someone else to. Instead, she decided to change the subject.

'Richard, this will be a whole new start for you—and for us both. There'll be lots to learn, but I'm sure you'll manage it all.'

A month later, they moved to Brisbane. She was thankful Mr and Mrs Martin, the previous owners, had agreed to continue running the business until they arrived and also to work with them for a while until they found their feet. While taking advice from them irked Richard, just as Mary's advice had, she was grateful for their help, especially in regard to the light refreshments. A surprising number of customers seemed to enjoy sitting at tables in a corner of the shop and feasting on Mrs Martin's delicious pumpkin scones, as they drank their tea—or the freshly squeezed orange juice that was Mr Martin's speciality. She hoped she would manage it all, but all she could do was try her best.

Richard was always busy, keeping an eye on their stock and heading to the Roma Street Markets twice a week to buy fruit and vegetables, which involved cycling into town early, then unloading and displaying the produce when it was delivered.

'This is all so slow and frustrating,' he told her one day. 'I wish I could afford our own horse and cart, but I'm a bit cautious about spending any more money just yet.'

She heaved a sigh of relief. She did not want to be any further in debt to her parents.

Soon her week began to take on a distinct rhythm. The regular customers kept coming and some quickly became her favourites, one being Reverend Fisher, the local Church of England minister, who dropped by most Mondays for tea and scones. There was something about his gentle, courteous manner that touched her. In the past month, they had begun attending his church and, whenever he preached, his face seemed to shine with an inner light that inspired her to listen much more than she ever had to John Trimble's sermons.

One day when they were alone in the shop, he told her about his wife—and her heart went out to him.

'Monday has always been my day off. My wife and I often used to walk here for our morning tea, then catch a tram to the city from the corner over there and stroll around window shopping. She passed away this time last year.'

'I'm so sorry,' was all she could think to say.

'Thank you, my dear—that's kind of you. She'd been unwell for some time and, towards the end, while she didn't want to leave me, she longed to be with the Lord. But I do miss her …'

His eyes clouded over under his bushy, white brows, but he managed to regain control.

'Each day when I wake, I imagine her painting away in heaven, so joyful and pain-free. She was a gifted artist, but we were often so busy, she didn't have much time to herself. I used to encourage her to paint more, but she always said "Later—I'll have time later". That can be a trap, can't it, to put aside something we love because we think other things are so much more important? … What do you love doing, Mrs McPherson?'

At first, she skirted around his question.

'Well, I don't have time for anything else much these days, apart from work. And soon I'll have even less, once the baby arrives. I try to do some sewing and knitting, but …'

He looked at her with his kind eyes—eyes that somehow seemed to see deep inside her.

'But what, my dear?'

She was on the verge of telling him about Jimbo and how she could not bring herself to paint, but just as she opened her mouth, Richard arrived back from town. Something told her Reverend Fisher would have understood—but now the moment was lost, as Richard steered the conversation in a different direction.

'Good morning, Reverend Fisher—nice to see you again. I enjoyed your sermon yesterday. I think you know we attended St Luke's in Rosewood before coming here. I've talked with our minister, John Trimble, about doing the lay readers' course and I'd like to discuss it with you too when it's convenient.'

They went on to other church matters then and her mind wandered. Perhaps it was for the best that her conversation with Reverend Fisher had been interrupted. She might have started crying and that would have embarrassed them both. With a sigh, she left them to it and went to serve another customer.

The next time Reverend Fisher came, she served him his tea and scones but was kept busy attending to other customers. As he left, however, he smiled at her and raised his hat.

'Thank you, Mrs McPherson—the scones were excellent. But I can see you're a little tired, so please look after yourself. I'll pray you can get some rest when Richard comes back from town.'

She felt tears pricking her eyes. It was only November, but already the weather was hot and sticky. She still had two months to go before the baby's arrival, yet she knew her legs would feel like lead by bedtime, after standing for most of the day. She needed to rest more, but she also wanted the business to be a success.

Richard was working his hardest too, yet she was amazed he still found the energy to study for his lay readers' course most evenings. He seemed to enjoy it, so she was surprised when he told he had put the course aside for the time being.

'I'd still like to do it—and, as soon as I can too, I'd like to audition for the Austral Choir. But right now, I think I need to help you get a bit more rest, Meg.'

Straight away, she wondered if Reverend Fisher had influenced his decision, but she did not ask. She was too thankful she could put her swollen feet up earlier each evening to wonder how it had happened. Besides, she wanted to believe Richard might have made his own decision, without any prompting from Reverend Fisher.

She was grateful too for their Christmas Day break from the shop soon after. It was wonderful to celebrate with Aunty Betty and the family and to be invited back for New Year's Day. She offered to help with the food on both occasions, but Uncle Harold would not hear of it.

'You need to look after yourself, Meg,' he told her in no uncertain terms. 'Soon your little one will be demanding your attention at all hours, yet you'll still be needed in the shop too. Will your mother come down to help when the baby arrives?'

She mumbled something about not being sure, but it was only half true. In reality, she had decided not to ask her mother to come. On the one occasion she had mentioned it to her father during one of his trips to Brisbane, he had obviously felt hesitant.

'I'm not sure that'd work,' he had told her, after a short pause. 'Your mother still isn't doing so well and, while she managed fine at the wedding, I don't think she'd be up to helping with a new baby—or in the shop, for that matter. Let's see how you go, shall we? Perhaps Isobel can come down for a while instead, if your mother can spare her.'

She would have loved Isobel to come, but her pride took over at that point.

'Don't worry, Dad. I don't want to be a burden to anyone, least of all Mum. I'd love to have Isobel here, but it sounds as if Mum might need her. Anyway, Richard will help—we'll get by.'

As her due date came closer, fear began to grip her. What if the baby was stillborn? What if something was wrong with it? She knew this happened often back home and even in Brisbane—several customers had shared such stories with her that did little to settle her spirit. She could not bear anything like that to happen—not after losing Jimbo.

One day, Reverend Fisher overheard a customer telling her a particularly sad story. Afterwards, he tried to reassure her as he paid for his tea and scones.

'Mrs McPherson, I want you to know I'll be praying for a safe and speedy delivery when your time comes. I think it's your sensitive nature that makes people share such things with you, but it's quite tactless of them. Please don't let them frighten you.'

Again, she had to stop herself from bursting into tears.

'I try not to, but sometimes I can't help myself. You see … I lost my baby brother not long ago and it was all so terrible. And I have trouble believing God could help me—or even want to. Anyway, how can God let such awful things happen, if He cares about us? Oh … I'm so sorry—I shouldn't be saying that to you. It just came out …'

She gazed at the floor, shocked at her outburst. The only person she had ever shared such things with was Isobel. What was it about this man that made her want to blurt out her inmost thoughts?

When she managed to look at him again, to her relief, he did not seem the least offended. Instead, the gentle compassion she saw in his eyes almost undid her again.

'I'm sorry you experienced such a terrible loss, my dear. Some things that happen in this world are impossible to explain—even the wisest among us have no answers at times. Yet I still believe with all my heart that God is loving and kind, rather than cruel and uncaring. But perhaps we need to leave that conversation for another day. … Tell me, are you having your baby at Lady Bowen Hospital?'

She managed to pull herself together enough to respond.

'I wanted to go to the hospital, but we thought it might be easier and cost less too, if a midwife came here. It's just that we don't know the best one to ask. My uncle, who's a doctor, suggested one lady, but she's very busy and might be away then too. That's one thing I've been worried about …'

'I might be able to suggest someone,' Reverend Fisher said after a slight pause. 'Mrs O'Doherty's a member of our congregation and has been a midwife for years. Several young mothers at church have said how kind and efficient she was. She doesn't live far from here either.'

She felt so relieved she could have hugged him but was sure that would not be appropriate. Just then, another customer arrived, so, after a quick promise to speak to Mrs O'Doherty on her behalf and a wave of his hand, he was gone.

The following Sunday, despite being busy with other things, Reverend Fisher found time to introduce her to Mrs O'Doherty. Then and there, she engaged her services—she sensed she could trust this warm, older woman with such a kind face and an air of calm confidence. She did not even wait to ask Richard's opinion.

And Mrs O'Doherty promised to visit her as soon as possible.

'I can see we'll get on like a house on fire, dearie. Don't you worry—I'll call in one day this week and we can chat then.'

She had never been more relieved to see anyone than she was to see Mrs O'Doherty when she knew the baby was on its way a little earlier than expected. She had been uncomfortable all evening and had tossed and turned in the hot, summer weather until the pains had begun in earnest around midnight. Richard had had a tiring day and she had trouble waking him, but once he realised what was happening, he set off straight away for Mrs O'Doherty.

'I'll be quick, Meg—I'll run the whole way,' he told her as he dashed out the door, still pulling on his shirt.

For a while, she thought the baby might come when she was by herself. She felt the same as she had in the floodwaters when Jimbo had been swept away and her whole body shook, as she relived the horror of that moment. In the midst of her fear, she found herself wishing she could pray like Isobel and Reverend Fisher—but that was impossible. Anyway, the only prayer she could remember was the Lord's Prayer. Besides, what could God do for her? He had done nothing to help her rescue Jimbo, so why would things be different now?

As another fierce pain gripped her, she cried out, her voice echoing through the empty house. If only Aunty Betty were with her. She had offered to come early, but Richard had made it clear he did not want her there any longer than necessary.

'Your aunt's welcome, of course. But I have to say I don't like being told how to run my own home.'

She understood. She could see how Aunty Betty, who was so skilled at arranging parties and organising everyone, would annoy him. Yet right now, she longed so much for her aunt's reassuring presence.

But as soon as Mrs O'Doherty arrived, she knew she was in good hands. At any other time, she would have laughed at how meekly Richard did whatever the midwife told him, then disappeared as soon as she waved him out of the room. But she needed all her energy to deal with the searing pain that soon eclipsed everything else and threatened to go on forever. At one stage, she noticed it was no longer dark—surely the baby would arrive soon? Then she became aware of the midwife's voice, urging her to push harder. With an almighty effort, she did just that, then fell back exhausted.

'It's a little girl, Mrs McPherson,' she heard Mrs O'Doherty say, as if from a long way off. 'She's a bonny one too—and she's a good, healthy colour. What will you call her?'

'Alice May,' she whispered through her tears, as she held her baby close. In an instant, a memory surfaced of her mother letting her hold Jimbo, not long after he was born, but she pushed it aside. She did not want to spoil this moment. And she would never let anything happen to this precious little one—ever.

When Richard was allowed in to see the baby, his response touched her.

'Oh Meg, she's so little, isn't she? I don't think I'll hold her quite yet, but she's perfect. Well done, dear! I hope you grow up to be just like your mother, Alice May.'

That evening, he fetched Aunty Betty, who soon had everything running smoothly. She even seemed to enjoy serving in the shop, although she kept pestering Richard to ask where things were. He bore it as best he could, but heaved a sigh of relief when her week with them was up.

'We'll manage, Meg,' he told her with confidence.

And they did, to a large extent. But as the weeks and months passed, life seemed to sap her of every ounce of energy she had, as she cooked and cleaned and served customers, often while holding the baby. On the evenings Richard was out at his lay readers' course, which he had taken up again, she would often head straight to bed, after feeding Alice and settling her in her cot. It was such a relief when the baby began to sleep through until morning at around nine months, but even that did not seem to ease her general lethargy or constant lower back pain. Richard supported her as best he could, but she tried to asked for his help as little as possible. She knew he did not enjoy housework—and he was so busy anyway, working to make a success of their business.

Towards the end of November, she discovered the reason behind her tiredness. She was pregnant again.

'Well, we might not have planned to have our children so close together, Meg, but Alice will love a little playmate,' Richard said at once. 'Maybe it'll be a boy this time. I'm sure you'll be doing much better in a few weeks. Don't you remember how you felt when you were expecting Alice?'

'I remember,' she told him, 'and it was quite different from how I'm feeling now. I have this constant pain in my back and I'm feeling more and more uncomfortable as the weeks go by. Mrs O'Doherty's remedies haven't made any difference either—and Uncle Harold can't seem to suggest anything other than bedrest.'

'That's a bit impossible with Alice around and I certainly can't look after her all day. Perhaps we should see if we can get someone to mind her. Even then, you wouldn't be able to rest because there's so much else to do. What about asking your mother …'

But she shook her head and responded with more vehemence than she had intended.

'*No*, Richard. Remember how Dad didn't think that was a good idea when Alice was born? And since then, Mum hasn't shown any great interest at all in her first grandchild. We'll have to get by ourselves somehow.'

She considered asking her father if they could spare Isobel for a while at least, but soon it was all too late anyway. One morning, as she got up to attend to Alice, she felt a sharp pain in her lower abdomen, followed by another. She shook Richard awake—she knew something was wrong.

'Richard, you'd better fetch Mrs O'Doherty straight away. I'm in quite a bit of pain and …'

But she could not put her fear into words. It was too awful to contemplate. She heard Richard's sharp intake of breath and then an exasperated sigh.

'Meg, you'll be fine. Maybe you've been carrying Alice around too much—let her crawl instead. Anyway, she likes trying to stand by herself. I'm sorry I have to head into the markets right now, but please sit down as much as you can. And don't pick up Alice!'

She could tell he was tired. He had come to bed late the previous night and she knew there was no point in arguing. Her legs were trembling as she climbed out of bed and began to dress. She was glad Richard at least had time to bring Alice to her in the bedroom before scrambling into his own clothes.

Eventually, she found the strength to walk to the kitchen and make some porridge, while Alice crawled around, playing with her toys.

'I'll be as quick as I can, Meg,' Richard told her, as he hurried out the door, 'but I have a fair bit to buy this morning. If you're still worried, perhaps one of our customers could get Mrs O'Doherty for you, but please try to rest. And Alice—be a good girl for Mummy, you hear?'

For a while, she stayed where she was, gulping down the hot tea Richard had managed to give her and too afraid to move. But soon Alice became fractious, so she bent down to lift her into her highchair. Straight away, another strong pain gripped her and she watched, almost mesmerised, as a small stream of blood trickled down her leg and onto the floor.

Panicking, she staggered to the bathroom, but nothing seemed to stop the flow of blood that now stained her clothes. With shaking hands, she tried to clean herself up, to the accompaniment of Alice's furious cries from the kitchen. She felt a mess—but first, she had to take care of Alice. After feeding her the porridge, she slid her out of the highchair, then onto her lap and down to the floor. But what should she do next? Perhaps if she opened the shop, she could send a customer to fetch Mrs O'Doherty, as Richard had suggested.

Taking her time, she moved to the bedroom and pulled on the first clean dress she could find. Then, with Alice crawling along beside her, she slowly made her way to the door of the shop and unlocked it. Then she sat down, rested her feet on a chair and tried to pray, as she waited for someone to arrive.

She did not have to wait long. To her relief, their first customer turned out to be an older lady from church who went to fetch Mrs O'Doherty straight away, taking Alice with her. Perhaps God had indeed heard her prayer this time around—but surely that was impossible. With an effort, she managed to serve two other customers, but as soon as Mrs O'Doherty arrived, she crumbled.

'You'll be all right, dearie,' the midwife reassured her. 'I'll stay with you until your husband gets back. Sit down—you can tell me where to find things for your customers. Now, I phoned Reverend Fisher before I left. He's going to town to look for your husband at the markets, so don't worry. And Mrs Chalmers says she'll mind Alice for the morning. Would your mum come and stay for a while—or perhaps your aunt again?'

She gave Mrs O'Doherty some sort of noncommittal response, then tried to work out what she should do. Perhaps Aunty Betty could come for a few days again, although she knew she was busy. But she did not want to ask her mother—and Caroline was too young to be any help. With a sigh, she closed her eyes. It was all too hard for her right now.

She was relieved beyond words when Richard and Reverend Fisher arrived at last. Yet, despite her own pain, she could tell how tired and worried Richard was as he came and put his arm around her.

'Meg, I'm so sorry—don't cry, dear. Perhaps ... perhaps if I'd gone to get Mrs O'Doherty earlier like you asked, this wouldn't have happened, but I knew I had to get to the markets.'

Mrs O'Doherty cut in then.

'Well, it's likely it would have happened anyway, given the pain and discomfort your wife's had all through. She needs rest now though—I hope she can get it.'

She felt Richard stiffen at Mrs O'Doherty's stern, almost rebuking tone and held her breath, but she need not have worried.

'We'll do our best,' was all he said in the end, his voice terse. 'Meg, I'll help you to the bedroom now and Reverend Fisher will telephone your uncle. Maybe your aunt can come and stay again for a while.'

She sighed, remembering how Richard hated having Aunty Betty with them, but she could not think what else to do. She knew he hated public displays of emotion too, so did her best to stop crying. Yet, however hard she tried, the tears continued to flow.

After she was settled in bed, he sat beside her for a few moments, holding her hand.

'Meg, I need to go and look after the shop now, but please don't worry. It's disappointing for us both about the baby, but you'll soon be well again. And we have plenty of years ahead of us when there'll no doubt be more children.'

She squeezed his hand and nodded, but it was all she could bring herself to do.

Throughout the days that followed, she felt almost lifeless—everything around her seemed shrouded in a haze of blackness. Sleep was her safest refuge, although more than once, she dreamed she was slipping down a deep, dark well, with nothing to grasp that would break her fall. She was conscious of Richard and Alice nearby at times, as well as Aunty Betty. Then one day, she thought she heard Isobel's voice—and another deeper voice too. Was it her father? How could they be here? Perhaps she was still dreaming.

She roused a little, as someone tiptoed into her room. The next moment, she was crying in her father's arms as he stroked her hair.

'Oh, Meg, don't cry. Look, Isobel's here as well to stay with you. You'll be much better soon. Come on, Meg—dry those tears, my dear.'

She tried to pull herself together—he had always hated to see her upset.

'Your mother sends her love,' he told her. 'She would have come, but she thought we should send Isobel instead, rather than leave her to manage Caroline and Harriet. You know what a handful they can be, even though they should know better. I'm sorry I have to go home tomorrow, but work's busy right now.'

Something in his manner told her there was more to the arrangement than he let on, but she did not have the energy to enquire further. She tried to listen while he told her about things back home, but only half heard him.

'Dad, I'm sorry I'm not such good company at the moment,' she said at last. 'But thanks so much for coming—and for bringing Isobel. I guess Mum can spare her more now, with only Caroline and Harriet at home …'

He made no comment when she stopped, but seemed to understand. She could not afford to let her mind stray to Jimbo. She was sad enough as it was.

# Chapter Seven

Many times, she wondered how they would have survived without Isobel's help. At first, she was worried Richard might resent her presence, just as he had Aunty Betty's. But Isobel's gentle manner and her quiet, efficient way of working seemed to reconcile him to the situation. Besides, she suspected Reverend Fisher had had a few words with him about it all too. One day when the door to the shop was left open a fraction, she had overheard them talking together.

'I'm sure Meg will be strong enough soon to manage by herself again,' Richard had said, with a slight edge to his voice.

After a short pause, Reverend Fisher had responded a little more firmly than usual.

'I hope and pray that's the case, Richard. Of course, I can't comment on her physical wellbeing, but I think she's still fighting some big mental and spiritual battles. And that's where Isobel comes into her own, in my opinion. She has such a warm, loving manner and also a strong faith in God. Besides, if she stays for a while longer, your wife may have time to pursue some interests of her own that will feed her spirit. We all need that, don't we? After all, you have your lay readers' course—and I have my garden and my books.'

She could sense Richard's annoyance when he responded.

'With all due respect, I wouldn't call my lay readers' course a mere interest. Besides, Meg seems to enjoy things like sewing and knitting and even baking. She used to paint and play the piano, but she hasn't wanted to for a while now. Anyway, we don't have a piano—and her art materials are still packed away somewhere.'

'That's interesting, Richard. Meg—I hope I have your permission to call her that—has always reminded me of my dear wife Frances, who was also an artist. She found such solace in her painting. Fran had several miscarriages too before our boys came along, but her faith remained firm. She always sensed God's comforting presence with her whenever she painted—and I pray Meg will soon as well.'

They must have moved further away then and her brain was too dulled to think much more about the conversation. But she was sure of one thing—she could never imagine God being any sort of comforting presence to her. Reverend Fisher often preached about God's love and mercy and grace and she could tell it was all so real for him. She even longed to believe in it all herself at times. Yet God had not loved her enough to rescue Jimbo—and now, after losing her own baby, God seemed even more cruel and unmerciful. Time and time again, she wondered if her miscarriage might even be a punishment for what had happened to Jimbo. As she felt herself slipping down that dark well in her dreams, she often thought she could hear God accusing her, over and over: 'You *were* to blame, Margaret, just like your mother says. You did *not* take care of your brother!'

And although she would never know, she wondered if the baby she had miscarried had been a boy. Wasn't there a verse in the Bible that talked about how God demanded an eye for an eye? Oh, there were so many horrible thoughts tumbling over one another in her mind. Perhaps if she talked to someone about it all, she would feel better. Isobel would always listen, but right now, her thoughts were too dark and shocking even for Isobel to hear.

They were not too dark or shocking for Reverend Fisher, however. She had not meant to tell him anything when he called in a few days later, but it was the gifts he brought and his whole manner as he gave them to her that weakened her resolve.

'How are you, my dear? May I call you Meg? It's good to see you sitting up and looking a little better. Can we perhaps chat for a while? Richard and Isobel are managing fine in the shop—with Alice's help, of course.'

She did not have the energy to talk much, but as he stood there looking a little like Father Christmas, with his white hair, beaming face and rather round stomach, she could not bring herself to rebuff him. Then she noticed he had a small, wooden case with him and another parcel as well which he placed on his lap as he sat down. A moment later, he leaned forward and smiled at her.

'I'm sure you don't feel like talking to anyone, so I'll be as brief as an old clergyman can. My wife Frances used to say I never knew when to be quiet, so please tell me if I'm tiring you out. But the other day when I was chatting with Richard, he mentioned you used to enjoy painting. Remember how I told you Fran was an artist? Well, I went home and rummaged in our back room where I had put some of her art equipment I thought I should keep. I understand yours is packed away somewhere and I thought it might be too hard to find right now, so … would you do me a favour and accept these as gifts from Fran and me? I know she'd be delighted for you to have them—and she'd be even more delighted if they helped you express whatever thoughts are running around in your head at the moment.'

She had not meant to say anything, but the words tumbled out.

'Oh, I don't think anyone would want to know about the sort of thoughts I've been having lately.'

Reverend Fisher sat back and looked at her with his piercing, blue eyes.

'You wouldn't have to show your work to anyone, if you didn't want to. Whenever Fran felt particularly sad, she would refuse to let me see what she painted. But I came to realise it was the process rather than the end product, including her conversations with God along the way, that helped her more than anything. We all need to express those things that are deep inside us, Meg. Otherwise, our hearts and minds can become so dark and muddled. The enemy has a field day too, feeding us all sorts of lies about ourselves.'

She could see he understood, but she still hesitated.

'I can't … I can't accept anything so precious, Reverend Fisher. What about your own family? Perhaps your children …'

'Oh, my boys are much more like me than their mother when it comes to art. I'm hopeless—although I'd love to have been able to paint like Fran. No, I sense these things were meant for you, my dear. I'd almost forgotten I still had them until God reminded me, after I talked with Richard. And I'd be delighted if you'd accept them.'

She knew she had to tell him the truth then.

'Reverend Fisher, ever since my little brother died, I haven't been able to paint. You see, I was with him when he drowned. I tried to save him, but I couldn't. If I'd have been less selfish and hadn't snuck out of the house that day, he wouldn't have been near the water. It had been raining a lot, but I decided to go down to the creek anyway to paint by myself. And Jimbo followed me. I didn't leave our gate open, as my mother still thinks I did—Jimbo told me himself he wriggled under it. … Isobel keeps telling me I wasn't to blame, but I still feel so guilty. And I know if I tried to paint again, I'd be reminded of that day. Besides, I don't deserve to do something I enjoy so much—I fell that's a sort of punishment for what happened. So I can't accept your gifts, Reverend Fisher— although at times when I see something beautiful, I long to be able to paint again.'

It had all come out so muddled, but as she talked, the heavy weight inside her seemed to shift a little. She found it hard to meet Reverend Fisher's eyes at first, but when she did, she saw no judgment, but instead, deep compassion and understanding.

'My dear, I wish my wife were still here to talk to you, but you'll have to make do with me, I'm afraid. Thank you for telling me all that, Meg. That was brave of you. What a difficult journey you've had—and I can see how much you're still grieving the loss of your little brother. … You know, all of us have pain and heartache in our lives one way or another, from what I've observed. But there are ways God can strengthen us to carry on and even bring some good out of these terrible things too. For you, I think that might well happen as you paint, so please do an old man a favour and open this first gift.'

She could not stop shaking as she unwrapped the parcel he had held on his lap. She gasped when she saw its contents—a beautiful, compact Winsor and Newton watercolour paint and brush pen set, complete with twelve vibrant colours and a mixing palette inside the lid.

'I gave these to Fran,' Reverend Fisher told her, his voice soft and a little tremulous. 'She'd wanted a set like this for a while that she could carry anywhere. As it turned out, she didn't even get to try them out, so I'd love them to be used now. And you might find this handy too.'

She held her breath as he lifted up the small case at his feet and handed it to her. She undid the latches to find a beautifully crafted, collapsible French box easel, with light, wooden tripod legs and a little drawer for storing paints and brushes.

Even though she had known what it might be as soon as she saw the case, she was still shocked.

'But … but I can't accept this! I know how expensive they are—a friend at college had one. Surely you could sell it somewhere?'

Reverend Fisher's eyes became moist, as he sat staring at the little easel. She knew she had sounded ungracious and tried her best to retrieve the situation.

'I mean … I absolutely love it, of course. I own two other easels, but one's big and clumsy and the other isn't the easiest to carry either. Both of them are packed away in the shed somewhere. … Oh, I don't know what to say.'

'Then don't say anything, my dear. As you can tell by these little scuff marks here, Fran did use it, so it's not brand new. But seeing it open again reminded me how she often used to set it up with a gleam in her eye, as she thought about what she wanted to paint. Please accept it as a gift from us both—but on one condition. And that is, that you start using it as soon as you feel well enough. I know Isobel will be more than willing to mind Alice to give you time to do just that. … And Meg, I have to tell you I agree with Isobel about your brother's death. Even though I don't know all that happened, I'm sure it wasn't your fault—and I think God wants you to know that too. So please don't allow all that guilt to keep you from doing what you were created to do.'

The tears poured down her cheeks then.

'I … I thought this miscarriage might be God's punishment—you know, "an eye for an eye", like in the Bible. … Oh, I'm so mixed up about everything right now.'

Reverend Fisher took a moment to wipe his own eyes before responding.

'You know, sometimes I suspect we tie ourselves in knots, trying to work out what God thinks and how God works. But one thing I know for sure, my dear, is that God loves you and wants you to know that deep in your heart. Where would we all be without God's love and forgiveness?'

'That's what Isobel says—but I still find it hard to believe.'

'I'm so glad you have a friend like Isobel. God doesn't mean us to walk through our pain and grief all alone. And Richard loves you and is here for you too, my dear, even though he's often so busy and expresses his faith a little differently from Isobel. … Look, I think I've talked more than enough for now—if you'd like, we can continue our conversation another day. But I want to see you through this time, Meg. And I believe God will reveal His love and forgiveness to you as you begin to paint again. Will you give it a try, my dear?'

She met his eyes then and saw such love and compassion in them that her determination to stand firm crumbled. It was as if, right then and there, Reverend Fisher was expressing God's own love to her, not only through his gentle words and manner but also through his precious gifts.

'I'll try,' she whispered after a while. 'I'll do my best.'

That evening, as she showed Reverend Fisher's gifts to Richard and Isobel, she could feel a small glimmer of hope beginning to well up inside her. Perhaps it might be possible to find a way through the darkness that had engulfed her since her miscarriage. Perhaps Reverend Fisher's gifts had indeed been prompted by God's love for her—perhaps everything Reverend Fisher and Isobel said about God was true, after all. Richard too had a faith in God that she sensed would never waver, although he did not speak of it often to her. She owed them all a great deal. And perhaps too, if God had created her to paint, as Reverend Fisher had said, then she might even owe it to God to do just that.

In the weeks that followed, she learnt to accept at least some of Isobel's offers to cover for her in the shop and head off to paint, while Alice had her afternoon nap.

'Just go, Meg,' she would say with a kind but mischievous smile, as she shooed her out the door. 'Quick, before any customers come and before Alice wakes up.'

Some days, she chose to paint scenes close to home, like the view down the valley from the front of the shop or the flowers in their own backyard—the bold, bright zinnias, the hardy gerberas and the dainty, little pansies. But sometimes, the deep emotions she had grappled with for so long surfaced with a vengeance, so that the end result bore little resemblance to what she had started out to paint. On those days, she knew her efforts were for her eyes alone. Yet, to her surprise, she came to value and even welcome such experiences. They would often leave her exhausted, but also somehow lighter and more hopeful, as she expressed things she could never put into words.

Reverend Fisher had been right. Little by little, God was bringing strength and healing to her through her art.

As time went on, she would sometimes paint down at Ithaca Creek, after following the rough paths the local children had made through the bushes and reeds to the water's edge. Then in February, just before Alice's first birthday, Isobel managed to persuade her to catch a tram into the city. Once there, she felt drawn to walk down George Street again towards the Botanic Gardens, where, to her delight, most of the magnificent, old poincianas were still in flower. She set about painting them with enthusiasm, but the nearby river also beckoned her. Soon she was seated beside it with brush poised, ready to start painting, but also happy to delay that first stroke, as she allowed the murmur of the waters below and the sunlight dancing on the rippling surface to soothe her spirit. At that moment, the ancient words of the Twenty-Third Psalm came to mind again, as if from somewhere outside and beyond her.

And, in the quietness, unbidden, she sensed God's presence at last.

Wherever she went to paint in the days that followed, she began to sense God more and more, holding her and comforting her. Often, she found it hard to tear herself away and head home, yet she was always anxious to relieve Isobel and not inconvenience Richard too much either. She was aware he had a lot on his mind with the business and, while he seemed happy that she was painting again, she knew he did not quite understand why she needed to.

'I'm glad you enjoy it, Meg,' he told her one night, as they lay in bed, 'although it's quite time-consuming, isn't it? I'm no artist, as you know, but if painting helps you feel better about everything, then that's good.'

She tried to talk with Isobel about it all too at times and, although Isobel was no artist either, she listened and did her best to understand.

'I think painting again has helped me a lot, Isobel,' she told her one night. 'I still have a way to go but I do feel more at peace—and somehow kind of softer on the inside. I don't understand why God lets bad things happen like Jimbo's death or losing our baby, but I know this world isn't how God meant it to be. And when I paint, I often feel God's right there with me—although I don't know why He would *want* to be. Sometimes I still feel so guilty, Isobel, but I try to remember God loves me and has forgiven me, as Reverend Fisher's always saying.'

Isobel reached out and patted her hand.

'It's so wonderful to see you enjoying your painting again, Meggie. And I'm sure none of us feels deserving of God's love and forgiveness. All we can do is accept it. And when we do, somehow it seems easier to love and forgive others too, don't you think?'

'Well … that's still hard for me, Isobel. I can't forgive my mother yet for blaming me for Jimbo's death, although I realise how terrible it must have been for her to lose him. I think my miscarriage helped me understand that a bit more. I'm sure God does teach us important lessons through our difficulties, as Reverend Fisher told me a while back.'

Isobel never seemed to judge her or expect more from her than she could give—but it was different with Richard. At times when she tried to talk with him about how she was feeling, he would shake his head and find it hard to grasp what she meant.

'You shouldn't feel like that, Meg,' he told her one evening when she started talking about something that was troubling her. 'It's only because …'

She knew he was only trying to help, yet it made her want to scream. Instead, she took a deep breath and forced herself to speak calmly.

'Richard, I'm sure what I'm feeling isn't logical, but it's how I *feel.*'

On another occasion when she tried to share some of her thoughts about God with him, he could not seem to resist setting her straight.

'But Meg, if you knew more theology …'

She managed to laugh it off—and no doubt he was right anyway. After all, she was so young in her faith and still had so many questions. But his words discouraged her, although she was sure he had not meant them to. On the other hand, whenever she talked about such things with Reverend Fisher, he was always so patient and encouraging.

'My dear, I've been listening to people for a very long time,' he told her one day, with a twinkle in his eye and a gentle smile, after she had tried to thank him for his help. 'I don't think anything could surprise me much these days, so I hope you'll always feel free to ask whatever questions you like about God. I'm sure God's big enough to handle them too.'

It was unfair to compare the two men, she knew that. Richard had so many strengths she valued—she would be forever grateful he had persisted and asked for her hand in marriage a second time. But Reverend Fisher had played a special role in her recovery and in her spiritual journey—and as soon as she felt her painting had improved a little more, she was determined to paint something special for him as a thank you gift.

Yet first, she needed to paint something for Will. He was twenty-three now and about to start his final year at university, so it was high time she fulfilled her promise to him. She still remembered the original painting she had been working on for him on the day Jimbo drowned—perhaps she could steel herself to produce something similar now.

In the end, she found a suitable scene to paint quite close by, on a bend in Ithaca Creek. The terrain was not the same as it was back home near Lockyer Creek, but she knew he would still approve of her choice. At times, so many dark memories surfaced that it was a struggle to keep painting, yet she sensed it was part of her healing and that God was with her in it all. She would tell Will that too, she decided, when she gave him his gift.

She was delighted when he managed to make it down from Helidon in time for Alice's first birthday, before he headed back to Sydney. She had invited her parents and sisters too, but they had been unable to come.

'Dad's busy at work and Mum still isn't all that well, so I've been trying to help out a bit more than usual these holidays,' Will told her. 'They send their love though—and I've brought a special present from them for Alice.'

Their gift turned out to be a handmade teddy bear that Alice took to straight away and named Johnno.

'At least she didn't call him Jimbo,' Will commented without thinking, before trying to hide his embarrassment by opening his belated twenty-first birthday gift. 'Wow, Meg … I'm almost speechless. This sure was worth waiting for—I love it. It'll take pride of place in my room when I get back to Sydney—and I can't wait to tell everyone my sister painted it. Thanks, sis.'

'I enjoyed painting it,' she told him. 'Of course, it's not the same as your original present, but I wanted it to be a creek scene at least. It was hard at times to keep going when I remembered what happened down at our creek that day, but I'm glad I did. … I'm not sure what you'll think about this, Will, but God seems to be using my art to help me work through some of the hard things that have happened to me. And our minister, Reverend Fisher, has been such a support, as has Isobel.'

Will was quiet at first, but then nodded.

'I'm pleased, Meg. Some of my friends in Sydney haven't given up on me either, as far as God's concerned. They don't badger me, but they're always hoping and praying I'll throw in my lot with them. I'm tempted, I must admit—they stand for something beyond just having fun and getting on in life. I still don't know what I want to do or what I believe, but I'm working on it. I'll finish my engineering degree, but I might do something different before going back to Helidon and joining Dad in the business. Anyway, I have to pass this year first.'

Reverend Fisher's gift took a lot longer to complete. In the end, she chose to paint their church, St Barnabas's, a wooden building perched on the side of a steep hill—and that provided some challenges, as she worked to get the perspective right and make the surrounding gardens as attractive as possible. She was aware Reverend Fisher was nearing retirement age and hoped it would be something he would treasure, not only as a thank you gift from her, but also as a reminder of his time at Red Hill.

When she gave it to him some weeks later, she saw at once how touched he was.

'Well … this is … this is so unexpected, my dear. How I wish Fran could see it—I know she'd love it. And she'd also know how much effort has gone into creating it. Imagine painting something like this just for me! Thank you so much. I'm going to put it on my mantelpiece in the rectory straight away and tell everyone I'm friends with the talented artist who painted it. Whatever happens, Meg, please keep painting—and please keep reaching out to God too.'

As the year unfolded further, they became much busier in the shop, which enabled Richard to pay back most of her father's loan, to her great relief. She was sure this was due in no small measure to Isobel, who often freed her up to work more in the shop by minding Alice and taking care of the housework. But Isobel was also adept at serving customers herself and often helped as well during their busiest times. The older folk in particular seemed to like her and often shared stories of family difficulties or physical ailments with her.

'Isobel always listens to me,' she heard an elderly customer tell Richard one day. 'She never seems too busy to stop and chat—and I feel much more peaceful afterwards.'

She sensed this comment was aimed at Richard himself, who was often rather curt with older customers, if he felt they were wasting his time. He much preferred working in the office, balancing the books and paying the bills. She was glad he did—she knew nothing about such things. Yet she suspected he did not value Isobel's help as much as he should have, which upset her. And one day when he quibbled at the cost of having Isobel with them, she could not hide how she felt.

'I don't care how much it costs,' she told him in a shaking voice. 'She's worth every penny of it, many times over. I can't imagine what I'd do without her and each day, I thank God for her. Besides, she's such a help in the shop as well—the customers all love her.'

Richard's face was red, but he came and put his arm around her.

'It's all right, Meg—don't cry. I can see how important Isobel is to you and I'm sorry I mentioned anything about it. It's just that I want the business to be a success, so I need to be careful how we spend our money.'

When her father visited them again in early June, she was worried he might tell her they needed Isobel back with them in Helidon. In the end, she decided to ask him about it straight out.

'Dad, how's Mum managing without Isobel? She writes to me from time to time, but she never asks about her. It was good of her to let Isobel come when I needed help, but we'd understand if she wants her back now—although I don't know how we'd get on without her.'

To her surprise, her father looked embarrassed.

'Well … I'm afraid I didn't quite tell you the truth when Isobel first came here, Meg, but your mother thought it was for the best. We were about to let Isobel go because there wasn't enough for her to do, what with Caroline and Harriet growing up and able to help more. And … well, of course there was no James to look after either. Besides, your mother felt we should save the money we were paying Isobel each week, on top of her board and keep, and put it towards sending Caroline and Harriet to boarding school in Toowoomba. I thought they'd both continue on at the convent like you did, but your mother changed her mind about that. Anyway, it worked out well that you could afford to have Isobel. And I know she gives most of her wage to her mother to help the family out.'

As she listened, she felt a huge stab of disappointment—and she also understood more why Richard had queried the cost of having Isobel with them. She had thought her mother had sent Isobel out of kindness and that her parents had continued to pay Isobel's small weekly wage out of kindness too. Yet now she realised Richard had been paying Isobel all along.

She could feel the old hurt and anger rising up in her. It was obvious nothing had changed—her mother had still not forgiven her for what had happened to Jimbo. But she tried to pull herself together as her father continued.

'I'm glad the business is doing well, Meg. It's a credit to you that you've been able to repay most of my loan *and* cover the cost of having Isobel here too. Before we know it, you'll be wanting to find bigger premises.'

Her heart lurched again—she hoped he did not plan to put any such thoughts into Richard's mind during his visit. She did not want to move anywhere, especially when she was just beginning to feel stronger and more alive than she had for a long time. Yet right now, her father's revelations about Isobel were threatening to undo what progress she had made and bring all her old, dark thoughts to the surface again. And she resented that.

'Sometimes I seem to take one step forward and two steps back,' she told Reverend Fisher, when he called in a few days later. 'I've felt so much better these past few weeks, but then something my father told me has upset me a lot.'

She had not meant to, but in the end, she explained what had happened.

'I can understand your anger and disappointment,' he said. 'But Meg—and I hope you don't mind my saying this—could you think about trying to forgive your mother? It always seems to me that, when we choose not to forgive, the person we hurt most is ourselves. The other person goes on with life, often unaware of or unconcerned about how we feel, while we tie ourselves up in knots and miss out on God's comfort and peace. Besides, we've all been forgiven so much, haven't we? So for that reason, as well as for your own sake, I'd encourage you to try to extend that same forgiveness to your mother.'

She knew he was right, yet it was not an easy step for her to take.

'Some things are so hard, aren't they?' she sighed. 'Just as well God's patient with me. I promise I'll try to let it all go. And ... well, when all's said and done, I'm so thankful to have Isobel with us, however it happened.'

Later, when she talked with Isobel about what her father had said, she saw even more clearly how gracious God had been to them.

'I knew your mother didn't need me any longer,' Isobel admitted. 'In fact, Mr and Mrs Percy over near Withcott had already asked me to work for them when your father told me you needed help. I hadn't felt settled about accepting the Percy's offer so, once I heard about you, I knew God wanted me to come here instead. I'd have come even if you and Richard hadn't been able to pay me anything on top of my board and keep. But I'm so grateful you can, as I give most of it to Mum.'

'But … but you're so much further away from your family than you would have been at Withcott, Isobel.'

'Oh, Meggie—as if I would have left you in the lurch. Besides … well … I like all your family …'

That night in bed, Isobel's last few words kept coming to mind. She had noticed Will chatting with Isobel often when he had visited them earlier in the year. Once or twice, she had even caught them deep in conversation about God and the Bible but had thought no more about it. After all, she was aware Will had questions about such things—and Isobel knew her Bible so well. But … could there have been more to it? She hoped so, with all her heart.

By the August holidays, she sensed change was in the air, whether she liked it or not. Richard had finished his lay readers' course and helped in their morning service from time to time, even preaching once when Reverend Fisher was away. And, despite being so busy in the shop, he had also managed to join the Austral Choir at last. But despite these extra activities, she could tell he was restless. As a result, when Will came to stay during the university holidays, she was not surprised when Richard told her he felt he should take a short break.

'I hope you don't mind, Meg, but I think I'll go back to Helidon with Will for a few days. Then I'll head down to Rosewood and visit Mary. Things will be a bit slower here in the school holidays, so you should be fine. I've organised for someone from the markets to deliver our Monday morning order and I've asked young Frank from church to come and help unload it. I know you and Isobel will manage everything. And Reverend Fisher's promised he'll pop in from time to time to make sure you're okay.'

'Well, I'm glad you can go home with Will, Richard—I think you could do with a break. Isobel and I will manage, especially since you've organised things for us so well. Then when you come back, you might feel a bit more settled.'

Yet that was not to be. When he returned, she discovered he had explored business opportunities in both Rosewood and Grandchester, as well as closer to Helidon.

'It was a good trip, Meg, and I enjoyed having Will tag along with me when I went looking around at what's available in those areas. He's thinking he might work alongside me in whatever venture I undertake next, so it was important to have him there as well.'

She was shocked. It was a few moments before she could respond and, even then, her voice shook.

'But … but couldn't you have told me what you planned to do? … And why leave here anyway? Besides, what would Dad think if Will decided not to join him at the quarries?'

'Look, we've done well here and built up the business,' Richard told her with a tinge of impatience, 'but that's the best time to sell, don't you see? Anyway, I feel I've mastered the running of this place—I like new challenges. … And this house is a bit small now, especially with Isobel living with us. Alice is growing up too—and I hope she'll have a little brother or sister someday soon. Isn't that what you want as well, Meg?'

The thought of another miscarriage terrified her, but she knew it was something she would have to overcome. She opened her mouth to respond, but Richard went on.

'As for Will joining me rather than working at the quarries, we talked about that with your father and he seems to think it might be a good idea—at least for a while. Will isn't sure what he wants to do after graduating, and it'd be a good opportunity for him to try something different. Your father doesn't want Will to feel trapped into doing anything—he'd prefer him to choose to work with him of his own accord, then give it his all. But I think he'd be disappointed if Will decided not to join him in the end.'

As Richard went on to talk about possible business options, she listened but could not take much in. It was daunting enough to think of moving at all—but the thought of moving back to Rosewood was even more daunting. Try as she might, she had been unable to get on with Mary, who was still at the school there. Still, if they did go back, Isobel would at least be with her for moral support this time.

Then another thought occurred to her. Was Isobel part of the reason Will wanted to work with Richard? And would Isobel be pleased about that? Well, time would tell.

By the end of the year, her head was in a whirl with all the changes happening in their lives. In November, she discovered she was pregnant again, which delighted them both, although she felt a little fearful too. Then to Richard's relief, they found a buyer for their business. And finally, after much searching, Richard managed to purchase a general store in Harrisville, twenty miles south of Rosewood.

'I think you'll like Harrisville,' he told her, after one of his trips there. 'It's a nice little town. The good thing is it's on the branch line from Ipswich to Dugandan, so it won't be too hard to get supplies from Brisbane by rail. It even has a hospital—and the school looks good too. Our store was started by the Harris Brothers themselves— their cousin's been managing it for many years. It's a bit run down, but the region's growing, so there should be plenty of custom. Once we've got the general store running well again, I'm thinking I could branch out into stockfeed and other farming supplies. Then Will could take on more responsibility for the shop itself. I'm sure we'll be able to make a go of it, Meg. … As for the house, I think you'll like that too. It's right behind the shop in Queen Street and has three bedrooms and a big veranda, with a sleepout at one end Will can use. There'll be plenty of room for Alice to play, both inside and out.'

She tried not to sound too cautious as she responded.

'It seems right for us, Richard—and I'm sure I'll be as enthusiastic as you are, once all the moving's over.'

In the remaining weeks at Red Hill, Richard's excitement seemed to spur him on, as he worked even harder to ensure everything was ready for the new owners. She did her best too to pack up everything in the sticky, summer weather, but was so thankful Isobel was there to help, before heading home to her own family for Christmas.

'You'll get through this time, Meggie,' she told her often, refusing to become ruffled when Alice pulled out things they had already packed. 'And we'll all have such fun in Harrisville together, won't we, Alice?'

Leaving Red Hill and Brisbane in general was hard for her, but saying goodbye to Reverend Fisher was even harder. And it seemed he did not find it easy either, judging by how often he dropped by on some pretext or other.

'Don't forget you're an artist at heart, Meg,' he told her during his last visit. 'I'm going to picture Fran's easel and paints being put to good use often there in Harrisville, perhaps down by Warrill Creek somewhere. I'll try to visit you after I retire, which will be in the next couple of years, Lord willing. Meanwhile, I hope you enjoy being part of St John's parish. I don't know the minister, but I understand he's a lot younger than I am, which might be good for you both, my dear.'

She could not stop the tears welling up but tried her best to say what she wanted to say.

'Reverend Fisher, I'm not sure where I'd be right now if I hadn't met you. I've appreciated our conversations so much, not to mention all your prayers for me. You've always listened and explained things in a way I could understand. And you helped me see that God is in fact loving and gracious, despite the bad things that happen in our lives. I'm so grateful too that you encouraged me to paint again and to know God's right beside me as I do. Thank you for everything, from the bottom of my heart.'

'It's been a pleasure, Meg—and it was all God's doing anyway. But I'm so glad you still have Isobel to talk to. God has great things ahead for you both, I believe.'

To her surprise, settling in at Harrisville turned out to be much less difficult than she had envisaged. With both Will and Isobel around to help, things seemed to sort themselves out much more quickly. The shop itself, with its bay windows on each side of the wide front door, was a little rundown, as Richard had warned her, but their cream-coloured wooden house with its red, corrugated iron roof and steep front steps was comfortable and roomy and she revelled in the extra space. She loved the large, airy kitchen in particular, with its big, wood stove in a recess at one end, and the wraparound veranda along the front and side of the house. But most of all, she was grateful for her own little corner of the veranda where she would be able to set up her art equipment. She had spied the half-enclosed area near the sleepout as soon as they arrived and hoped Richard would be happy for her to take it over.

'Well, I suppose that'll be all right, Meg,' he had responded, to her relief. 'I know your art's important to you—although I think you'll probably be too busy with everything else to spend much time there. I'll need your help in the store quite a bit until I get everything set up how I want it.'

She relaxed then, happy that she would have her own space to paint. And, once the first months of her pregnancy were past and the threat of another miscarriage over, she began to relax even more and look forward to their baby's arrival.

'Alice will love having a little playmate,' she commented to Isobel one day, as they unpacked Alice's old baby clothes. 'I don't mind if it's a boy or a girl, but I hope it's a boy for Richard's sake—although I'd have to try not to think of Jimbo every time I looked at him.'

She had not meant to voice this fear to anyone, even Isobel, yet it was too late to take the words back. But all Isobel did was reach out her hand and speak in her usual gentle, reassuring way.

'Meggie, please don't let your fear spoil things for you. You're so much stronger now in every way. You know God's with you—and I'll be here to help too, no matter what.'

# Chapter Eight

Robert Richard McPherson was born on a cold evening in May 1913, just as the midwife Mrs O'Doherty had recommended arrived from Ipswich. He was perfect—and her heart filled with joy as she watched Richard tenderly cradling their son.

'He's a McPherson, for sure,' he announced with pride. 'He has the same wide forehead as my father and me—and the McPherson nose. I think my dad would have been proud of his namesake—I'm only sorry he isn't around to meet him. And look at all that hair! Perhaps he'll have a thick mop like mine too when he grows up.'

She felt too exhausted to remind him how Alice had also had thick, dark brown hair when she was born, which had soon disappeared. Instead, she gazed into their baby son's eyes as she held him close and wondered what colour they would become. Would they be grey like her own?  She hoped so, with all her heart. That way, they would not remind her of Jimbo's big, brown ones.

She was so grateful for Isobel's constant help, as she learnt to cope with two young children and also find the time and energy to relieve Richard or Will in the shop. Each week, there seemed to be a steady stream of new customers, which kept them all busy.

'Things seem to be going well—and Will's shaping up well too,' Richard told her one night in a pleased tone. 'I'm hoping he'll want to stay with us for a long while yet, to free me up for other things.'

'What … what other things? Do you plan to expand the business more already?'

'No, no—at least, not quite yet. No, I understand I'm to become the local reporter here for the Ipswich Queensland Times soon—they apparently liked the few articles I've sent them so far. It'll take time out of my already busy week, of course, but I enjoy writing things here and there when I can.'

'Oh, Richard, I know you do. And you do it well too,' she told him. 'I remember those interesting, newsy letters you used to write to me when I was in Brisbane at Aunty Betty's.'

She felt proud of him when his role with the newspaper became official and, whenever she had time, she enjoyed reading his regular reports on their local community dances and sporting events. Soon, he was also asked to submit occasional feature articles which, while interesting, were sometimes a little too complex for her. Some weeks, he spent many hours writing, yet it was not long before his church commitments began to take up even more of his time. Reverend Gillespie seemed delighted to have a willing lay reader in his congregation, what with two services to conduct each Sunday at St John's, as well as others in nearby towns. But her head spun when Richard was also elected to the local School of Arts committee.

'Don't you have enough things to do in the community, Richard?' she asked him when she found out. 'I know you'd be an asset to them, but you're so busy with everything else already.'

At first, he had looked a little annoyed, but then his face had softened.

'It's all right, Meg—don't worry about me. I like to be busy and have lots of things to occupy my mind. I'm sure you've noticed that before now. But I'll try not to make you any busier, my dear.'

She had to let it rest there. After all, if he was happy, she was happy too.

She was also happy to hear how pleased he was with Will's efforts—and she was sure Isobel would be too. As they sat around the table after dinner in the evenings, she would often catch Isobel glancing at Will. And several times, she had noticed Will gazing at Isobel. Now and then, their eyes would meet—at which point Isobel would often look away. But her tell-tale flush always betrayed her.

Yet would they truly suit? Will was still trying to work out what he believed, whereas Isobel had grown up in a minister's family where God was at the centre of everything. And Isobel had told her several times she could never marry anyone who did not have a firm faith in God. But what did she mean exactly? Perhaps she should talk more with Isobel about it all—and about Will too.

The opportunity came that same evening, as they sat together sewing. Richard had gone out, Will had disappeared to his room and the children were asleep at last. Taking a deep breath, she decided to seize the moment.

'Isobel, do you ever think about what the future might hold for you? After all, you're twenty-three now. I don't mean to pry, but I've seen how well you and Will get on when you work together in the shop. You both find things to laugh and chat about with the customers. And I've noticed how you sometimes look at each other across the dinner table ...'

She broke off, as Isobel put down her sewing and covered her face with her hands.

'Oh, Isobel, I'm so sorry—I didn't mean to upset you. It's just that I love you and want the best for you. Some days, I hate to see you stuck here with us, running after Alice and minding Robbie so I can work in the shop or have some time to myself. You have your own life to lead.'

Isobel's face was pale but determined.

'I knew you'd notice—we've been friends for so long now. Anyway, I owe it to you to tell you what's happening, since this is your home. Will and I do enjoy each other's company and we think the same about so many things. We've had quite a few serious talks, sometimes after you're in bed or on weekends when I don't go home to my family. Will's told me he cares for me a lot and I feel the same about him. But … well, you know how important God is to me, Meggie—and Will's still thinking through all that. I'm glad he's so honest about it, but until he decides what he believes, nothing can happen between us.'

Isobel wiped her eyes and cleared her throat, then went on.

'I don't want to push Will into anything—I'm sure I couldn't anyway. He has to make up his own mind. He's happy to go to church with us sometimes, as you know, but he doesn't want to be a hypocrite either. And right now, he also needs to decide whether to work with your father next year or stay here, so he has lots to think about.'

Her heart went out to Isobel and she patted her on the shoulder.

'You know, Isobel, sometimes I wonder if we think too much about everything rather than just going with our hearts. It's good to know what we believe about God and why, I suppose. But what's made the most difference for me over the last couple of years is knowing God loves and accepts me as I am. Remember how Reverend Fisher used to talk about that often? That's what I try to hang onto, especially when I feel I'm not managing too well.'

'I understand what you're saying, but I think people come to God in different ways, Meggie—and we have to allow them to do that in their own time. Anyway, I'm hoping and praying Will experiences God's love for himself soon too and knows for sure that God's real, whatever anyone else might say.'

'I hope so too, for both your sakes, and I don't want either of you to leave. For some reason, I feel something different will happen for Will next year, although I can't imagine what. He's always been up for an adventure—it's a wonder he settled down enough in Sydney to make it through university. Perhaps his Christian friends had more influence on him than we know.'

As 1914 began to unfold, Richard became more and more

involved in managing the stockfeed and farm supplies aspect of their business. She was thankful Will had decided to stay on, but she could tell he felt unsettled. Often when Isobel headed home for the weekend, he would accompany her, especially after a cyclone damaged so many properties in Helidon in April.

'I'll go home to Mum and Dad again this weekend, Meg,' he often told her. 'Isobel likes company on the train. Anyway, the folk at the Methodist Church still have lots of repairs to do on their building—and I don't mind helping them.'

On other weekends, he sometimes visited friends on a nearby farm, but mostly, he would saddle his horse and ride off somewhere by himself for the day.

'It gives me space to think,' he explained to her one day, without elaborating any further.

Yet soon, the events unfolding in Europe gave them all much to think about, including Will. By July, Richard spent time each day reading every news report he could lay his hands on about the situation on the Continent and the troubles in the Balkans.

'It looks like everything will come to a head soon,' he told them more than once.

He was right. Once Britain declared war on Germany on 4th August, things moved swiftly, with many Harrisville locals needing little encouragement to join up. And it did not surprise her when Will announced to them all one evening that he too had decided to enlist.

'I'm going to volunteer for a Light Horse Regiment—I might as well make the most of all those hours I've spent riding. They want us to take our own horses too, so I'll be fine. I've told Dad already and he supports me one hundred percent. He said he'd do the same if he were younger. But Mum's worried, of course.'

She could see Richard was unhappy about losing him, but also proud of his decision.

'Well … good on you, Will—although we'll miss you for sure. If I were younger and didn't have family responsibilities, I'd think about it too, although my poor eyesight might rule me out. Besides, someone has to keep the economy ticking over here. I guess Meg and Isobel will have to spend more hours in the shop then after you leave, unless we can find someone else to help out.'

True to his nature, Will did not waste any time after that. He enlisted that week and soon discovered he would most likely be sent to Egypt to fight the Turks and help guard the Suez Canal.

'That'll suit me,' he grinned. 'Sounds like we'll see plenty of action.'

Yet his face became serious again, as he glanced across at Isobel. And later, as she settled the children for the night, she could not help overhearing the two of them talking on the veranda.

'Isobel, I've thought a lot about God while I've been out riding, you know. And I sometimes read the Bible at nights, especially the Gospels. My university friends were always telling me to do that, so when you suggested it too, I thought I'd better listen. The more I read, the more convinced I'm becoming that Jesus was God's Son. I can't say I believe it all yet—but I'm on my way. I wanted you to know that because … well, if anything happens to me, I'm thinking I might just squeeze through those pearly gates after all. What do you think?'

She heard Isobel's quick gasp and the quiver in her voice as she responded.

'Don't talk like that, please, Will—we'll all be praying nothing happens to you. As for squeezing through those pearly gates, it's what *God* thinks that really matters, isn't it? But I'm so glad you're reading the Gospels. And I'll pray you soon come to a place of certainty about it all. God never gives up on us, so wherever you go, Will, don't you give up on God either.'

She admired Isobel for her firm faith in God—and her firm stand in her relationship with Will. One day, she hoped to have a faith like hers, but she knew she had a long way to go. Still, she loved how she could often sense God's presence now as she sat painting. And she was learning to rest more in God's love and forgiveness each day. The church services at St John's helped too, especially Holy Communion. Some Sundays when she received the bread and wine, the enormity of Jesus' sacrifice would almost bring her to tears, although Reverend Gillespie's sermons often failed to impact her. But some Sundays too, the bitterness and grief she still felt would well up inside her, causing her to feel shut off from God. She hoped and prayed nothing would happen to Will to give them any further pain—she could not bear that.

In the months after Will left, she felt for Isobel and tried to support her, despite her own concerns. Isobel's faith was strong, but she was only human, after all. Richard had taken over some of Will's tasks but was stretched even further when the young man he had employed to help with the farm supplies joined up too. And as the war escalated, he often stayed up even later at night, writing extra reports for the newspaper, which had also lost staff to the war effort.

They all rejoiced when they received postcards from Will, featuring scenes of pyramids or camels or palm trees. The brief greetings he scrawled did not give much away, but at least they knew he was still alive somewhere in Egypt. She could well imagine him laughing and joking with his mates, even in the most dangerous situations. But it was no laughing matter to see the terrible, ever-growing list of young men from Harrisville and other parts of Queensland killed at Gallipoli in April that year, 1915, and in the months that followed.

'I'm so glad Will joined a Light Horse Regiment instead of some infantry unit,' she commented to Richard one night. 'Otherwise he could well have been among the poor souls trying to get up those cliffs in Turkey.'

'Well, I hate to say it, Meg, but I read today how some Light Horsemen were in fact sent to Gallipoli, although they had to leave their horses behind in Egypt. Still, even if Will's among them, he'll make it, you'll see. He's a resourceful young man. Besides, knowing him, he won't want to leave his horse anywhere without him for too long. He'll find a way to get back.'

She hoped and prayed he was right, but she decided not to tell

Isobel what Richard had said.

By June, she suspected her tiredness was due not only to working more in the shop in Will's absence—and she was right. She was pregnant again. They were all delighted, especially four-year-old Alice.

'I'll be almost five when she's born, Mummy,' she told her often, convinced the baby would be a girl. 'I'll take good care of my little sister.'

She knew that was true too. Sometimes she would take the children with her to the post office, a little further along the main street. They both loved old Mr Atkins, the postmaster, and liked to wave to his wife, who often greeted them from her bedroom window when they walked past. On these excursions, Alice would always behave like a little mother, holding Robbie's hand as he trotted along beside her. But it was in church each Sunday that she was most grateful for her help, especially on Isobel's weekends off. Richard expected them to attend both the morning and evening services and would not budge, whatever she said.

'It's too much for the children, Richard—and for me. And it's extra hard when Isobel's away and you're busy helping Reverend Gillespie or sitting with the choir,' she told him after one particularly tiring Sunday.

'I realise it's not easy, Meg, but the children need to learn to be quiet and respectful in God's house,' he told her, his voice firm. 'And when they're older, they'll go to Sunday School too.'

'Well, at least Alice is usually happy to share her books with Robbie during the sermon. She even tries to tell him in a whisper what the story's about to keep him quiet. But sometimes nothing works, as you know. In the end—and especially if you glare at us from wherever you're sitting—I have to march Robbie out and scold him or even smack him. And I hate doing that.'

But her pleas fell on deaf ears. And she knew that, once Richard made up his mind about something, he was unlikely to change it, even for her. All she could do was hope that, when the new baby arrived, they would find a better way of managing things each week. Whenever the children were quiet enough, she tried to focus during Reverend Gillespie's sermons, but sometimes her mind would wander to her special corner of the veranda where she had set up her easel or even to certain spots along Normanby Gully or Warrill Creek where she loved to paint by herself. She often felt closer to God there than she did at church. Yet those precious moments painting alone were hard to find and would become even more so in the months ahead.

She particularly dreaded harvest time when Reverend Gillespie's asthma often flared up and Richard had to preach instead, as well as conduct the service. She had enough trouble following Reverend Gillespie's sermons, let alone Richard's. His voice was clear and he seemed able to hold the congregation's attention well enough, yet she often wished he would stop using so many theological terms she found hard to understand. She felt disloyal even thinking such things, but decided to talk about it with Isobel anyway.

'Isobel, do you like our church services? They're not what you're used to, are they?'

'I don't mind them, even though they're different from our Methodist ones. We don't celebrate Communion as often as you do and we don't use as much liturgy either. Each week, the minister decides what to include in the order of service and we often make up our own prayers too. But I like your liturgy, Meggie—it keeps us all involved. Most of it is based on the Bible and I like hearing the Old and New Testament lessons read each week too.'

'What about the sermons? Do you find them helpful?'

Isobel hesitated.

'Well … I hate criticising anyone, but I find Reverend Gillespie's sermons a bit confusing. Sometimes he seems to lose his place in his notes, which doesn't help. Still, I'm sure he tries his best.'

'What about when Richard preaches?'

Isobel lowered her eyes and took a few moments to respond.

'Meggie, please don't ever tell him I said this, but … well, sometimes I find him hard to understand too. My father used to say his own sermons needed to be intelligible even to the youngest or least educated in the congregation. Then again, he didn't have the opportunity to read as many theological books as Richard has.'

She could not help laughing at Isobel's apologetic manner.

'You don't have to make excuses for Richard—I know what you mean. Even when I'm not trying to keep Robbie quiet, my mind sometimes wanders when he preaches. But, like you, Isobel, I don't mind our liturgy—and I enjoy the organ music and the hymns. Even the choir isn't too bad, although Richard's the only real tenor they have. Still, I often struggle to feel close to God in church, which is a strange thing to say, isn't it?'

'We're all different, Meggie. Some people enjoy church services like yours, whereas others prefer something simpler. And I think creative people like you may well feel God's presence just as much when they're alone painting as they do in church, especially out somewhere in nature. But I also think what's happening in our own lives can affect how we connect with God. I remember a stage just after Dad died when Mum used to recite the Twenty-Third Psalm out loud, over and over again. It was all she could do—so don't be too hard on yourself.'

'Oh Isobel, I don't know what I'd do without you. You're so good to talk to—and you're always here for me. Richard says church is important because it's a way of encouraging one another, as well as worshipping together, but sometimes I feel more exhausted than encouraged after our services.'

Isobel leant over and patted her hand.

'Don't give up, Meggie—I'm sure you'll feel more positive about it all soon.'

Yet would she? As her pregnancy progressed, she began to wonder how she would cope with three young children, on top of helping in the shop. She wished Richard could find someone else to replace Will, but even many of the young women from the area had gone to Brisbane to take up jobs left vacant when the men enlisted. She could not blame them—this was their opportunity. And they were needed to keep the hospitals and factories and shops going. Yet it made life so much harder for those in country towns like theirs.

Christmas that year turned out to be a rather sober affair, given all the food shortages—and the fact that there had been no recent news from Will. They had been invited home to Helidon and also to Aunty Betty's but decided to stay in Harrisville, since there was no one else to look after the shop. Anyway, she did not feel like travelling in the hot weather, with the baby due in a matter of weeks. Isobel had gone home for Christmas, but had promised to be back in time for the birth. And she knew Isobel would keep her word, even if it meant missing out on time with her family. She had not bothered to ask her mother to come and help—and her mother had not offered either, which hurt. But that was how it was and no doubt always would be.

The children still loved walking with her to the post office and waving to the postmaster's wife, but it was Alice who realised one day not long after Christmas that they had not seen her for a while.

'Mummy, where's Mrs Atkins? Do you think she's sick?'

'I don't know, dear. Tell you what—let's ask Mr Atkins next time we go to the post office,' she told her, her mind on other things.

She almost forgot when the moment came, but Alice soon prompted her.

'How's your wife, Mr Atkins? We often wave to her, but we haven't seen her for a while.'

His face softened, as he looked at them from under his bushy, white eyebrows.

'She hasn't been too well, to be honest, Mrs McPherson, but she's on the mend now. I know she likes waving to you all too. She loves children—we weren't able to have any of our own.'

He paused then, looking thoughtful.

'Tell you what, why don't you come and say a quick hello to her now? It's lunchtime, so I can close the post office for a while. Just follow me. She'd love to see you—it'll cheer her up.'

'Well, if she won't mind …'

'Not at all,' he beamed, as he ushered them into the house in his courteous way, then along the hallway to the bedroom. 'Hettie, my love, you have some visitors. The children have missed seeing you wave to them, so we thought you might enjoy saying a quick hello today. This is Mrs McPherson. And this young lady here is Alice. Last but not least, this young man here is Robbie.'

'Please call me Meg, Mrs Atkins,' she told her. 'We're so pleased to meet you, but we don't want to intrude.'

'And please call me Hettie,' the older woman responded, as she smiled at them all. 'I've been a little unwell, but I'm a lot better now. The hot weather doesn't suit me—it seems to sap all my energy. I'm sure you must find it tiring too, Meg. When's your baby due?'

They chatted for a while, until Alice and Robbie became a little restless.

'Don't worry about them,' Hettie told her, 'but I expect you'd like to head home and put your feet up. Before you go though, children, I might have a little something here for you.'

She picked up a small bowl from her bedside table and held it out.

'Please take a barley sugar, Alice and Robbie, providing your mother says it's all right. I eat too many anyway. And please call me Aunty Hettie—I'd like that.'

'Say thank you, both of you,' Meg prompted them. 'It's so good to meet you at last, Hettie. Perhaps we can call in again another day.'

'You'd be most welcome. And after the baby arrives, I'd love to have a nurse sometime. God bless you all—and I'll be praying for the baby's safe arrival too.'

She was surprised at Hettie's final words but tried not to show it. They had sounded sincere—and she had also noticed a well-worn Bible on the bed. She wondered which church the Atkins belonged to. Or maybe Mr Atkins needed to look after Hettie on Sundays and did not go anywhere. Richard would know—as the local reporter, he seemed to have learnt so much about everyone in Harrisville.

When she asked him, his answer intrigued her.

'Cliff's Church of England, but his wife's Presbyterian. He used to come to church before our time, I understand, but can't manage it now because of his wife's health. I think Len Gillespie visits them when he can—although I suspect he doesn't get there too often. … By the way, Meg, I may have to do more in the services again soon. Len's thinking about enlisting as an army chaplain. I don't like his chances, given his weak chest, but you never know. If the war goes on much longer, they may take anyone—even someone like me.'

Her heart skipped a beat.

'Richard, I can't believe you'd even *think* of enlisting. Soon you'll have three children to provide for. Besides, your eyesight's not good enough.'

She was sorry she had reacted the way she had,. as soon as she heard the irritation in Richard's voice.

'I know, I know, Meg—you don't have to remind me. And we need people here to keep the shops open. I don't warm to the idea of staying here while everyone else heads overseas to fight for us, but … well … that's how it is, I guess. Anyway, if Len's accepted, I'll have to stand in for him, unless a locum becomes available, which I doubt.'

She would have liked to ask him more about the Atkins and also about Reverend Gillespie's plans, but she left it at that. Better to choose a time when he was not so tired. Yet those moments did not seem to come often these days, with all there was for them both to do.

And soon there was even less opportunity to talk, when Elizabeth Grace, Alice's longed-for little sister, arrived safely at the end of January, weighing a hefty ten pounds. She felt a warm glow spread through her once again as she sensed Richard's delight and watched him hold his new baby daughter with such pride.

'This one's going to be like you, I think, Meg—she has your pretty nose and chin. She seems so strong and healthy too. Look how she's holding onto my finger!'

Baby Elizabeth was indeed strong and healthy, with what seemed like an almost insatiable appetite. For the first few weeks, she found it exhausting, having to wake so often in the night to feed her. Things became easier once the baby could manage some thin porridge and milk custard, but the days still passed in a blur for her.

At times, Richard tried to help out in the kitchen, but his efforts tended to create even more work for Isobel or her. She often had to hide a smile, as she watched him retreat to his office with a mixture of exasperation and relief or head out to yet another meeting. Yet she felt proud of him for his achievements in so many other areas. He had become a leading figure in the town and was often required to attend committee meetings and community events in the evenings, particularly with so many men absent. And even after he came home late from these, he would tend to stay up, writing his newspaper reports.

In early May, they were relieved to hear from Will again at last. She heard a faint gasp from Isobel when Richard came in for lunch brandishing a postcard from him, which she could see featured another desert scene.

'Look what turned up at the post office,' he told them with a grin, as he handed the precious postcard over.

She tried to read what Will had written, as she sat feeding Elizabeth, but her tears made it impossible.

'Oh, it's such a relief to hear from him. If I know Will, he's probably been too lazy to write before this. Perhaps you'd better read it out for us, Richard.'

'He hasn't written much. All he says is he's well and still with his Light Horse regiment. No doubt he's helping to fend off the Turks again near the Suez Canal, from what I've read in the papers—and having the time of his life doing it.'

'Well, at least we know he's still alive,' she managed to say.

'Yes, which is good news these days,' he said in the vague tone he used when his mind was elsewhere. 'Look, if you ladies don't mind, I'll take my sandwiches back to the office and get on with wading through the rest of this mail.'

After Richard left, she glanced across at Isobel. She had noticed her turn away when she saw the postcard and wipe her eyes.

'Are you all right, Isobel? I'm so relieved for you. I hope and pray God continues to keep Will safe and that things work out for you both when he comes home.'

'I … I don't have any right to react like this,' Isobel said in a shaky voice. 'Will knows where I stand and … well, there was nothing decided between us when he enlisted. But I pray each day that God will watch over him and that he'll grow in his faith.'

'There's nothing I'd like more than to have you as a sister-in-law, but I honour you for sticking to what you believe. I'm sure Will would always respect your faith in God, even if he didn't see things quite the same as you, but I know that wouldn't be enough for you. You're so strong, Isobel—and you've helped me grow so much in my own faith too.'

'I'm not always as strong as you think, Meggie. Sometimes when I see how hard Mum works and how much our family misses Dad, I feel so angry and wish with all my heart that things were different for Mum and the others—and for me. But I'm trying to rely on God more and trust Him with my future. I don't know what that will be, but God does, so I know I need to stay close to Him.'

Her heart went out to her friend. *Please God*, she found herself praying, *make the path ahead smooth for her—and may Will soon join her on that same path.*

Several weeks passed before she managed to visit Hettie Atkins again with the baby, as promised, along with Alice and Robbie. Mr Atkins's lined face lit up when he saw them and he immediately ushered them into the house, where they found Hettie seated in a comfortable, old, wicker chair at a big, oak desk in the lounge.

'When Hettie's feeling a little better, she enjoys spending time writing,' he explained. 'I'll leave you to it then, if you'll excuse me.'

She could see Hettie looked better than she had on their first visit. Today, she was wearing a pretty, blue dress the exact colour of her eyes and a soft, white shawl that matched her wavy hair. Her gentle smile lit up her whole face, as she turned to welcome them.

'What a wonderful surprise! Now … who have you brought to meet me today? I can see by this beautiful, pink dress that she must be a girl. Congratulations, my dear. Alice and Robbie, perhaps you can tell me your sister's name. … Elizabeth Grace? You must be so proud of her. Could I hold her, do you think?'

For a moment, she thought she detected mixed emotions on Hettie's face, as she laid Elizabeth in her arms. But then Hettie seemed to pull herself together, as she stroked the baby's cheek.

'Oh, what a sweet little thing—and I do love her name, Meg.'

'My husband chose it. His mother's second name was Elizabeth. But I like it too.'

'And Grace—such a beautiful name to give a child. Yes, my little one,' she said, as she held the baby close, 'may you always experience God's amazing grace in your life and come to know the wonderful lovingkindness of God for yourself. Amen, Lord.'

She noticed how quiet the children were, as if sensing something special was happening. Hettie's gentle, heartfelt blessing seemed much more real than the words Reverend Gillespie had read out at Elizabeth's christening the previous Sunday. They had felt so formal and impersonal, whereas Hettie's words had been simple, yet so full of God's love and grace.

The moment passed, as Alice and Robbie began fiddling with the shiny handles of the desk.

'Do you have any barley sugars left, Aunty Hettie?' Alice asked at last in a hopeful voice.

She tried to shush her, but Hettie only laughed.

'Don't worry, dear. Alice, be a good girl and take Robbie to my bedroom. You remember where you came to see me last time? You'll find some on the bedside table again. I know I can trust you to take just one each, can't I? Thank you.'

Hettie turned to her then.

'Now that they're gone, my dear, how are you *really*? I prayed for a safe delivery for you and I've kept praying for God's strength for you during these past few weeks too.'

The words were spoken with such love that she found it hard not to cry.

'I … I'm doing fine, Hettie—thank you for praying for me. I need those prayers so much. My friend Isobel who lives with us has been a huge help. I don't know what I'd do without her, to be honest. Richard's so busy …'

Her voice trailed off and she was thankful when Hettie started talking again.

'I'm sure you're run off your feet, Isobel or no Isobel. I wonder—I don't want to make you any busier, but do you think Isobel could look after Alice and Robbie now and then so you could spend a little time with me? You could bring the baby. It might help you, my dear—and I'd enjoy it too. I've felt burdened for you—and I wonder if God's prompting me to share a few things with you that I've learnt in my own life. Of course, it's up to you, but please know you'd be welcome anytime. And if I'm not well enough, Cliff will tell you.'

At first, she had been reluctant to take up Hettie's offer, but in the end, Isobel's encouragement won out.

'Do it, Meggie,' she told her. 'You need someone older to talk to—and Mrs Atkins could be just the right person. Don't worry about Alice and Robbie. They'll be fine.'

Hettie's comments soon reassured her too.

'I feel God's brought us together for a reason, my dear, so let's listen to Him and find out what that could be. Perhaps it's merely that I'm someone older to talk to, given you don't see your mother often. But I'm sure God will show us.'

Every few weeks, she tried to make time to meet with Hettie— and soon she began to wonder what she would have done without these meetings. After arriving, she would settle herself in a chair beside Hettie's bed or next to her desk in the lounge. Then they would sit in silence, sensing God's presence with them, which in itself brought such peace. Sometimes she would come with questions for Hettie, only to end up talking about something quite different.

Yet these unexpected conversations often turned out to be the most fruitful of all.

'How do you have such wisdom, Hettie? And how can you be so at peace, with all your health problems?' she burst out on one occasion.

'One day, I'll tell you my story,' Hettie told her with a small sigh. 'But all I can say is, any wisdom I have comes from what God's taught me over the years. I haven't always been at peace with the way my life has unfolded, my dear—and sometimes even now I'm not. But I've learnt that, whatever happens, God will always give me the strength to handle it.'

'I try to believe that, Hettie, but sometimes it's hard not feel bitter about things, isn't it? Sometimes I feel so angry and sad. It feels like a big, tight knot deep down inside that I can't undo. I don't like talking about it, but perhaps I should tell you what happened …'

She took a deep breath and plunged on, spilling out the whole story of Jimbo's death and how hard it was to forgive her mother for blaming her. She talked about her miscarriage too and the dark days afterwards and how Reverend Fisher and Isobel had encouraged her to open her heart to God's love and forgiveness. And finally, she told her about taking up her painting again and how healing that was.

'I love my corner on our veranda where I paint, but I don't have much energy for it right now. Besides, I suspect Richard thinks it's a waste of time, when we're so shorthanded in the shop and when I have so much else to do. But Hettie, sometimes when I'm sitting in church, trying to keep the children quiet, I find myself wishing I was back home painting—or, better still, outside in nature all by myself. It might seem strange, but that's where I feel God's presence the most.'

Hettie did not respond straight away, but when she did, her voice was firm.

'Meg, I know you have so much to do, caring for your little ones, as well as supporting your husband in the shop and at church. But in order to stay close to God through it all, our spirits need to receive real nourishment, don't you think? I used to love our church services, yet when I couldn't attend anymore, I found I could meet with God in other ways—and that includes listening to Him as I write. Someday, I'll tell you more about that too. But for now, I'm going to pray you can find those special times of refreshment with God—and that might well be when you paint. … Please look after yourself, my dear. And thank you for sharing your story with me. That took courage.'

# Chapter Nine

To their amazement, Len Gillespie was accepted as an army chaplain early in 1917.

'I hate to be unkind,' Richard commented, after hearing the news, 'but the army must be desperate to accept someone with … well, with his health record and fitness level.'

'Not to mention his muddled preaching or his lack of organisational ability,' she added, without thinking.

As soon as the words left her mouth, she regretted them—especially when Richard frowned at her in disapproval and glanced in Isobel's direction. He was always so loyal when it came to Len Gillespie and church matters in general. She tried to retrieve the situation as best she could then and rushed on.

'Well anyway, he has a good heart—and perhaps army life will suit him better. But … have they found a locum to fill in for him?'

'I suspect there aren't any available, although I'm sure the bishop will do his best to find one. In the meantime, as the only church warden around, I'll have to see that things run smoothly. And I'll be busier in the services too, of course.'

Her heart sank, but there was no point in saying anything. Besides, she knew he enjoyed his church commitments.

By Easter, Len Gillespie had gone, and Richard was left to care for the parish, with occasional help from one of the ministers in Ipswich. The church members did their best to support him, but she soon discovered how much they looked to him to make the final decision about so many things—including even the cleaning and flower rosters.

She was always glad of Isobel's help when it was their Saturday to clean. As they polished the brass crosses and candlesticks and dusted everywhere, they would often let Alice and Robbie run in and out of the pews, something Richard would never let them do on Sundays. But she was thankful she could leave all the flower-arranging to Isobel.

'I might be an artist, Isobel, but I'm hopeless with flowers,' she laughed. 'Aunty Betty tried to teach me, but it didn't take her long to give up.'

'I don't mind. I had plenty of practice helping Mum when Dad was alive.'

It was good to see Isobel smile, as she filled the vases with fluffy, white chrysanthemums or colourful gerberas from their own garden or sometimes red poinsettia from the churchyard, depending on the season. She had seen that smile less and less as the war dragged on, with no further word from Will. It had been many months since his last, scrawled postcard had arrived.

'Don't worry,' Richard told them often. 'From what I've read, I suspect his regiment's somewhere in Palestine now, so communication could be difficult from there.'

She knew her parents had not heard from Will either—her father wrote from time to time and Caroline and Harriet had visited them during the August holidays. She had also been pleasantly surprised and touched when her mother had sent a little knitted jacket with them for Elizabeth, along with a brief note, but there was still no real communication between them.

As the year wore on, she seemed to be in a constant whirl of busyness. Yet she was determined to take Hettie's advice and find time to paint and be alone with God. Sometimes when Robbie and Elizabeth were having their afternoon naps before Alice came home from school or when all the children were asleep in the evenings, she would tiptoe out to her special corner of the veranda, even though she was tired herself. It was always a struggle at first to quieten her spirit, but she was beginning to glimpse what Hettie meant when she talked about connecting with God heart to heart. Sometimes the grief and remorse she still felt at times would threaten to rob her of her peace, but, little by little, she was learning to hand it all over to God and receive God's deep love and reassurance in return.

She also still treasured her times with Hettie and was grateful for Isobel's ongoing efforts to help her get there. Sometimes when she arrived, she sensed Hettie was in pain, but Hettie rarely referred to her health problems that confined her to the house or the ongoing pain she suffered.

'Don't let's talk about me, dear,' she would say. 'This is *your* precious time. Now, how are you really?'

She shared all sorts of issues and concerns with Hettie, including her frustration at having so little time to herself.

'I often feel so guilty when I take time to paint, Hettie. I keep thinking of all the jobs I should be doing. And sometimes I hear a little voice whispering, "you don't deserve any time to yourself—you don't deserve ever to paint again". I know it's the enemy, trying to accuse me all over again about what happened to Jimbo—and I know in my head at least I wasn't to blame. But sometimes when I'm tired, my thoughts get muddled and I forget how much God loves and accepts me, whatever happened.'

'That's good you realise what's going on, Meg. Satan's always out to accuse and deceive us. I've seen that in my own life, as well as Cliff's. For many years, he felt so responsible for my health issues, most of which stem from injuries I received in an accident soon after we were married. Cliff blamed himself for that accident, but that's just what it was, my dear—a terrible accident. Poor Cliff was devastated. Eventually God got through to him and he realised it wasn't his fault. Yet sometimes even now, if he's aware I'm in pain, I see tears in his eyes and I know what he's thinking. But do you know what we do, dear? We hold hands and pray together and praise God until that old enemy slinks away. And we sing hymns too—especially the ones that remind us of the day when we'll be with God and there'll be no more pain and suffering.'

'Oh Hettie, I need to do that too. At least, I don't think Richard would want to pray and sing with me—or have time to, for that matter—but I could do it by myself. Richard's faith is strong and he loves our church and all it stands for, but … well … it's more of a private matter for him in many ways, even though he enjoys preaching. Sometimes Richard and I seem to like different things when it comes to worship and church.'

'We're all different, Meg—that's how God made us. Cliff grew up in the Church of England and I was brought up as a Presbyterian. But nowadays, we've grown used to having our own little service here by ourselves each Sunday, although Cliff still goes to church on occasions. I know it's important to meet with others, but God has sustained us anyway over the years and taught us so much. Sometimes we have such joyful times here together, just Jesus and Cliff and I.'

'That sounds wonderful, Hettie. Your faith's so strong and resilient, like Isobel's—I'm so glad God brought you into my life. I don't know what I'd do without Isobel and you.'

Hettie became serious then.

'I'm humbled you should say that, Meg. But I won't be here forever—and I'm sure God has other things ahead for Isobel too. None of us knows what the future will hold. That's one reason we need to be sure of our faith, so that, whatever happens, we can still stand firm.'

She heard what Hettie said, yet part of her did not want to take it on board. She would hate to lose Isobel, yet she loved her and wanted those 'other things' Hettie believed God had for her—perhaps even marriage to Will. But as for Hettie's leaving …

One afternoon in September, Richard came into the house grinning and waving a letter.

'I think I might have good news for you, Meg. The bishop's found a locum for St John's at last—and you'll never guess who it is.'

'I've no idea, but I hope it's someone good,' she said a little wearily, as she picked up Elizabeth.

'Consider it done, my dear—it's Reverend Fisher!'

She could not believe it.

'Oh, that's such wonderful news, Richard! But … but how is he free to come to Harrisville?'

'I understand he retired a while back, but apparently he's happy to do some locums while the war's on at least. What a godsend. I haven't minded filling in, but I'll be glad to hand things over to him. Perhaps I can be more involved in other community groups then.'

She sighed. She would have liked him to be at home more instead, but knew he enjoyed his involvement in the various organisations around town. And she was proud of his efforts and of how well-regarded he was everywhere. Besides, if he continued to feel so valued in Harrisville, he might decide to stay put there longer than they had at Red Hill.

When Reverend Fisher arrived, she was touched at how delighted he was to see them again. He looked older and more stooped, but still had that same gentle, understanding manner that had warmed her heart and brought her so much healing back at Red Hill. He was also delighted to meet Robbie and Elizabeth and to catch up with Isobel again.

'It must have helped a lot, Meg, having Isobel here with you,' he told her. 'But how's your painting going? I'd love to see what you've produced since I saw you last.'

She looked at him ruefully.

'I haven't had much time for painting, what with the baby's arrival and needing to fill in for Will in the shop. But Isobel's always encouraging me to get back to it. And so is Hettie Atkins, an older friend I've made here. I'm sure the two of you would get on well.'

'Hettie Atkins … now where have I seen that name before? … Is she a writer? I seem to remember reading a story by a Hettie Atkins in a church magazine not long ago—and an excellent poem too.'

'I know she writes, but I didn't realise her work had been published. What a dark horse. I'd be happy to introduce you to her sometime.'

Reverend Fisher soon proved a blessing to her in more ways than one. She was grateful Richard could now hand over many of the tasks involved in keeping the parish running. She understood and appreciated his sermons. And she loved the way he would call in on occasions to see how she was and to chat with Isobel and the children. But most of all, she was thankful he was there when they received the news they had been dreading for so long.

Will was dead. He had been killed during the Battle of Beersheba in Palestine at the end of October.

One look at Richard's face as he entered the kitchen and she knew something terrible had happened. The thin, cream-coloured paper clutched in his hand confirmed her worst fears and she could see his hand was shaking.

'What … what's happened, Richard? Is it Will? Is he dead?'

Richard nodded, then came and held her close. But after a while, she wrenched herself away and went to Isobel who was standing at the sink as if turned to stone. She put her arms around her and could feel her whole body shaking.

'Oh Isobel—I'm so sorry.'

They clung to each other, sobbing, while Richard tried to console them both. Then she met Richard's gaze and saw that his eyes were filled with tears too. Yes, she had lost her beloved older brother, but he had lost a brother-in-law who was also his trusted friend and business partner. Worse still, her parents had lost their one remaining son—and that was too awful for her even to think about.

Isobel tried to wipe her eyes and began to make a cup of tea for them all.

'I'd better get back to the shop, Meg,' Richard managed to say after a while, his voice husky. 'We'll talk about what to do later. Your parents know already—the telegram was from your father.'

By then, Robbie and Elizabeth were pressing around her legs, their little faces puckered with worry. She sat down, gathered them close and tried to comfort them, although, in reality, she was the one who needed the comfort of their small, loving arms. Yet today, those little arms also reminded her of Jimbo's, as he had held onto her when the waters raged around them. He would have been eleven, if he was still alive—almost a young man. And now there would be no young Porter men to join the family business. How cruel it all was—how utterly cruel and senseless.

'Oh Isobel, what are we going to do?' was all she could think to say, as their tears continued to flow.

'I guess all we can do is grieve, Meggie. And somehow, with God's help, we'll get through this—although it seems such a terrible, terrible waste. I loved Will and I'd hoped and prayed ... but it's too late for all that now. God's brought us through other big losses and He'll give us the strength to keep going now.'

Reverend Fisher said much the same when he visited them later that day, after hearing the news from Richard, but he kept his words to a minimum. Just as he had done at Red Hill, he seemed to know how to sit and be present with them, comforting them even in the silence.

'There's little one can say that will be any great comfort, I've found—but I know God can do that without words,' he said, as he rose to leave. 'I've experienced these times far too often lately to blunder in with any trite comments. I'm here whenever you need to talk—and I'll be praying for you all. But try to allow yourselves to grieve. And Meg, remember how your painting helped you work through things when you were at Red Hill, my dear.'

Will had been well-liked by their customers and the news that he had been killed in action travelled fast. Later that week, she received a beautiful card from Hettie, with a hand-written poem that touched her heart. She wondered about sending the poem to her parents, in the hope that it would comfort them too. Or should she perhaps go and see them? Yet as she thought of how they must be feeling, guilt threatened to overwhelm her all over again. ... If only Jimbo had not followed her to the creek that day. At least they would have one son left.

Her head was so muddled—she needed to talk it all over with Richard.

'I don't know what's the best thing to do,' she told him that night. 'I feel so sorry for Mum and Dad. I've been wondering if I should go and see them, but I think it'd be too much for Mum to have all the children there—and I don't think it's fair to leave them here with Isobel when she's so sad herself. Anyway, I'm not sure I could face seeing them right now. I keep thinking how they'd still have *one* son at least, if Jimbo hadn't drowned ...'

She could not go on then. Richard held her close, patting her and stroking her hair.

'Meg, you don't have to keep feeling responsible like that, but I've been wondering about paying your parents a quick visit myself next week. I need to take Will's things to them sometime, along with some money of his. I know you'll be extra busy if I'm not here, but I think it's the best option.'

She did not say anything at first, as she rested in the safety of his arms, but soon realised the wisdom of what he had suggested.

'Thanks, Richard—I think that's probably the best idea. I'll write them a note for you to take—and perhaps I could write out Hettie's poem for them too.'

She was sure they had made the right decision when she discovered she was pregnant again, just before Richard set off for Helidon.

'I've been extra tired lately and a bit nauseous, but I thought it might just be a reaction to losing Will,' she told Richard when she gave him the news. 'I know you'll be delighted, but I don't know how I feel, to be honest. It'll be lovely for the children to have another little brother or sister. But it's hard for me to be happy about the baby when I still feel so sad about Will. And … well, I'm not sure how I'll manage everything either, with another little one to care for.'

'You'll be fine, Meg. When I come back, I'll try to get someone else to help out in the shop. Surely the war will be over soon—then we'll have lots of young men looking for work.'

'But we won't have Will,' she blurted out, her eyes filling with tears. 'And Richard … I suppose you should tell Mum about the baby, but it might remind her of Jimbo all over again—and how she's lost both Will and him now.'

'Well … I don't suppose we need to tell them quite yet—you can write to them further down the track. It might even give your mother something nice to look forward to, now Will won't be coming back.'

'I don't know,' she gulped, as she wiped her eyes. 'She hasn't made much effort with her grandchildren so far—although she did send that pretty jumper for Elizabeth.'

In the days that followed, she tried to be strong for Isobel's sake, as well as the children's, but it was difficult—especially when Richard returned from seeing her parents.

'I hate to say it, Meg, but I think it'll be a long time before your mother gets over Will's death. She refused to look at his belongings that I took back, so your father packed them away. All she wanted to do was stare at a photo of Will in his army uniform, taken just after he enlisted. And she had one of James next to it too—I think it was at his third birthday party.'

She could not bear to hear anything more. Instead, with a stifled sob, she went to their room and flung herself on the bed. Yet she knew she could not stay there for long. The children needed her— and Isobel did too. Will's death had hit them all hard, but somehow they would have to find the strength to carry on.

'You'll get through this time, Meg,' Reverend Fisher told her when he next called. 'Right now, it must be extra hard to deal with it all, given you're expecting another little one. But God hasn't forgotten you. He can give you the strength you need. And … well, I know this might sound impossible, but you must paint again, my dear. God will bring healing and comfort to you as you do, just as He has in the past.'

In the end, it was Hettie Atkins's story that inspired her to start painting again. When she managed to visit Hettie not long before Christmas, she found her writing at her desk.

'Come in, Meg—I'm so pleased you could get here today. How are you? … My dear, I was so very, very sorry to hear your sad news. I never met your brother, but I used to see him sometimes from my bedroom window. And Cliff always spoke highly of him.'

'We're managing, Hettie, but it's been hard. Thank you for your beautiful card and poem. I've put them in a safe spot where I can look at them whenever I need to. You have a wonderful way with words—it must be so fulfilling to be able to express yourself in that way and bless others in the process.'

'Yes indeed—and it's healing too, just as painting is for you, I'm sure. But Meg, I'd like to tell you how I started writing, if you have time. I remember promising I'd share my story with you sometime and I've sensed God wants me to today.'

'I'd like that, Hettie. Isobel will be fine with the children for a while.'

'Just after we were married way back in 1870, Cliff was appointed to a small post office at Beenleigh. It had opened a few years earlier to meet the needs of the sugar cane farmers in the area. One weekend, we decided to visit friends on a farm a little north of Beenleigh. To get there, we had to cross a creek that flows into the Logan River. When we'd visited them another time, there was only a trickle of water in the creek, but this time it was much deeper. We were never sure what spooked our horse—perhaps he was afraid of the water or maybe he slipped in the mud—but the buggy tipped over and I was thrown onto some rocks. Cliff ended up in the water, which cushioned his fall. But when he checked on me, he couldn't rouse me, so he ran to get our friends. They carried me back to their home and eventually I regained consciousness. But I was in a lot of pain and, when the doctor arrived, he said I had broken my hip and pelvis and had internal injuries. When I could be moved again, they took me by boat down the Logan River, then up the Brisbane River and, from there, by horse and cart to the hospital. There was no train line back then and that was the safest way for me to travel, even though it took so long. The doctors patched me up as best they could, but afterwards, it was hard to walk by myself. And … well … they also told me I'd never be able to have children.'

She was shocked and put her hand on Hettie's arm.

'Oh Hettie, that must have been so terrible for you—and for Cliff. And I hate to think how much pain you had to go through. … Please don't feel you have to tell me anymore if it's too upsetting for you.'

'I'm fine, dear—I wanted to tell you. But yes, poor Cliff suffered so much too. You see, as I told you once, he blamed himself for trying to take the buggy through that creek. He knew our horse could be a bit skittish around water. And he also felt things might have been different if he hadn't hit the creek at such a pace—but I doubt it, as I've told him often. Anyway, after several months, I was allowed home and, ever since, Cliff's been such a wonderful help. As well as doing a full day's work  wherever we've been sent, he's looked after my every need.'

'I can see he's devoted to you, Hettie. And he's so proud of you and your writing.'

'Yes, I know—although I have to admit I wasn't always easy to get on with in those early days, my dear. I wasn't angry at Cliff. After all, I'd wanted to cross that creek as much as he had and I would've done the same. But I was angry at God—especially because we couldn't have children. We'd both wanted a large family, you see. And I'd always been very active, so to be confined indoors day in and day out seemed unbearable. Yet what could I do? Cliff and I had a strong faith in God and were regular church attenders, but this was a huge test for us both.'

Hettie fell silent, a faraway look in her eyes. Then she gave herself a little shake and continued on.

'After a while, my mother came to stay with us for a few weeks, while my two younger sisters cared for my father. She didn't say much, but she sat by my bed, holding me when I cried, praying hard and reading the Psalms to me. Sometimes I didn't want to hear them. Sometimes I even shouted at her to stop. But one day—I'll never forget it—I knew God was right there in the room with us. My heart was beating so fast and it was as if the words she read were piercing right into me.'

She held her breath as she watched Hettie reach for her old, battered Bible.

'The words she read were from Psalm 116—and I feel I should read them to you today, Meg. Do you have time?'

She nodded and Hettie began:

*I love the Lord, because he hath heard my voice and my supplications.*

*Because he hath inclined his ear unto me, therefore will I call upon him as long as I live.*

*The sorrows of death compassed me, and the pains of hell laid hold upon me: I found trouble and sorrow.*

*Then called I upon the name of the Lord; O Lord, I beseech thee, deliver my soul.*

*Gracious is the Lord, and righteous; yea, our God is merciful.*

*The Lord preserveth the simple: I was brought low, and he helped me.*

*Return unto thy rest, O my soul; for the Lord hath dealt bountifully with thee.*

*For thou hast delivered my soul from death, mine eyes from tears, and my feet from falling.*

*I will walk before the Lord in the land of the living.*

A sweet presence seemed to surround them then, as Hettie finished reading. She closed her eyes and felt a wonderful, healing balm flow over her, almost engulfing her. At first, she could not understand what was happening, but then she knew, beyond the shadow of a doubt, that it was God's love pouring over her and bringing with it such comfort and peace.

She did not want to move, but opened her eyes when Hettie began speaking again.

'That day, God gave me the strength to accept what had happened and begin to move on with my life. It wasn't always easy—sometimes I slipped back into complaining and feeling sorry for myself. But always, always, God picked me up again and helped me find those things I could still do—things that turned out to be so fulfilling, like my writing and spending time with people like you, Meg. That day, I realised that, even though I had experienced trouble and sorrow, God had preserved my life and would continue to help and comfort me, just like the psalm says. But I had to decide to trust God and claim that final sentence of the psalm for myself: *I will walk before the Lord in the land of the living.* ... And that's God's challenge for you today as well, I believe, my dear.'

She stayed silent for some time. Then she squared her shoulders and reached for Hettie's hand.

'Hettie, *I will walk before the Lord in the land of the living* too, as God helps and strengthens me. I know God's been with us today. I don't know how to describe what happened, but I feel so comforted and blessed.'

'That's wonderful. Remember this day, Meg—and remember your promise to God too. I ... well, I suspect there could be more changes ahead that may be hard for you at first. But whatever happens, remember God will help you through it all.'

She decided not to ask what those changes might be. Instead, she bowed her head as Hettie held her hands and prayed for her.

When Hettie had finished, she knew she should go home and relieve Isobel, but she wanted to ask one more thing.

'Hettie, what about your writing? You haven't told me how you started doing that.'

'I'm sorry—I forgot. Well, I'd always loved to write, but after that day, it was as if God lit a flame in me and I began to write all sorts of stories and poetry. I found it so rewarding—and it also helped me make sense of my difficulties. Then, when some of my writing was published, I began to see how others could be helped as well. So that's why I encourage you to find time to paint, Meg. God's given you such a wonderful gift and I believe that, as you express yourself in this way, you'll receive even more healing and fulfilment and bless others too.'

She felt as if she was treading on air as she hurried home. She had been gone longer than she had meant to, but as soon as she opened the door, she could see the children had had a wonderful morning with Isobel. They were all crowded around the kitchen table, making scones and laughing together. Robbie was covered in flour and Elizabeth was sitting on the table, licking dough off her chubby hands.

'We're doing some baking, Mummy,' Robbie told her with pride. 'Isobel says we're helping a lot. We're having our scones for lunch.'

'Are you going to leave some for Daddy and me too?'

'If you're good,' he told her, his cheeks dimpling as he laughed up at her.

She laughed as well—he had spoken in the same tone she herself often used. But her breath caught in her throat too. For a fleeting moment, he had reminded her so much of Jimbo. Then she steadied herself, thanked Isobel for entertaining them and promised to tell her what had happened at Hettie's as soon as she could.

That evening, she tried to tell Richard all about it. He listened, but she could see he did not quite grasp how much it had meant to her.

'I didn't know the details of Hettie's accident and how they couldn't have children as a result—that's very sad. But I knew about Hettie's writing. She's had a couple of poems printed in the Queensland Times over the years, I understand, and one or two short stories in magazines. But I think she mostly writes for small Presbyterian publications. … As for Psalm 116, Meg, I think you need to remember it was written at a very different time in history and for a different purpose too. But the words are beautiful and I'm glad they helped you.'

She winced at the dismissive tone in his voice as he talked about Hettie's writing. He had used the same tone once or twice about her own paintings, which had annoyed her at the time. But to hear Hettie's work denigrated even a little was hard to take. She swallowed, wishing she knew how to defend her friend, but in the end, decided to say nothing. After all, as a writer himself, Richard was no doubt well able to judge such things. Yet she felt she had to respond to his comments about the psalm Hettie had read out.

'I'm well aware I don't know anything about when Psalm 116 was written or why, Richard, but I found the words so powerful and comforting. They meant a lot to me, right here today in Harrisville, and I hope I never forget them.'

She left it at that, but was glad she had said something at least. Those precious moments at Hettie's had been so wonderful—she did not want them spoilt in any way.

It was a relief to speak freely with Isobel about it all the next day when they found a quiet moment to talk.

'Isobel, I know in my heart God's Spirit was right there speaking to me through that psalm. I know something happened to me yesterday that I can't quite explain. And I want to grow and become stronger in my faith so I'm ready to face those challenges Hettie mentioned, whatever they might be.'

'That's wonderful, Meggie—and I'll be praying for you too. … Do you know that verse in Hebrews that talks about God's Word being powerful and alive and sharper than a two-edged sword? I think that's what you experienced with Hettie, don't you?'

She could tell Isobel understood and she was so thankful for her support. But several times during the following weeks, she caught Isobel staring into space in the middle of some mundane task, as if lost in another world. In the end, after saying her name several times one day and receiving no response, she decided to find out what was happening.

'Is everything all right, Isobel? You didn't seem to hear me …' she said gently, as she put her arm around her shoulders.

Isobel jumped and her face flushed with embarrassment.

'I'm so sorry, Meggie—I was miles away. I'm fine, but … I guess it's just taking a while for it to sink in that Will's never coming back. Not that we had any definite understanding between us, as you know. And it's far worse for you, having lost a wonderful big brother. But I'm also trying to work out what God might want me to do with my life now. I know I'm needed here, especially with your baby due soon—I won't let you down. But I want to be open to whatever God has for me to do in the future too. I don't know for sure yet, although … well, I'm thinking about applying to become a missionary. We have a dear family friend serving in China and I've always been interested in her work with women and children there.'

She was stunned but tried to keep her voice steady as she responded.

'Oh Isobel, what can I say? You have every right to do what you want with your life, but … well, I can't imagine how we'd manage without you—and I'd miss you so much. … Please don't do anything in a hurry, will you? Please think about it long and hard. Besides, while you and Will would have made a wonderful couple, there'll be plenty other young men around when the war's over who'll be bound to want to snap you up in a trice!'

It was good to hear Isobel laugh, yet she soon became serious again.

'I can't see that happening, Meggie, but I promise you I won't doing anything rash. I talked with Mum when I was home at Christmas and she encouraged me to keep praying about it and to make sure I want to do it for the right reasons. … Anyway, nothing can happen until after the war's over, so don't worry.'

Richard said much the same when she told him about it in bed that night.

'Put it out of your mind, Meg—if it happens, we'll sort something out. You have enough on your plate with the baby due soon. … But I must admit, if any of our children ever wanted to do something like that, I'd be the first to discourage them. As far as I'm concerned, that's throwing your God-given life away. I'm afraid I agree with the old saying, "Charity begins at home"—there's plenty to do right here. Anyway, I'm sure God can look after the heathen Chinese and others like them without our help.'

'Well, I have to say I admire Isobel for being prepared to give up everything and go to the ends of the earth to save others, if that's what God calls her to do. But she cares a lot about everyone here too. For a start, she's taught me so much about God. And she's wonderful with children. You've seen yourself how the whole Sunday School loves her—it wouldn't run anywhere near as smoothly as it does without her help and guidance.'

She was annoyed but not surprised when Richard said nothing and turned his back to her—he never liked losing an argument. But Isobel was the last person anyone should accuse of not helping others and she wanted to defend her, no matter what. Well, no doubt he was tired, given all he had to do, so she gave up and turned over herself. Perhaps, given time to think about it all, his response would be different. At least, she hoped it would.

She was never more thankful for Isobel than she was on the evening of 20th May, when baby Margaret Jane decided to arrive early. She felt the first sharp pains at around ten, but put it down to standing up in the shop all afternoon. It was far too soon for her to go into labour—the baby was not due for over a month. Yet the pains continued and became more and more frequent. What could she do? Richard was out—and often his meetings went quite late. All she could do was wake Isobel, but she felt terrible disturbing her. At least Harrisville now had a midwife who lived close by, but how could she ask Isobel to go for help in the freezing cold and rain?

Isobel took only seconds to come. She did not need to be told what to do and ran for her shoes and coat, stopping only long enough to reassure her as best she could.

'Don't worry, Meggie—hang on! I'll get Mrs Paterson, then try to find Richard too.'

By the time the next pains hit, Isobel had gone. With a cry of anguish, she bit her lower lip and pressed her legs together, willing the baby not to come. *Lord, please look after us—please keep our little one safe.*

She was so relieved when she heard Lena Paterson's heavy footsteps at last and her deep voice calling out to Isobel to boil some water and bring more towels. She knew Lena would know what to do.

In the end, there was little time to do anything. She did her best to answer the questions Lena put to her, before another huge wave of pain engulfed her. She cried out, trying hard not to give in to the desire to push, but the next moment it was all over. Their tiny, baby girl had been placed on her chest and Lena was covering her with towels.

# Chapter Ten

At first, she thought the baby was dead—her skin had a bluish tinge and she lay so still. But then there was a flicker of movement, accompanied by pitiful, little cries.

'Oh, she's alive! Oh, the poor little thing. Don't cry, my darling. Oh Lena, she's so tiny—will she be all right?'

'Well, time will tell. But I think she's a fighter, so we'll all do our best to help her win through, won't we, little one? … There you go—now you're nice and warm. We'll let you stay close to Mummy—that's best. It's all we can do anyway, for now at least.'

She placed her hand on her tiny daughter and patted her gently.

'You're going to be fine, dear—Mummy's here,' she told her, as she stroked her forehead. 'Your name's Margaret Jane, but most of the time you'll get Jane because my name's Margaret too. Welcome to the world, little Jane. I love your name—it means "God is gracious".'

The tears were running down her cheeks and then she found she was praying out loud. *Dear Lord, please be gracious to us and to our little one here. Please keep her alive and help us know how best to care for her.*

She knew she was in good hands with Lena there, but the baby looked so small and fragile.

'Lena, when my husband gets here, do you … should we go for Doctor Waters?'

'To be honest, I think I know more about these little mites that insist on coming too soon than any doctor around here. All the same, in the morning, I suggest you get your husband to take you and the baby to Doctor Brown's hospital in Ipswich—it's in Milford Street. She'll have the best chance of survival that way and you can stay there with her. … Is that your husband now?'

She heard footsteps coming towards the bedroom, but they were too light to be Richard's. Then Isobel opened the door, tiptoed over and pressed her hand, as she took a quick peek at the baby.

'Meggie, I found Richard at the School of Arts, but all I could do was leave a message for him with another man. He said Richard was chairing the meeting and they were about to vote on something important, but he promised to tell him as soon as it was over. It's the best I could do—I'm so sorry.'

'Isobel, I'm the one who should be sorry. Fancy sending you out for a second time on a night like this—you're dripping wet all over. I hope you haven't caught a cold.'

'I'll be fine—I'll go and dry myself off now. And Richard should be home soon, so don't worry.'

Richard arrived around half an hour later. Despite her exhaustion, she could not help thinking how handsome he looked in his best suit, as he came to the bedside. Yet however important his role at the meeting had been, she had needed him too. She reached for his hand then as he bent to kiss her cheek—she felt so responsible for the little mite lying on her chest and longed for his reassurance.

'Richard, I couldn't seem to do anything—the baby just decided it was her time to come. And it was so quick too. This is Margaret Jane, but Lena says not to pick her up. She's warmer where she is, right next to my skin.'

She watched his face soften, as he lifted the blanket covering the baby and saw her small head.

'Well, what a night you chose to arrive, Margaret Jane. She's very tiny, isn't she?'

'Lena says we need to take her to Doctor Brown's hospital in Ipswich as soon as we can tomorrow, but I know it's such a busy day for you.'

She heard his sharp intake of breath and saw him stiffen.

'But … do you think that's necessary? I mean, couldn't we look after her ourselves? I remember my mother caring for Charlotte at home when she was born premature. Or what about our own hospital here?'

She was thankful Lena came back into the room at that precise moment.

'Mr McPherson, as an experienced midwife, I'm telling you this baby will need special round-the-clock care for the first few weeks. She's fighting hard to breathe and her little chest's quite congested. I'd advise you to get her to Doctor Brown's hospital as soon as you can—it's much better equipped to care for premature babies.'

She held her breath. Richard did not like being told what to do, especially by a woman. But Lena Paterson was no ordinary woman. She was a force to be reckoned with, when it came to anyone questioning her opinion about the babies she delivered. And she seemed extra determined to have the final word with Richard.

'So, sir … it's up to you. You can keep this little one here and risk having her death on your hands or you can take her to the hospital in Ipswich. I'll go and clean myself up while you decide.'

There was silence in the room for some time after Lena stomped out. Then Richard heaved a sigh.

'It seems we have no choice, Meg, if that woman's to be believed. Isobel will have to look after the children and I'll have to find someone to mind the shop, at least for tomorrow. After that, well … perhaps we should ask your mother if she could help out.'

But she was past thinking about such matters.

'Don't bother,' she sighed. 'I don't think she'd come anyway. But we should at least let her know about the baby.'

The next day, Richard made her as comfortable as possible in the buggy, putting pillows around her and covering both the baby and her with blankets. But the journey seemed to take forever, as he tried to steer them slowly around the worst bumps in the muddy roads. She clutched Jane to her chest and prayed, as the rain fell and the wind whistled around them, but at last, over two hours later, they arrived at the hospital in Ipswich. The baby appeared to be sleeping, but she could see how her little chest heaved with every breath, as she handed her over to the matron.

She turned to say goodbye to Richard, but he started speaking first.

'Well, Meg, I'll need to go back almost straight away, so I'm afraid I'll have to leave you now. I've got another long, inconvenient drive ahead—and a meeting tonight too. I only hope it was the right decision to bring you here.'

He had sounded so brusque that her heart sank and her eyes filled with tears. She had wanted to ask him to help Isobel out with the children, but decided not to. She could see how tired he was. He kissed her then and his voice softened a little—she was sure he had seen her tears.

'It's just that I have a lot on my mind right now, with the shop and other things, Meg. But take care of yourself, my dear—and of our little girl. Perhaps you could tell the hospital they can phone Bill Fisher when they want to contact me. He'll pass any message on. And I won't forget to let your parents know about the baby when I can.'

'Thanks, Richard,' she managed. 'I hope the trip home's a bit easier.'

After he left, she dried her tears and did her best to focus on what the matron was telling her. She tried not to resent Richard's comments—no doubt he was worried about her and the baby, on top of everything else. Well, all she could do was take care of herself, as he had said, and pray Jane would soon be doing well enough for them both to go home.

But it was three weeks before Doctor Brown was satisfied enough with the baby's breathing to agree to discharge her.

'Remember she's always likely to be prone to chest infections,' he told her in his morose voice, 'so make sure she's rugged up in cold weather. And don't let her exert herself too much.'

She was thankful the trip back was quicker and easier—and so thankful to be home at last.  At times in the hospital, she had wondered if they should have asked her mother to help out after all. She had even started to write to her once or twice, but had found it impossible. Anyway, Isobel seemed to have managed everything so well, as she always did. And she was also modest about her efforts.

'I'm glad I could help, but Alice was wonderful too. She's not even eight, but she did such a good job with the younger ones. And when Mrs Atkins heard about the baby and everything, she insisted on sending her own house-help May to do some cleaning and cooking for us.'

She was touched Hettie had done something so kind and thoughtful for them and was quick to thank her, when she visited her a few weeks later with the baby.

'I know Isobel would have managed, Hettie, but I'm glad she had some extra help. Richard … well, Richard's forte isn't housework.'

Hettie laughed.

'It's not Cliff's either. That's why he's always tried his best to find a house-girl to help us out, wherever we've lived. And we wanted to do something for you all. Can I hold the baby—or is she still too fragile?'

Hettie's face was rapt, as she placed Jane in her arms.

'Oh, she's so tiny and light, isn't she? I remember holding Elizabeth not long after she was born, but she must have been double the size of this little one. … Well, God bless you, Margaret Jane—although I'm glad we can call you Jane, because I believe it means 'God is gracious'. May the Lord indeed be gracious to you, Jane. … But how are you, Meg? You have your hands full now, but I know you'll manage.'

'I don't think I would without Isobel's help—or yours either, Hettie. I know you pray for me a lot—and having you nearby to talk to is so reassuring as well.'

'I'm glad I can support you and I'm sure Isobel is too. But neither of us will be here forever, my dear, as I mentioned once before, so keep your eyes on the Lord. Whatever happens, He'll never leave us or forsake us, as the Bible says.'

Three months later, the war was over at last. On 11th November 1918, the armistice was signed and, along with everyone else, she celebrated the moment with great joy and relief. As the weeks passed, the young and not-so-young men who had left Harrisville and the surrounding farms to enlist began to arrive home and try to resume their normal lives. Yet things would never be normal again for so many families, including their own. They had lost Will, which was hard enough. But some parents had lost two and even three sons— and these sons were often husbands and fathers too. Her heart felt so heavy for these grieving families, as they tried to cope with the huge, gaping void left in their lives and somehow find a way to carry on.

Richard wrote several eloquent articles for the Queensland Times about the huge toll the war had taken on their area—she was proud of the way he was able to find just the right words and phrases to use. She was proud too of all the extra roles he had taken on in Harrisville during the war, but she hoped and prayed he could soon hand these over to some of the men returning home. Yet her heart sank when she realised Len Gillespie would also be returning soon. And a few days later, Richard confirmed this.

'The parish council just received a letter from Len, Meg. He plans to visit his mother in Brisbane for a month, then head back up here, so I guess we need to arrange some sort of farewell for Bill Fisher before then. I'll be sorry to see him go—he's a good man.'

She could not bear the thought of saying goodbye to Reverend Fisher again. He had been such a support to her and, despite having to care for the children during church, she had still managed to gain much from his sermons.

'I hate the thought of not having him here,' she burst out. 'Whenever he preaches, I feel he truly means what he says.'

'I'm sure Len Gillespie means what he says too,' Richard responded in a disapproving tone.

'Yes, but I understand Reverend Fisher better—and he preaches with such heart. I've always loved how his face lights up. It's like God's Spirit is bursting out of him.'

'I grant you Bill Fisher's sermons are easy to understand— although sometimes I'd prefer a little more food for thought, to be honest. But as for his face lighting up, that's just his manner, Meg—or his personality, if you like. God's Spirit is present in us all, whether our faces shine or not.'

'I guess you're right, but I'm always touched by his warmth and kindness whenever he preaches or comes to chat with me. And I'm thankful he was still here to take Jane's christening service too. I felt he meant every word of it and I loved how he prayed for her. Did you notice how the sun shone through that stained-glass window behind the font, just as he put his hand on her head? It made his white surplice and hair all rosy too—it was such a beautiful picture.'

She was even more touched when he made time to visit her again, just before handing over to Len Gillespie in January. He caught her in a rare, quiet moment one afternoon when Alice and Robbie were playing at a friend's house and both Elizabeth and Jane were asleep.

'I wanted to say a personal goodbye to you, Meg—is this a suitable time to talk? I've been praying for you, as you settle in with little Jane and try to cope with everything. How are you *really*?'

It was the same question Hettie often asked her—and she knew it was sincere. He always seemed to see beyond the surface things she mentioned, although he never pressured her into sharing anything deeper. And today, she wanted to honour that and be honest with him in return.

'Reverend Fisher, I'm so glad the bishop sent you here as our locum. You've been a big encouragement to me once again and I've gained so much from your sermons, even though I'm often busy with the children. I'm much stronger in my spirit now than I was at Red Hill. Isobel's helped me a lot—and Hettie Atkins has been a tower of strength too. Hettie's tried to prepare me for the day when I'll need to stand on my own two feet more, without her support or Isobel's, but I don't even want to think about that. It's bad enough saying goodbye to you, let alone them.'

He was silent for a moment, then seemed to make up his mind about something.

'Isobel came to see me the other day about writing a reference for her. She said she's already told you what she's considering doing. It does seem God could be calling her to missionary work, despite what a hard road that might be, especially as a single woman. But Isobel's determined to do whatever God wants her to do. I know how much you'll miss her, Meg, if she leaves. Yet life will go on. And God's been preparing you for a while now to be able to stand firm in your faith and stay close to Him. God's Spirit is with you and in you, my dear—God will never leave you or forsake you.'

'I know,' she told him, with tears running down her cheeks. 'God *is* so much more real to me now. I don't often get time to myself to read the Bible and sit with God these days, but I've learnt I can pray as I do other things like feeding the baby or cooking or even serving in the shop.'

'And what about your art? That must be hard to fit in right now too, but don't forget it altogether, will you? It's a special gift from God, as I've told you before—and I know how often you sense God's presence as you paint, just like my Fran did. But I've been wondering too, Meg … how are things between you and your mother now?'

'Well … I haven't seen or heard from her for a while now, although Dad always keeps in touch. I did try to write to her when I was in the hospital in Ipswich, but I just couldn't seem to find the words to say. She hasn't even met Jane yet—as you know, she couldn't be at the christening. If and when Isobel leaves, Richard thinks it might be a good idea to ask her to help out with the children for a few weeks, but I don't imagine she'll want to. I do feel my miscarriage helped me understand how she must have felt when Jimbo died, but I still can't seem to forgive her for blaming me, even though I promised you I'd try to. Yet I know God's forgiven me so much, so I need to have the grace to forgive Mum too.'

'I'll pray you will soon, Meg—I won't forget to. How could I, when I have that wonderful painting you did of our church at Red Hill to remind me of you? That'll be one of the first things I put up when I move to my son's house. They've made a little flat for me downstairs, but I still plan to do some locums wherever I'm needed.'

Len Gillespie seemed more organised at first when he returned, although she still felt his sermons tended to ramble. But she soon noticed how often he glanced at Isobel after the Sunday services and at other times too.

'He must be lonely,' Richard said, when she mentioned it to him one night. 'After all, every minister needs a good wife. And Isobel would be perfect for him, don't you think? Anyway, she'd be much more use here than somewhere in the backblocks of China, in my opinion. And she'd still be near us too for a few more years then. She could even keep helping us out until her own family comes along.'

She wondered if Isobel had noticed Len Gillespie's interest in her, but soon discovered she had—and that she was more than a little upset about it.

'Meggie, I … I think it might be better if I don't clean the church or arrange the flowers by myself anymore,' Isobel burst out one Monday night when they were alone. 'It's just that on Saturday, Reverend Gillespie saw me there and … it was all quite embarrassing. At first, I thought he just wanted to chat, but he … he put his arm around me, told me he'd always admired me and asked if I'd like to get to know him better. He even talked about getting engaged, Meggie. I hated hurting him, but in the end, I had to tell him I'm planning to head to China as a missionary and didn't want to get engaged to anyone right now. Then he said something about what a waste that would be and that, once we got to know each other, he was sure I'd change my mind. He wanted to talk more, but I told him I had to help you with the children. I hated lying to him, but I couldn't think of any other excuse.'

She could see how upset Isobel was and put her arm around her shoulders.

'Oh, you poor thing—what an awful experience. I *thought* something was wrong yesterday when you stayed so close to us at church. I have to say though I'm not altogether surprised, because I've seen him glancing your way often. I should have warned you, Isobel—I'm sorry. But … how could he talk about getting engaged? Surely that's taking things far too much for granted? Anyway, he's far too old for you, Isobel. He must be close to forty.'

'I don't care how young or old he is—I could never marry him. He's … all I can say is he's not the sort of man I'd want as a husband. Besides … well, we're just different. Maybe I was spoilt by having such a wonderful father and seeing how close he and Mum were. They both loved God so much and always worked so well together in our church. But I know I couldn't do that with Reverend Gillespie.'

'Don't worry about it, Isobel. I'll make sure one of us is with you whenever you need to do anything at church. And perhaps if I tell Richard, he could have a word with Len Gillespie too and warn him off in no uncertain terms.'

She tried to end on a light note for Isobel's sake, but her heart was heavy. Whatever Richard thought, Isobel and Len Gillespie did not suit at all, in her opinion. Isobel had known and loved God for so long—and that love showed in everything she did. She was like Reverend Fisher and Hettie, always so caring and sensitive to others' needs. But Len Gillespie was different. He tried his best and was no doubt sincere, as Richard had already pointed out to her. Yet his faith still seemed more a matter of the head than the heart to her— and she knew that would never satisfy Isobel.

On the other hand, she did not want Isobel to head overseas to the mission field either. And, from what Isobel had told Len Gillespie, that still seemed to be what she had in mind.

'It isn't all cut and dried with my mission organisation yet about going to China,' Isobel told her then, as if reading her thoughts. 'They're still considering my application. They may want me to go to Bible college or get some other qualification here first. But I haven't changed my mind about it all, Meggie, so I wasn't lying to Len Gillespie about that anyway. I still want to go to China, if the mission accepts me. But I hate the thought of leaving you all—and my own family too, of course.'

'You don't *have* to go, you know,' she decided to risk saying. 'After all, we know how loving and gracious God is. He'd understand what a huge sacrifice that'd be for you.'

Isobel looked straight at her then.

'Yes, I know He would, Meggie. But I do feel God's called me to go—and I need to be obedient and respond to that call, whatever doubts I have. Besides, how will those women and children in China hear about God's love unless someone tells them?'

She knew Isobel was right, but that did not make it any easier to accept the fact that she might soon be leaving.

'I don't even know how to pray for Isobel,' she told Hettie in exasperation, when the two of them next met. 'I want her to be happy and at peace, whatever she does—and I know she'd make a wonderful missionary. But I hate the thought of her leaving. If she goes, I hope the folk in China truly appreciate her. And I hope she never feels she's missed out or opted for second best by becoming a missionary.'

She was glad Hettie did not respond at once. She loved the little silences that often fell between them. They provided a quiet space to think about what they had shared and to listen to what God might want to say. And this time, Hettie seemed to wait longer than usual, as if she wanted to be sure she had listened well to God.

'I can understand how hard it would be to contemplate not having Isobel around, Meg. She's been part of your life for so many years, first at Helidon, then at Red Hill and now here. Perhaps that's a good way to look at it, my dear—to thank God for the way Isobel's been such a true friend to you over all those years and helped you draw nearer to God.'

'Yes, even way back when I scoffed at believing in God, she prayed for me and showed me what it means to be a Christian. I owe her a lot, Hettie. She put up with me too when I couldn't understand how a God of love would allow Jimbo to die and when I was in such a dark place after my miscarriage. I'm sure she felt exasperated with me at times, but she kept on loving me through everything, which in itself helped me realise that God truly is gracious and forgiving.'

'As for what happens for her in China,' Hettie continued then, 'God will look after her, I know. Just this morning, I read some wonderful words in Psalm 139 about how God holds us fast, even if we settle on the far side of the sea. So, while this might be a difficult time for you, Meg, remember that, whether we're right here in Harrisville or far away in China, God will never lose sight of us.'

She tried to hold onto this truth in the months that followed, as Isobel liaised further with her mission, then travelled to Brisbane for interviews. And in September, word came through from the Home Council at last. Isobel had been accepted to join the China Inland Mission and would set sail from Sydney after Christmas, along with three other women candidates, bound for the mission's headquarters in Shanghai.

'They did have some reservations about my application, because I don't have any real educational qualifications or formal Bible training,' Isobel told her. 'But when they tested my Bible knowledge, they seemed satisfied—and I have my parents to thank for that. Every evening after dinner, my father used to read the Bible to us and explain what the passage was about. Mum did the same after Dad died—and all that helped me understand the Bible for myself.'

'If it had been me, Isobel, I'd probably have been bored to tears and wriggled around on my chair, annoying everyone else!'

'Oh, I used to get into trouble at times for that, don't you worry. Then Mum and Dad would tell me I should set a better example, being the oldest. But now I'm thankful they persevered. The Council seemed to like Reverend Fisher's reference too, especially his comments about my Sunday School work. I've always loved teaching kids about God—I started that back when I was still at school. I'm sure it'll be a much harder challenge in China, but I'll do my best.'

'It's good to see Isobel so happy,' she said to Richard that night. 'She's looking forward to it all—even to learning Chinese. But I don't know what we'll do without her.'

'I reckon Len Gillespie will be downhearted when he hears her news. I warned him, but I'm sure he still held out hope. Well, it's Isobel's decision, of course, but I think it's a big waste.'

She did not tell Isobel what Richard had said—it was too late to dissuade her anyway. Instead, she did her best to support her and not to cause her to feel uncertain about her decision. Each evening, she tried to help her finish sewing the different items of clothing she needed to take, but as she did, her spirits sank lower and lower.

'I hope you remember me in China, whenever you see my terrible sewing,' she joked one night, to try to lighten her mood. 'Aunty Betty wouldn't be impressed, after all her efforts to teach me—although I think I've improved since then.'

Straight away, Isobel tried to make her put down what she was working on.

'Meggie, please leave it. Mum can help me when I'm home at Christmas, if I don't have time to do it myself before then. To be honest, I'd love to see you go and paint for a while. Could you … do you think you could perhaps paint something for me instead, as a farewell gift? Of course, it'd have to be small to fit in my luggage, but I'd treasure it so much.'

She wondered why she had not thought of the idea herself. Then again, it had been so long since she had painted anything, let alone a special gift. And Isobel's gift would need to be special indeed.

'Well, if that's what you want, Isobel, I guess I could—although it might take me a while to come up with an idea.'

In the end, she decided to paint a picture of a spot in Normanby Gully where the water formed a little lagoon. The previous Saturday afternoon when Richard had gone to report on a cricket match, the rest of them had walked there together. Isobel had paddled and swum with the children, while she herself minded Jane in the shade of the trees on the creek bank. She remembered how Isobel had stood waist-deep in the water laughing, her head thrown back and her hair streaming wet, as the children splashed her from every direction. The scene seemed to ooze happiness and joy, yet it was etched in her memory for another reason too. For a moment as she had gazed at them all, another image had surfaced in her mind—an image of a swollen, fast-flowing creek and a little boy holding onto her tightly. She had started trembling, but God had strengthened her and enabled her to refocus on the scene before her, where the water was calm and where everyone was having such fun. She had felt so grateful—and she knew this was the scene she needed to paint for Isobel.

It took several attempts and quite a few late nights before she was happy with the little painting. She showed it to Richard before wrapping it, keen to gauge his response.

'I feel it's one of my better paintings, even though I'm out of practice,' she told him as she held it up. 'It was such a joyful scene—and I'm so glad I've been able to produce something I think Isobel will like.'

'It's nice, I guess—but are you sure Isobel will want to take a picture all the way to China? She might have to leave it at home, after all your work.'

She had hoped his response would be a little more enthusiastic. And she had wanted to tell him how God helped her as she watched the children swimming with Isobel, but he had already turned away. So she swallowed her disappointment, answered his question and left it at that.

'Isobel was the one who suggested a painting—and I think it's small enough to take with her.'

To her relief, Isobel's warm reaction more than made up for Richard's cooler one. After unwrapping her gift at the dinner table the next night, Isobel stared at it for some time, before turning to hug her with tears in her eyes.

'Oh Meggie, that's just the sort of scene I hoped you'd paint for me. Thank you so much—I'm sure I'll be able to fit it in my luggage. And if I can't, I'll carry it all the way in my handbag.'

Later, after the children were in bed, she saw Isobel holding her painting again and smiling. She went to sit beside her—she was sure Isobel would understand what had happened as she had watched them swimming that day.

'Isobel, I'm so glad you like our gift. I felt God wanted me to paint this particular scene, as I sat watching you all having such fun in the creek. But then, a picture of that awful day Jimbo drowned flashed into my mind. It almost overwhelmed me, yet a moment later, I sensed God saying in a firm but loving voice, "That was then, Meg—this is now. You won't ever be overwhelmed—you're so much stronger now. I'm delighted Isobel's going to China. It's what I've called her to do and I'll always be with her. But I'll never leave you either—I'll be with you forever." I won't forget this scene in a hurry, Isobel, or the joy of painting it for you.'

'Oh, that's wonderful, Meggie. That must have been so reassuring to hear—and it is for me too. Isn't God amazing?'

The following week, she watched on as Isobel wrapped her little painting and stowed it in a corner of her suitcase. Early the next day, Richard drove them all to the station in the buggy, with the children taking turns to sit next to Isobel. When the train arrived, Richard took care of the luggage while she tried to comfort Alice and Elizabeth. Then Isobel turned and hugged them all—even Richard, who seemed a little teary himself. Then, after one final flutter of her handkerchief out of the train window, Isobel was gone.

As she stood on the platform with the children around her and waved until the last minute, she remembered again the words God had spoken to her down by the creek. Alice and Elizabeth were sobbing—and even Robbie seemed about to cry. But instead of being overwhelmed herself, she did her best to console them. They would miss their beloved Isobel and she was determined to provide the comfort they needed.

It was hard to find time to meet with Hettie now that Isobel was gone, but one morning after school had started again for the year, she set out, taking plenty of things to occupy Elizabeth and Jane.

'How are you, Hettie? It's so good to see you. I've wanted to come for ages.'

'I'm fine, my dear. Yes, it's been a long time—but you must be busy, with Isobel gone.'

'We were extra busy in the shop over Christmas. Then Len Gillespie's having time off for health reasons, so Richard's had extra responsibilities at church again, including preaching. We've missed Isobel in so many ways, but the thing I've missed most is not having her there to talk to anymore. At times I turn around to share something with her, then realise I can't. But I'm so glad you're still here, Hettie—and I have so much to tell you.'

She noticed how Hettie looked down then and a sudden, horrible thought occurred to her. What if Hettie left too? Her heart plummeted. She had other friends in Harrisville, but no one who understood her like Hettie. Well, better not to say anything while the children were with her at least. Better to put it right out of her mind and enjoy their time together today.

It was good to be able to tell Hettie about her experience down by the creek and to hear her response.

'That's wonderful to receive such reassurance just when you needed it. I wish I could have seen your painting, but I can picture it in my mind from what you've told me. I'm sure Isobel will treasure it. And I know you'll treasure those words God spoke to you too. Whatever happens in the future, Meg, God will never leave you, even though others may come and go. You *are* so much stronger now and you won't be overwhelmed. You know God loves you. You know how to listen to God's voice. And you know how to rely on God and stand firm in your faith. I'm so proud of you, my dear.'

It was encouraging to be affirmed in such a warm, heartfelt

way. But it also made it harder to entertain the thought that Hettie Atkins, who had been like a mother to her, might leave too one day.

In the end, that day came sooner than she had expected. One morning in June, she managed to find someone to mind Elizabeth and Jane, while she went to see Hettie by herself. She headed off with a light heart—it was a beautiful, crisp, winter day and the sun warmed her as she walked to the post office. She wanted to discuss some passages in the Bible about women with Hettie and how they served God. And she had a recent letter from Isobel with her too— she knew Hettie would be interested to hear what it said.

She thought she might be imagining it, but Hettie seemed quieter than usual as they enjoyed a cup of tea together. Then Hettie lit a candle on the table nearby, as she always did, and they both sat in silence, enjoying God's presence. She felt her breathing become more even—it was wonderful to sense God's Spirit with them and to know God held them both safe in His loving arms.

After a while, Hettie broke the silence with a soft 'Amen', then reached for her hand.

'Meg, before we go any further, I have something to tell you. Cliff's due to retire in September—and … well, that means we'll be leaving Harrisville. Maybe we could find somewhere else to live here, but we feel it's time we moved back to Brisbane to be closer to my sisters and to doctors. I've hated the thought of telling you, my dear—I know how much you value our times together. But I also know you'll continue to stand firm, as you face life's challenges with God. He'll always be with you—remember that.'

She could not say anything at first. Instead, she closed her eyes and held on to Hettie's hand, feeling its warmth and strength. Her brain was swirling and the tears were threatening, but she willed them away. As they sat together, she became aware of various sounds nearby and in the distance—the ticking of the grandfather clock in the hallway, children's laughter, a dog barking. But she sensed too the gentle presence of God—and, even in her grief, she felt comforted.

When she opened her eyes, she saw Hettie had tears in her own.

'God's been preparing me for this moment, Hettie,' she told her, as she tried to stop her voice shaking. 'Last time I was here, I sensed this might happen soon. And now that it has … well, what can I say? I'm so happy for you both—you deserve a wonderful retirement together and many years of being nearer your sisters. But oh, I'll miss you so much.'

The tears coursed down her cheeks then and she let them fall. After a while, she leaned over and hugged Hettie, who was wiping her own tears away.

'I'll never forget what you've done for me, Hettie. You've helped me grow in God and as a person. You've been like a mother to me—and I thank you so much for that.'

'I'll never forget you either, Meg. And wherever I am, I can pray for you, my dear. We must write too—I love writing letters. I know how busy you are, but if you get time to answer them now and then, that will be wonderful. Of course, I'll want to hear all your family news, but I'll also want to hear what God's teaching you and what's happening with your painting.'

'I'll try—but I think I'll always be a better artist than I am a writer.'

They laughed together, as Hettie poured another cup of tea.

'I'm so glad God promised you that day at the creek that those past events will never overwhelm you again, Meg. That must give you such hope for the future.'

'Yes, I won't forget that experience. But you've also given me so much strength and hope, as we've read the Bible together and prayed and as you've shared your wisdom with me. I love the way God's Spirit shines out of you, Hettie. I hope someone can say that about me one day.'

'You've come so far, Meg—I'm so proud of you. You know … you mentioned before how I've been like a mother to you. That was a wonderful compliment and such a comforting thing to hear, given we don't have children of our own. I haven't met your mother, but I suspect in her own way she'd be very proud of you too. And I believe

God wants you to know you'll hear her say that to you one day.'

'Oh Hettie, right now I can't imagine that happening, but I'll tuck it away in my mind. I've written to her a couple of times since Isobel left and she replied too. Just short notes, but still … Richard wanted to ask her to come and stay with us for a while to help out, but I didn't want to. I think in some ways I couldn't bear to hear her say no again, like she has in the past. But maybe one day things will change between us.'

'It might take a while, Meg—and God might have more things for you to learn too about understanding her and forgiving her. So stay close to God, dear, and listen to Him.'

She read Isobel's letter to Hettie then and they spent a few moments praying for Isobel, before delving into the Bible together. Soon it was time to leave but, as she walked home, an idea came to her. She would ask God to show her just the right picture to paint for Hettie too as a special farewell gift.

# Chapter Eleven

In the weeks that followed, she began several paintings, but none of them seemed quite right. Then one night, she woke with a clear image in her mind of a young girl with jet black hair, holding her skirts wide and laughing, as she danced for joy in the middle of a field of purple flowers. She knew Hettie loved purple—but was this the right scene to paint for her? It seemed tactless, given Hettie could barely walk unaided.

She began working on it every spare moment she could find and, as she did, she sensed she was indeed on the right track. Yet she felt afraid too. What if Hettie did not connect at all with the painting? The battle raged on, as she added some finishing touches, but instead of letting her fear overwhelm her, she prayed for the strength to remain calm and not change her mind.

A week before Hettie and Cliff were due to leave, she completed it. She wrapped it with extra care, then walked to Hettie's house. She was glad the children were with her—their chattering kept her mind off the butterflies she always felt in her stomach when she shared her work with anyone. But this was not anyone. This was Hettie.

'I so hoped you'd paint something for me, but I thought you mightn't have time,' Hettie exclaimed, as she unwrapped the gift the children presented to her with pride.

She held her breath as the moments ticked by. Hettie sat gazing at the painting, her hands trembling a little. Then at last she looked up and held out her arms.

'Meg, thank you so much, from the bottom of my heart! But … but how did you know what I looked like when I was growing up? I loved running and dancing barefoot in the paddocks around our farm too, even though my parents warned me not to. I thought all the purple wildflowers that grew everywhere in spring were wonderful—and I remember how I felt so alive and joyful as I danced and so in awe of God that He could create such beauty. Oh, thank you for bringing it all back to me in such a special way.'

'I hoped it wouldn't make you feel too sad, Hettie. … And I had no idea what you looked like back then. I would never have guessed you had black hair, for a start. I chose that picture because I saw it in my mind one night and sensed that was what God wanted me to paint. But to me, it symbolises your spirit now—so free and joyous and alive, even though you've been through many dark times and can't dance like this girl. That thought stayed with me and touched my heart as I painted, so without even knowing it, you've helped me all over again.'

Even the children were quiet, as they watched Hettie gaze at her painting with joy and awe. Then, when Jane became restless at last, Hettie reached out her hand to her.

'Let's join hands and thank Jesus for this beautiful painting, shall we? *Lord Jesus, we love you. Thank you for showing Meg what to paint—and thank you for giving her the ability to do so. Please bless and strengthen her in the months and years ahead. And bless Elizabeth and Jane too. Amen.*'

She relaxed then, as Hettie chatted with the children and gave them some treats. And her heart filled with thankfulness when she noticed Hettie peeking at her painting again and smiling, just as

Isobel had with hers.

'I'm so glad you like my gift, Hettie. I'll never forget painting it. I felt God was right there beside me, guiding me and giving me inspiration.'

'Keep painting like that, dear, that's all I can say. But I'd also like to share some wonderful words with you that I read in Psalm 121 this morning:

> *The Lord shall preserve thee from all evil: he shall preserve thy soul.*

> *The Lord shall preserve thy going out and thy coming in from this time forth, and even for evermore.*

That's the truth, Meg—whatever happens, that's the truth.'

The departure of both Isobel and Hettie left a huge hole in her life—and she missed Reverend Fisher so much too. Although she tried not to, she found herself becoming even more critical of Len Gillespie's sermons, as she endeavoured to keep the children quiet each Sunday and follow his train of thought.

'I know he's not a well man,' she said to Richard in exasperation one Sunday night, 'but I find his sermons so confusing.'

'I don't think we should criticise him, Meg. After all, he went through some terrible experiences on the Western Front. He saw so much pain and death everywhere and must have felt so helpless at times.'

'But Richard, he was like this even before he enlisted. Do you think he's really suited to parish ministry?'

'It's not for me to say—or any of us at St John's. It's the bishop's role to decide such things. Anyway, I'm doing my best to support Len and I hope everyone else will too.'

She knew there was no point in arguing with him. In a sense, Richard was right—it *was* unhelpful for her or anyone else to focus on Len Gillespie's shortcomings as a preacher. At least she still found the liturgy helpful and the Bible readings and hymns. And she remembered how Hettie had been unable to get to Sunday services at all, yet had stayed strong in her faith.

'Well, I don't know what Len Gillespie would do if you weren't here,' was all she said in the end. 'You seem to have to fill in for him more and more these days. And where would the parish council be without you? Or the choir?'

'I don't mind—and I like things to be done well. But I suspect old Mrs Stubbs is thinking of retiring from playing the organ in the new year. It's beyond her anyway—especially playing for the choir anthems. *You* could do better than she does.'

She laughed, but suspected he was half serious too.

'It's a long time since I played anywhere—and I've never played the organ. I don't want to either, to be honest. I've tried out the old piano in the hall once or twice when we were cleaning and I was thinking I could perhaps use it to start teaching Alice next year. But it's hard when we don't have a piano here at home. ... Remember how I used to play at the dances in Helidon to help Mrs Watson out? It seems such a long time ago, doesn't it?'

'It *was* a long time ago, Meg. Anyway, perhaps I can see about buying a piano of our own after Christmas. Business seems to be looking up, now the war's over. ... By the way, I've been thinking of getting a car in the new year. That'd make it easier for me to do my reporting and also get to my meetings at night. We might even be able to visit our families more often too.'

She was taken by surprise and did not know how to respond at first. But then she realised he was waiting for her reaction, so pulled herself together.

'I think having a piano would be wonderful for the children at least. Maybe then I can put all those lessons with Mrs Watson and Miss Lang to good use and teach them myself. As for me, I'd still much rather paint than play the piano—and I don't have time to practise anyway. ... But Richard, are you sure we can afford a car? That seems almost too good to be true! I never ever thought we'd be among the first in Harrisville to own one. I can see how much easier it would make things for you, but as for visiting our families more often …'

'A car would make our trips to Brisbane and Helidon a lot quicker. I thought you'd like that, Meg.'

'I'd love to be able to visit Aunty Betty more, of course—and Charlotte's happy to see us any time, I know. Dad's always welcoming when we go to Helidon too, but … well, there's often so much tension in the air whenever Mum and I are together. And I always seem to say the wrong thing when we go to Rosewood to see Mary.'

She could tell by the tone of his voice that he had not liked her final comment.

'It's just an idea, Meg. I won't have time to look into it properly for a while anyway, so don't worry about it.'

But Richard did find time to buy a good, second-hand piano for them at least, not long after Christmas.

'Now you can practise whenever you like,' he told her with pride. 'And playing the organ's not so different. With young Annie Armstrong coming to help in the shop and at home here, you should have more time to play, once she learns the ropes.'

Had he forgotten what she had said about not wishing to play the piano—or the organ? Or was he choosing not to believe her? She had always sensed he did not see the need for her to spend so much time painting. Now it seemed that time would be eroded even further—at least until Annie settled in.

Richard had told her about Annie only a few days earlier.

'The Armstrongs need a bit of help, Meg,' he had announced one lunchtime. 'Alf hasn't been the same since he came back and Elsie's finding it hard to keep everything going. I've let them run up quite an account at the shop, but I think it's time we did something more. Their Annie's almost thirteen now and seems to get on well with the children at Sunday School and church. She wants to stay on at school this year, so I thought she might live with us during the week. Then she can help in the shop in the afternoons—and with the children too. Anyway, I told them we'd try it until Easter and see how things work out.'

Again, Richard had caught her by surprise, but this time, she knew what she wanted to say.

'Richard, I know you mean well—and that's good of you to let the Armstrongs run up an account. But don't you think we should have talked about having Annie here before you arranged it all with her parents? I know she gets on well with the children, but she's so loud and tomboyish and …'

Richard had interrupted her then—and she could see he was nettled.

'I decided it was best to sort it out then and there—and after all, I was thinking of you too. Besides, this is our best chance of finding anyone in Harrisville who can help in the shop and with the children. I know Annie can be a bit boisterous on Sundays, running around the church grounds with her brothers, but the children like her. … Anyway, let's try it until Easter and, if things don't work out, then so be it. But I hope you'll do your best to make Annie welcome, Meg—for all our sakes.'

She had felt she had no choice then except to acquiesce. Yet she had sighed as she thought of those quiet moments she enjoyed at home, especially when the children were in bed. There were always so many jobs to do, but as often as she could, she would steal out to the veranda to paint and be with God. Isobel had known what she needed and had encouraged her to take time to herself, but she could not expect Annie to do that. And her heart sank too when she remembered what a chatterbox Annie could be at church.

Her fears were soon realised. As the weeks passed, she tried to make it clear to Annie she needed time to herself, with little success. She did not want to discourage her too much—after all, she was only thirteen. All the same, her constant chatter irked her.

'I don't mind being interrupted if she needs help with her homework,' she told Richard one day. 'I don't think her parents have had the time or energy for things like that. She seems way behind where she should be at school. But she comes and finds me so often when I'm painting and just wants to chat about anything.'

'Then I guess you'll have to decide which is more important, Meg. Your painting—or having Annie's help around the place. And I happen to think it's the latter,' he told her, his voice tired. 'You can do your painting when the children are older, after all, but we need Annie's help right now.'

She had not expected him to offer a solution, but his curt response upset her.

That evening, she tried to express her frustration about it all in a letter to Hettie. She did not find letter-writing easy, but she knew how much Hettie loved to receive any news from her. Often Hettie would reply almost at once, although her letters were always thoughtful and never rushed. And, on this occasion, the lengthy one that arrived from her a fortnight later turned out to be particularly meaningful. Along with news about life in Brisbane and some interesting insights from Hettie's own reading, it contained a paragraph that changed her whole perspective on Annie.

*My dear Meg*

*It was so good to hear all your family news, as always. We're doing well here in our little cottage by the river, but we miss you all in Harrisville. And I of course miss our special times together.*

*I'll tell you all our news and comment on yours in a moment. But first, I feel I should pass on something God seemed to impress on me regarding Annie and her wanting to chat. Could it be that Annie senses God's Spirit in you and the peace and joy you have as a result? Could it be that she wants to know more about listening to God? I'm sharing this for you to consider, my dear, and to be faithful to God's prompting. My comments are not meant to judge you in any way.*

*And as I prayed for you and the situation with Annie, I believe God gave me a picture of someone else you may be able to help in the near future—someone who will understand the need for those times of quietness, just as you do. I did not recognise her—perhaps she's moved to Harrisville since we left. She seemed to be single and around your own age and I think she has dark brown, bobbed hair. Of course, I could be imagining all this, but I know you will pray about it and be sensitive to any nudges from God. And please be assured I'll be praying for you as you do.*

She pondered Hettie's comments about Annie for some time. She had never considered helping Annie in anything other than practical ways like checking her homework or showing her where things were. Yet maybe Hettie was right. Maybe Annie *was* searching for something more. If this was the case, could she help her come to know God better, just as others had helped her in her own journey? She remembered her teenage years in Helidon and how much Sister Mary Margaret's encouragement had meant back then. And she remembered Isobel's quiet presence a little later, challenging her to take life more seriously and to think about God. Should she forget her own needs more often and reach out to Annie instead? There was no harm in trying at least. But she would need God to show her how to go about it.

As for Hettie's picture, she could not think of anyone who fitted the description she had given. There were a few single women her age in town and on nearby farms, but none with dark, bobbed hair. Most still preferred to keep their hair long. And, as far as she knew, there had been only a few newcomers to the district in recent times. Had Hettie imagined the whole thing? Or was she just plain wrong? Yet she trusted Hettie's insights, so all she could do was wait and be ready for that nudge from God Hettie had mentioned.

A few evenings later, she discovered much more about Annie. Richard was at a meeting and the children were all asleep, so, after making sure everything was ready for the next day, she tiptoed out to the veranda. She wanted to finish a scene she had begun weeks earlier of a spot in Warrill Creek where the willow trees overhung the water. And she had so much to think and pray about, including whether to keep Annie on after Easter. Richard had recently organised for electric lighting to be installed and she was so thankful for the large globe that now shone right along the veranda and onto her easel. She switched the light on and, as she set about mixing her paints, she could feel herself relaxing. But soon the sleepout door creaked open—and there was Annie, her old nightdress barely covering her stocky figure and her fine, fair hair all on end, wide awake and eager to talk.

'Can I see what you're painting? Oh, it's another picture of a creek. That's Warrill Creek, isn't it? It looks great, Mrs McPherson. … I wish I could paint. I like that spot too where the willows go right down to the water. … You paint lots of pictures of creeks, don't you? … Why do you do that? I suppose it's because they're the nicest places around here, is it?'

'That's half right, Annie. There are some pretty spots in the creeks near here, but I've always liked painting rivers and creeks, ever since I was about your age. And when I studied art in Brisbane, our teacher used to take our class through the Botanic Gardens and down to the river to paint.'

'I'd like to live in Brisbane one day. It's boring in Harrisville— and on the farm.'

'What would you like to do in Brisbane, Annie?'

'Well … I used to want to be a nurse, but I'm not clever enough for that. Perhaps mind children somewhere. But Mum and Dad want me to leave school after this year and help out at home.'

'Perhaps if you keep trying hard at school, you could get into nursing.'

'I don't know. I'm not much good at anything really. The others at school reckon I'm dumb—and my two older brothers are always telling me I'm useless.'

'You're very good with children, Annie. And we appreciate all your help around the house too. Besides, no one's useless. God created us with different gifts and strengths—and God doesn't make mistakes with any of us.'

Annie stared down at her hands then.

'I … I know you like reading the Bible and all that, Mrs McPherson. I've seen you praying here too—or at least sitting with your eyes closed. I like helping out at Sunday School when we can get there, but … well, I don't really know all that much about God.'

She could feel her heart pounding as she prayed for the right words to say. Now was the moment. She took a deep breath and ploughed on.

'Would you like to know more, Annie? Perhaps some nights when you've finished your homework, we could read a few verses from the Bible together and pray about things. How would that be?'

Annie sent her a shy but glowing look.

'I think I'd like that, Mrs McPherson. I've always wondered if God truly is real and I reckon you're the one who'd know. But I don't want to be a nuisance or anything. I'm such a chatterbox—Mum's always telling me that.'

She remembered then how she had planned to pray about whether to keep Annie on after Easter. Yet how could she not, when Annie seemed to be reaching out to her—and to God?

'Let's have Annie stay on after Easter,' she told Richard the next day, before she could change her mind. 'It's not that my painting doesn't matter—it's very important to me. And I love my times to myself on the veranda. But Annie needs help with her schoolwork— and she also told me last night she wants to learn more about God, so I promised to read the Bible with her some nights. If that works out, perhaps I could ask her not to bother me on other nights when I want to be by myself.'

Richard's face softened and his initial response was gentler than she had expected.

'That's good of you to do that for her, Meg, when you like to be alone so much. I suspect her parents can't read all that well, so they wouldn't be much help to her. But actually, I've … well, I've already told them we'll keep Annie on. I decided to seize the opportunity when they came into the shop yesterday. I know I should have waited to see what you thought, but Annie's done well in the shop and I think she fits in around the house too. Anyway, it seems it's all worked out.'

Straight away, her hackles rose. Once again, he had not consulted her first, but she could tell by the look on his face and the way he avoided her eyes that he felt guilty about it. Better not to say anything—and at least she had managed to point out how important her painting was to her. Besides, she was looking forward to reading the Bible with Annie. It was what Hettie had done for her, after all.

As the year progressed, her times with Annie began to fall into a regular pattern and, to her surprise, they turned out to be profitable for them both. Twice a week, they would read a Bible passage together and discuss what it meant, unless Annie had too much homework. She was glad she had begun with Luke's Gospel—her personal favourite—because the passages she chose turned out to be ones Annie had vaguely heard already. But whenever Annie discovered something new about Jesus and what He had taught, her own spirits lifted too.

'Wow, Mrs McPherson,' Annie exclaimed one night. 'I didn't know Jesus said that. To be honest, I don't think I believed He was real at all. I thought he was kind of made up, like Santa Claus. … I'm a bit like the lost sheep in this story, I think—it's so great how Jesus loved me enough to come and rescue me too.'

Another night, after deciding to tackle some of the psalms, she felt moved when Annie pointed out a verse in Psalm Three that was one of her own favourites.

'Oh, I love this—*But thou, O Lord, art a shield for me; my glory, and the lifter up of mine head.* My brothers often tease me and tell me I'm stupid, but now I know I don't have to feel ashamed. God can help me hold my head high.'

She opened her mouth then to share something of her own journey—how God had enabled her to hold her head high, despite the guilt and shame she felt over Jimbo's death—but changed her mind. Annie was too young yet and it did not seem appropriate. Instead, she prayed God would lift any shame Annie felt off her and that God would always protect her.

Yet later, she could not help thinking how much she missed talking over things with another adult, as she had with Hettie. There were women at St John's who seemed to have a deep faith in God, but most of them were already too busy with their families and farm life. Perhaps the person in Hettie's picture was the answer. But had Hettie simply dreamed it up? Well, there was nothing for it but to wait and pray.

There was plenty to occupy her anyway. She had started teaching Alice and Robbie the piano, with mixed success. Alice tried hard and was improving but, while Robbie was more naturally gifted, he was far less inclined to want to practise. Then too, in the end, she had felt obliged to fill the gap left when Mrs Stubbs resigned as church organist.

'Just do it, Meg, for goodness sake!' Richard told her one night, after returning from another disastrous choir practice. 'There's only one anthem this Christmas, but do you think Mrs Stubbs can get it right? No. She stopped dead so many times tonight. And even when she managed to make it through the whole thing, there were so many wrong notes. ... Look, I know you've never played the organ, but *anyone* could play better than Mrs Stubbs. She should have resigned months ago. I've got enough on my mind without having to put up with someone like her. Surely Annie can mind the children while you come to choir practice and play for us.'

He looked so tired and exasperated that she could not find it in her heart to say no. Yet she did not relish the idea of trying to play the organ—or of having to accompany the choir with Richard as choirmaster. She remembered how exacting he had been on past occasions when she had played for him to sing a solo. And she felt a little sorry for Mrs Stubbs too. She hoped the faithful, old soul had not been pushed into resigning. Anyway, all she could do was try her best—and hope and pray someone else would soon be available to take over.

She managed to struggle through the Christmas services with minimal mistakes, despite having to keep an eye on the children— although these days, Alice, at almost eleven, was a great help. Annie had headed home for the holidays, with an excellent school report clutched in her hands and a strong recommendation from the school that she be allowed to stay on for another year.

'You've done so well, Annie—and not only in your schoolwork,' she had told her, as she hugged her goodbye. 'I'll pray your parents let you come back next year. After that, perhaps we can talk to them and see if we can find a training course for you in Brisbane. My aunt might be happy to have you stay with them. I lived with her years ago when I was going to art classes—she might like to have someone young with her again.'

Annie had stood open-mouthed, before bursting into tears and returning her hug.

'Wow! Thanks so much, Mrs McPherson—for everything. I'll help wherever I can all holidays at home, so my parents will say yes. Please, God, let them say yes.'

In November, Richard at last bought the large T Model Ford he had talked about purchasing all year, which made it easier for them to get home to Helidon for a few days after Christmas. She felt proud, driving up the familiar, old lane in their brand-new car. Yet, while everyone seemed pleased to see them, she could still sense some tension beneath the surface as she chatted with her mother.

'Let me take care of Jane, Margaret, while you sort things out— she looks like she's doing well now at least. She's almost as big as James was when he …'

She decided to pretend she had not heard her mother's last remark or noticed her sudden silence.

'Yes, she's grown a lot this past year,' she almost gabbled. 'She does her best to keep up with Elizabeth now in everything. And she idolises Robbie, although he doesn't always want her around.'

'Well, that was how you were with William, after all,' was all her mother said, before turning away. 'Here, Harriet, please look after Jane while I see to the dinner.'

Over the next two days, she tried her best to involve her mother in little ways with the children and to be warm and friendly towards her, but she often felt as if she was treading on eggshells. As a result, she was not too upset when a message from Len Gillespie reached them via the Church of England minister in Helidon. She guessed what it would be—and she knew what Richard would decide too.

'I'm sorry, Tom and Pearl and all of you, but we need to get home today. Len's unwell again and there's no one else to take the services. We had to be back by Monday anyway, so it's not so bad.'

She tried to shush the children when they protested. They always loved playing down by the creek, which was quite deep and fast-flowing this year—yet another reason she was happy to head home early. But it was the undercurrents in her mother's words that disturbed her far more than any undercurrents in the creek. She would have to write to Hettie and ask for some advice about it all again.

Towards the end of the school holidays, Richard decided they would head to Brisbane for three days to make up for cutting short their time in Helidon. And on their last day, with Aunty Betty's help, she managed to arrange some time alone with Hettie.

'Go and visit your friend, Meg,' her aunt told her in no uncertain terms. 'It's time you did something for yourself. I'll help Richard with the children. She doesn't live far away, so it won't take all day.'

She caught a tram to New Farm and had no trouble finding Hettie's white, weatherboard cottage, with its green window shutters, cheery little garden and beautiful views of the Brisbane River. Hettie looked frailer, but she still greeted her in her usual warm, gracious way.

'It's so good to see you again, Meg—welcome to our place. Now … how are you *really*, my dear?'

It was wonderful to be asked that question again and to feel she could respond with complete honesty. They went on to talk about so many things, including the recent family visit to Helidon, but after a while, she noticed Hettie beginning to tire.

'I think it's time I headed home, Hettie,' she told her. 'Aunty Betty might have had enough of the children by now. I hope I haven't worn you out with all my talking.'

'I won't press you to stay, Meg—I do get a little tired these days.

But before we pray together, tell me, have you come across the young woman in my picture yet?'

She felt her face redden—she had concluded long ago that Hettie must have been mistaken.

'Well … not yet, Hettie. But I guess there's still time.'

Hettie patted her knee and smiled.

'I understand, dear. Of course, I could be wrong, but I still believe you'll meet her one day. And when you do, you must write and tell me all about it. Now let's pray, shall we?'

She felt she was floating along as she made her way back to the tram stop. God had been so close to them as they prayed—what a priceless gift her times with Hettie always were. Perhaps in the coming year she should try to find someone else to meet with and encourage in the same way.

On Elizabeth's first day of school, she had planned to go with her to meet her teacher and settle her in, but Elizabeth was having none of it.

'No Mummy—I'm big now. Anyway, I want to walk with Alice and Robbie and Annie. They'll show me how to find my teacher.'

She had thought of her all morning as she served in the shop, with Jane close by—and now she could hear the children chattering together as they arrived home. They clattered down the hallway, eager for some afternoon tea, but Elizabeth darted ahead and reached her first, waving a big piece of paper.

'Mummy … I drawed this picture in class and my teacher loved it. She's nice. I'm going to draw a picture of her on the back and give it to her tomorrow.'

'That's wonderful, Elizabeth—I love your picture too. … Did you have a good day, Alice and Robbie?'

She cut them some thick slices of bread and spread them with butter and jam. Soon they were all seated around the table, devouring their treats and telling her their news.

'I've got Mr Hemmings again,' Robbie mumbled, in between mouthfuls of bread, 'but I don't mind. He's always fair—and he likes playing cricket too.'

'I've got Miss Newman again,' Alice added. 'At least she's better than Mr Hemmings.'

'And what's your teacher's name, Elizabeth?'

'Um … I think it's Miss Webby or something.'

'It's Miss Wetherby, silly,' Alice corrected her. 'She's new, Mum, but she told us her name when we took Elizabeth to her class. She's pretty—and she doesn't look very old.'

'How about you, Annie? Did you have a good day?'

'Yes thanks, Mrs McPherson. I'm so happy Mum and Dad let me stay on for another year, although I know I'll have lots of homework. Miss Newman's looking after the older pupils again—she'll give us extra work to do on our own while she's busy. She's going to let us help out with the beginners too—I'll like that.'

She was relieved they all seemed happy enough after their first day. As they chattered on, she made a mental note to try to meet Elizabeth's teacher the next day. Then, as she glanced down at the picture Elizabeth had already started drawing for her teacher, she caught her breath.

Miss Wetherby seemed to have dark brown, bobbed hair that curled over her cheeks a little and a long, straight fringe.

'Are you sure your teacher wears her hair like that, dear?' she asked, her mind whirling.

'Yes, Mummy—I think it looks pretty, don't you?'

She left it at that. She would meet Miss Wetherby soon enough—and it was silly to jump to any conclusions. But the next morning, she discovered Richard had to drive into Ipswich for a meeting and she was needed in the shop again. Each day that first week, as it turned out, he had pressing jobs elsewhere or produce to pick up, so there was no opportunity to meet Elizabeth's teacher as she had hoped.

She had more than enough to think about anyway. It was good to have Annie with them again, but that also meant fewer quiet evenings to herself. And she still had to play for their church services, which meant finding time to practise. The first Sunday after school started, she sat down at the organ in a rather disgruntled mood and put her music in order, all the while hoping the children would behave. She did not want them to disturb Richard as he helped conduct the service—or anyone else, for that matter.

To her relief, there were no real disasters. But as she was packing up her music, Elizabeth ran up to her.

'Mummy, my teacher's here—come and say hello to her.'

Elizabeth tried to drag her towards a young woman standing near the door and smiling at her. But before they could reach her, Richard had taken charge and begun introducing her to everyone else.

At last it was their turn.

'Meg, let me introduce Emma Wetherby to you. She's the new teacher at school and has moved up here from Brisbane. Miss Wetherby, this is my wife Margaret—or Meg, as everyone calls her.'

'It's so good to meet you at last—and yes, please call me Meg. I've been trying to come to the school all week, but I couldn't get away from the shop. I understand you know Elizabeth already—she's enjoyed being in your class.'

'And please call me Emma—although I guess we'd better not let Elizabeth hear that!'

Before either of them could continue, Richard interrupted.

'Meg, Emma tells me she's a music teacher as well. Isn't that wonderful? Would you be interested in playing the organ for our services at all, Emma? I know Meg would be relieved not to have to, particularly when I'm involved in the services, as it's hard to keep an eye on the children at the same time. What do you think?'

She could see Emma looked a little taken aback, so decided to intervene.

'Perhaps we should give Emma a bit more time to get to know us before asking her anything like that. This is her first time here, after all. Maybe we could have dinner together one night this week—it'd be easier to talk then. Richard, will you be home Friday night? And would that suit you, Emma?'

She held her breath as the arrangements were finalised. Already, she longed to talk more with Emma and when Friday came, she was not disappointed. Emma chatted with them all over dinner as if she belonged and, after the children were in bed, she shared a little of her story with them.

'I've been living with my parents, down near the river at Toowong, not far from the Regatta Hotel. I taught at the local school and I also had a few private music students. I … I became engaged almost eight years ago, but Vernon signed up soon after. He was sent to Gallipoli and never came back. It's … it's taken me a while to come to terms with it all, but this year, I felt it was time to move on with my life, so here I am. I love Harrisville already—everyone's been so welcoming. In Brisbane, I attended St Thomas's Toowong with my parents—that's where I met Vernon. I've been one of the organists there for quite a few years, so I'd be happy to play at St John's whenever I'm needed, as long as you don't mind, Meg.'

Richard laughed and looked delighted.

'That's wonderful news—and I know Meg won't mind at all, will you, my dear? … Look, I have to leave you now, I'm afraid. I need to check with Len Gillespie about the Sunday services. It's been good to meet you, Emma, and I'll catch up about playing at church as soon as I can.'

She was glad to be alone with Emma, because she had begun to feel more and more convinced God had indeed brought them together. They talked about all sorts of things, but it was when Emma shared her struggles to hold onto her faith after her fiancé's death that her heart went out to her the most.

'Emma, I think I understand—at least to some degree,' she told her. 'Just before I was married, my little brother drowned in Lockyer Creek near our home in Helidon. I found it so hard to believe in God after that—and I almost stopped painting for good too.'

She heard Emma gasp.

'Oh, that's just like me! For a long time after Vernon was killed, I couldn't bring myself to play the piano. But in the end, it became such a comfort to me—and it still is. It feeds my soul more than anything, except perhaps reading my Bible and being alone with God.'

She knew then she needed to tell Emma about Hettie's picture. When she had finished, she wondered if it had all sounded a little crazy, but then she noticed Emma wiping her tears away. She put out her hand to comfort her and Emma held it tight.

'I truly believe God's brought us together, Emma. Perhaps if we could catch up sometimes, I'd love to share with you some of the things my friend Hettie taught me, because they might help you heal as well. And I'm sure you'd bless and encourage me too in all sorts of ways.'

Emma managed to find her voice at last.

'I can't believe it—how amazing that God would bother to give your friend a picture of me before I ever came here. That means so much to me, Meg. And yes, I'd love to meet with you, but perhaps let me settle in a little first. Then we can arrange something that suits us both.'

# Chapter Twelve

After Emma left, she lay awake for some time. She felt so relieved that she would not have to play the organ anymore. That would give her more time to paint—and she could also sit with the children in church and make sure they behaved. But beyond that, she could not get over how gracious God had been to bring Emma to Harrisville and to give Hettie a picture of her beforehand.

'I used to wear my hair long—Vernon loved it that way,' Emma had explained. 'But last year, I had it cut as a kind of tangible reminder that it was time to move on with my life. My class all loved it and thought it was very modern, so I decided to keep it like this. Just as well—or you might never have recognised me as the girl in the picture.'

It was never easy to find time to catch up, but they did their best. Some nights when Richard was out and the children were in bed early, Emma would come for an hour or so and they would talk and pray together. And this soon proved fruitful for them both.

'Sometimes I still feel angry at Vernon for volunteering, just when we were preparing to get married,' Emma told her one night, as she sat curled up on the lounge. 'And then he ended up getting killed. At first, I raged inside for hours at him—and God—because of the injustice of it all. But after a while, I realised Vernon couldn't have lived with himself if he hadn't enlisted. … And I guess I was looking for some sort of scapegoat for all my grief too. Then I began to see that, when we don't forgive, the person we hurt most is ourselves— all that bitterness inside stops us from moving forward in our lives. But this past year, I chose to let it go and let God in again and I'm so glad I did. Now I know God more in my heart, rather than just in my head. … And I've started to realise too that all the pain I've felt could well have made me a better musician, because it's taught me to play from my heart as well as my head.'

'I understand, Emma. I believe I'm a better artist now than before our Jimbo died. Like you, I found it hard to forgive God for what happened—and, while I hate to admit it, I'm still trying to forgive my mother for blaming me for Jimbo's death. I'm sure she still feels bitter towards me over it all too, but from what you've said, I can see I might perhaps be a scapegoat for all her grief. It helps me understand her a bit better at least, so thanks for sharing that with me.'

'Well, you've taught me so much yourself, especially about listening to God and being aware of God's presence with me throughout my day. And the way you paint, letting God's Spirit guide you, has inspired me to write some music of my own again, which I haven't done for ages.'

As soon as she could, she wrote to Hettie, telling her about her times with Emma.

*I hope they're helping her as much as they're helping me, Hettie. She says they are—and I must admit it's wonderful being able to pass on some of the things I learnt from you.*

Hettie wrote back, her handwriting even shakier now.

*It was so special to hear about your meetings with Emma. But you know, I have a sense there are others in Harrisville who are eager to talk about the things of God too. May you both continue to listen to*

*God—and may God open your eyes more and more to see who else needs encouraging.*

Once again, Hettie proved to be right. One by one, God seemed to bring people across their paths to talk and pray with, even if only for a short time. Emma drew others to her in such a natural way—the children in her class, other teachers at school and the music students who came to her house. Even Robbie, who now learnt from Emma, loved his lessons and practised hard for her, as did Alice. But it was Emma's warm, gentle way of drawing close to women who had lost husbands in the war that seemed to bear the most fruit.

'You know just what to say, Emma,' she told her often, as she watched her talk with some of the war widows at church. 'It's like God's taking something that was so painful for you and using it to help others so that it's not wasted.'

Her own opportunities were fewer, but she found herself reaching out more too, often in unexpected ways to the most unexpected people—a lonely customer in the shop, a farmer's wife at church worried about her family, the new couple at the post office. But it was Annie's friend, May, who touched her heart the most, with her long, untidy hair, thin face and shy smile.

'She doesn't like going straight home after school,' Annie had explained when she asked if she could bring her home with her. 'Her dad drinks and her mum's often out doing her cleaning jobs. We can make sure they know where she is though.'

She was intrigued at how much May loved watching her prepare dinner and helping her at times.

'Do you cook with your mum, May?' she asked one day.

Her question was met with a definite shake of the head and a resounding silence which she sensed she should not break.

'I don't think they have much food at May's place, Mrs McPherson,' Annie explained later. 'She doesn't bring any lunch to school, so I sometimes give her half my sandwich.'

In an instant, she saw what little effort it would take to provide

Annie with extra food for May and to help May learn to cook. Soon she also found odd moments to talk about God with her and to pray—and each time she did, she thought of Hettie and what she had written in her last letter.

But as the months passed, something else began to occupy her mind. By Christmas, she knew she was pregnant again. At first, she had mixed feelings about another baby—she had hoped she would soon have more time to paint, with Jane turning five in May and off to school the following January. Yet when she told Richard, he was delighted, as he had been at the news of each of their children.

'That's wonderful, Meg—and I'm sure the children will think so too. Jane will love to have a baby brother or sister to play with while the others are at school. And perhaps it'll be another boy to keep Robert company.'

'Yes, they'll all like the idea, Richard, but … well …'

'Well what?'

'I'm happy about it too, but … oh, it sounds so selfish, I know, but I was looking forward to Jane going to school soon. Then I'd have more time to paint, once I'd finished everything else.'

She could see Richard was taken aback.

'Oh Meg, you can't put your painting before our family like that. I know it's important to you, but you'll have time after the children grow up to paint to your heart's content. I mightn't understand completely, but I know how it feels to put thing aside for a while at least. Look at me with my singing, for example. I used to enjoy performing a lot, but I don't have time anymore, except at church. We all have to make sacrifices, my dear.'

'I'm well aware of that, Richard. I think I've put my own desires aside a lot over the years for our family—and others. It's just that I had hoped … but I know you're right, so don't worry. I'll be fine when I've had time to get used to the idea—my head's a bit mixed up at the moment.'

She considered talking with Emma about how she felt, but decided against it. Perhaps writing to Hettie would be enough—she would understand, despite not having children of her own.

As usual, Hettie's response was brimming with love and acceptance, but also honest and direct.

*Meg, my heart goes out to you—but I feel so delighted for you too. I keep thinking of those verses in Isaiah 55 that we used to read together often:* For my thoughts are not your thoughts, neither are your ways my ways, saith the Lord. For as the heavens are higher than the earth, so are my ways higher than your ways, and my thoughts than your thoughts. *Be brave, my dear, and hold onto the truth that God will work things out in the best possible way for you. Somehow too, I feel this baby will teach you more about God and bring you even greater healing, Meg. So may God enable you to welcome him or her into your family with great joy when the time comes.*

Stephen William James arrived hale and hearty in the middle of the night on 3rd August 1923. She was grateful their doctor had managed to convince Richard she should go to the local hospital this time around. She had not wanted everyone disturbed if the baby came at some unearthly hour, which was what happened in the end. And she was grateful too for a few days of relative peace and quiet in the hospital while she regained her strength.

At first, Richard had wanted to ask her mother to come down and help.

'I'm sure she's stronger now, Meg,' he told her. 'I could easily call your father today, now that we have the phone on in the shop. After all, I can't be everywhere at once.'

'I know, Richard—and of course that bothers me. But … well, I'm still reluctant to ask Mum to come. When she and Dad were here for Robbie's tenth birthday, she was quite critical at times. And she didn't say anything either about wanting to help out when the baby was born. Then in her last note, she mentioned how busy she is helping Caroline make her wedding dress and the bridesmaids' ones as well. The wedding's not far off now. No, don't worry—I'm sure Emma and Annie can manage. Emma's promised to come and cook dinner each evening and help Annie get the children to bed.'

'But … well, I'd be a bit uncomfortable with Emma here—and she doesn't have any experience putting children to bed.'

She had laughed then.

'Oh Richard, she mightn't have any of her own, but she loves them and she's quick and efficient. She won't get in your way. Some of the women from church have offered to care for Jane during the day too—and I think it's good for them to help out, after all you've done for St John's.'

He had seemed happy enough then with what she had arranged—and also relieved. He had always hated household chores and was often too busy anyway to notice what needed to be done. Yet she knew he loved his family. And when the moment came for her to leave the hospital with Stephen, she was touched by the care he took of them both and the pride evident in his face, as he carried the baby to the car and settled him on her lap.

When they arrived home, there was great excitement all round.

'Mrs McPherson, Miss Wetherby let us make you a cake,' Annie and May called out, even before she had made it inside. 'And Alice has set the table for a special afternoon tea.'

As Richard had predicted, Robbie was delighted to have a little brother at last, while Elizabeth and Jane covered the baby's face with gentle, butterfly kisses. He was a firm favourite with them all from the outset and remained so as the months passed. Sometimes after the children came home from school, she would even manage to paint for a while, as they took turns to play with him. But she loved to hold him close herself too at feed times and play with his little fingers as they lay on her breast. Often, she would sense God's presence so near as she did. Then she would remember what Hettie had said in her letter and pray for him and for them all. *Dear Lord, thank you so much for this child. Please give us wisdom as we raise him. Please help me learn what You want me to learn through him too—and may the healing I receive enable me to bring healing to others.*

The rest of the year seemed to fly by and, as the Christmas holidays drew near again, she knew she needed to help Annie make one of the biggest decisions of her life.

'I'm so proud of her,' she told Richard one night. 'Her schoolwork's improved even more and she's grown so much in her faith as well. When I think how uncertain I was about having her with us …'

'I don't like to say "I told you so", but it all worked out, didn't it? … Still, I have to say you've done a wonderful job, Meg, spending time with her when you would much rather have been dabbling in those paints of yours.'

'Thanks, Richard,' she said, choosing to take his words as a compliment. 'I admit I was reluctant to talk with her some nights, but it's paid off. Now I can't wait to tell her about Uncle Harold and Aunty Betty's offer.'

The moment came the next day, not long after the children arrived home from school.

'Sit down, Annie—I've got some exciting news for you. Remember how I said you might be able to stay with my aunt and uncle in Brisbane and do some sort of training course next year? Well, they'd be happy to have you—and Aunty Betty thinks they might even be able to get you a job at a nearby kindergarten. Then later, if you want to, Uncle Harold says he'll look into some nursing or child welfare training for you. I think it'll be good to have some wider experience with babies and young children first—and, with a paid job, you might even be able to help your family out too. We've already talked to your parents, but what do *you* think, Annie?'

She watched Annie's face turn pink with excitement.

'Oh, Mrs McPherson … oh, I can't believe it! I never thought in a million years I'd be able to do something like that. But … are you *sure*? What did Mum and Dad say? Wow, that would be so wonderful. I've always wanted to be a nurse or look after children—I can't believe I might get to do both.'

'Your parents weren't so sure at first, but now they seem to think it's a good opportunity for you. They've noticed how much you've changed, Annie, and how hard you've worked. So well done to you, dear.'

'I … I couldn't have done it without you, Mrs McPherson—and God. Thank you so much for everything,' she managed to say through her tears.

'I know you'll be happy with Aunty Betty. … And you never know, in a year or so, Alice here might be able to join you, once she decides what she wants to do and works hard like you have, Annie.'

She glanced at Alice then and noticed her quick flush and downcast eyes, so did not press the matter. After all, there was plenty of time, with a whole year of school to go yet. But she made a mental note to pray for her oldest daughter more in the coming months. In some ways, Alice reminded her of Isobel. She never drew attention to herself and was always happy to care for her younger siblings. Her faith in God was strong too and she enjoyed helping out at Sunday School—and reading Isobel's newsletters that arrived every two or three months.

She was particularly glad Alice was there to hold Jane's hand, as all four children headed off to school together in the new year. Alice understood Jane—both were quieter souls than Robbie and Elizabeth. The house seemed so still after they left and she paused right where she was for a moment, drinking in the stillness. Her whole body seemed to relax—and soon after, an idea for her current painting came to mind. For a few moments, she contemplated heading to her easel straight away, but then she heard Stevie's plaintive cry from his cot, signalling he was hungry.

As she sat down to feed him in the lounge, she noticed Richard had put some mail from the previous day on the small table nearby. And right on top was what looked like a personal letter from Isobel—her first for many months. She opened the slim envelope and began reading, as Stevie nestled against her.

*Meg, I wanted you to be the first to know outside my family—I'm engaged! Not long after arriving in Shanghai, I met a man from New Zealand, Henry McDonald. We were sent to different inland towns, but we would occasionally meet up at conferences and other gatherings. He visited our station once too and we kept writing to each other after that.*

*Now he's asked me to marry him and our colleagues here are delighted for us. I wanted to tell you earlier but didn't think I should until it was all settled. Please forgive me. I know if this had happened at home, we would have talked about it for hours.*

*Anyway, we are to be married in Shanghai in six weeks. Of course, my family can't be here, but we have good friends among the other missionaries who are helping us. One lady is lending me her wedding dress and it's beautiful. I'll try to get someone to take a photo on the day, but you might not see it for some time.*

*Meg, I'm so happy. God has been so gracious and faithful. I love Henry very much and I think you'd like him too. He's godly and wise— and funny as well. I hope you can meet him when we come home on furlough in a couple of years. I think of you all often. And I look forward to meeting little Stephen one day too. God bless you all.*

It took her a while to take in Isobel's amazing news. Then the tears came, dripping down on Stevie's little head as she cuddled him. *Thank You, Lord,* her heart cried out with joy. *You're so faithful in every way.*

All through that day, she could not get Isobel's wonderful news out of her mind. She remembered a time, not long after leaving school, when they had talked about what they wanted to do in life. Even then, Isobel had been sure God would work things out for her. She remembered too how Isobel had said she would love to be married and have children. Yet she had been prepared to trust God and leave her future in His hands.

'God's been so faithful and kind to Isobel, don't you think?' she said to Richard when he came to bed that evening. 'Who would have thought she'd end up falling in love with a New Zealander in China? But Isobel's been faithful too in doing what she believed God wanted her to do. I'm so happy for her.'

'Yes, of course it's good news, Meg. But remember, Isobel might have married Len Gillespie right here and had a brood of children by now. As it is, he's still single—and no doubt still lonely too. Isobel would have made a good minister's wife. And she would have been much closer to her family than she is now—and to us.'

'Well, I think it's perfect how things have worked out for her—except, of course, for her being so far away. And I'm sure Mr Henry MacDonald, whoever he is, will make a much better husband for her than Len Gillespie ever would. I can tell how much Isobel loves him from her letter—and that was never how she felt about Len Gillespie.'

All she heard in response, as Richard turned over, was a muffled 'hmph'.

She lay awake for some time, reflecting on the many conversations she had had with Isobel and how certain they had been that Len Gillespie was not the man for her. No doubt he *was* lonely, as Richard had said. She could feel sorry for him for that reason. Perhaps she should even pray he would find someone to marry. After all, if God had found Isobel a husband in the middle of China, surely God could find a wife for Len Gillespie too, right there in Harrisville.

She remembered this thought one evening several months later, as they celebrated Richard's birthday with a special dinner and birthday cake. Richard had invited Len Gillespie, but the children had insisted on inviting Emma too. She was grateful Emma arrived early and was happy to mind Stevie for a while—she still often became flustered when she had to serve a baked dinner for guests. And she was even more grateful when Emma offered to help the older children wash up afterwards, while Richard and Len moved to the lounge room.

During dinner, she had noticed Len's eyes straying in Emma's direction. Now, as she returned from putting the three youngest children to bed, she caught him glancing towards the kitchen where Emma was laughing with Alice and Robbie as they worked. Could he be interested in Emma? And … was Emma interested in *him*?

She decided not to say anything to Emma until the subject came up of its own accord. Whenever they could, they still liked to talk and pray together in her little corner of the veranda. With Annie gone, it was quieter and more private there. She was touched Emma still wanted to meet, despite how busy she was at school and with her music teaching. And before the Christmas holidays arrived, she was determined to tell her that.

They managed to catch up again one evening in the final week of term.

'I'm so glad you were still prepared to come, despite how busy you are,' she told Emma straight away.

'Oh Meg, I love our times together—particularly in your own special, creative corner. It may not be palatial, but I always seem to sense God's presence here. And that encourages me to keep listening to God as I write my music.'

'I'm amazed you have time to write at all. You seem to get more and more music pupils. Next year, I hope you'll be able to take on Elizabeth—and Alice and Robbie want to continue on too.'

She held her breath, as Emma hesitated.

'Meg, that's one thing I'd like to talk about tonight. I'd be happy to teach Elizabeth, but … well, I'm not sure what next year will hold yet for me. Um … this might come as a surprise, but Len Gillespie and I have been seeing a little of each other in recent weeks. I've … I've wanted to tell you for a while now. We've tried to be discreet—although that's almost impossible in Harrisville. We enjoy each other's company and we like similar things—Len loves music, even though he doesn't play an instrument himself, and we both like reading. He'll be back here at St John's next year, as Richard might have mentioned, although he's not sure for how long. … Meg, please don't tell anyone this, because I don't think even Richard knows yet, but Len's planning on leaving the ministry.'

At first, she was unsure how to respond.

'Well, you're a dark horse. But … oh Emma, I can see in your face how much Len means to you and I'm so happy for you. That's wonderful for Len too—Richard's commented quite a few times how lonely he must be. But … if Len leaves the ministry, what would he do? And … and I guess that means you might leave Harrisville too.'

'Whoa—hold on! It's early days yet, but … we do like each other very much. And I know I want the best for Len, which for him might mean leaving the ministry. He's tried so hard. Of course, he wants to do what God wants, but he does find running a parish overwhelming at times, especially since the war. And he's not such a well person either. At first, he thought he might become a chaplain again, but now he feels a secular job might suit him better. In fact, we've already talked to my uncle in Brisbane about that. He's friends with George Barker from Barker's Bookstore and he thinks they might have a job there for Len soon. They're about to expand again, so he might be offered a place in their new technical books department. Or perhaps he could run the library they're thinking of opening. He'd love that.'

'That sounds so right to me, Emma, but I'm sure no one leaves the ministry without a lot of thought and prayer. Maybe he could help out at a parish and work at the bookstore as well. Would that be possible?'

'I don't know what Archbishop Sharp would say to that, but we'll see. We think it's best to hasten slowly with everything, Meg, even though we're not so young anymore. It's a big step for us both— and of course, if we marry, I'd have to give up school teaching. But at least I could still have my music students come to our house, wherever that might be.'

Her mind raced, as she thought about the big decisions ahead for Emma. She wanted to ask her a hundred and one questions, but instead, leant across and gave her friend a warm hug.

'Whatever happens, we'll still be friends, Emma. I know God brought us together to support each other. And I think the best thing I can do is to pray right now that God will guide and watch over you both in the months ahead.'

She prayed for Emma then with all her heart. She did not want her to regret any decision she made and hoped upon hope she had not turned to Len out of mere loneliness. Yet, as she thought about it afterwards, Emma and Len Gillespie did have things in common. And they seemed to respect each other too, something she had come to see was so vital in her own marriage. Well, it was not her decision, but she was sure it was her responsibility to pray for Emma and provide a listening ear when needed.

The school year had finished before they saw each other again—and then there was time for only the briefest of goodbyes.

'My parents are expecting me in Brisbane for dinner, Meg. And my sister and her husband are up from Sydney with my niece and nephew, so no doubt I'm needed to entertain them too. See you in the new year, dear friend—and I'll write if I have any news before then.'

Two weeks later, she smiled when she noticed how soon Len Gillespie left after their Christmas morning service.

'Looks like Len can't wait to get away from us all,' Richard growled. 'I'm a bit sorry I said I'd fill in for him on Sunday now. We all need a holiday—and he's always said his mother doesn't mind if he's not in Brisbane until Boxing Day, so why the rush? Did you ask him to join us for Christmas lunch?'

She was sure she could guess why Len had hurried away but decided not to enlighten Richard.

'Yes, I did, but he said he had other plans this year and would need to be in Brisbane. Perhaps it's just as well anyway, with Annie and her family coming.'

They had no sooner arrived home than Richard came into the kitchen to talk more with her.

'Meg, I know you're busy now with everything, but I've been thinking we could all go away somewhere after Sunday. Len will be back next week and I've already told him we're likely to be away. I've enquired about camping down at Cribb Island for two weeks— that's the longest I can trust Tom to look after the store, with some help from his son.'

For a moment, she was stunned.

'I can't believe you're telling me this right now, Richard, when I'm in the middle of getting everything ready for our Christmas dinner,' she blurted out. 'Going *camping*? I don't know what to say.'

'You don't have to say anything, Meg. I know we should've talked about it earlier, but there's been so much else to do. Anyway, it's almost organised now. I've already found an old tent and I'm sure the children will all enjoy the experience.'

'I'm not sure *I* will though. I'll have to think about food to take and so much else. I guess Alice can help me get things ready, but … oh Richard.'

In the end, despite her misgivings, they had a relaxing holiday together. To her relief, Richard found a good, dry spot in the camping ground and they all managed to squeeze into their big, old tent to sleep. At times, it was a battle to cook everything on the two small primus stoves Richard had bought, but she persevered. And often, everyone seemed happy to make do with sandwiches and fruit instead—even Richard. The children swam for hours, played cricket and rounders on the beach with other families and built endless, ornate sandcastles. It was good to be away from Harrisville in the height of summer and she enjoyed the cool sea breezes, as she kept an eye on Stevie and chatted with some of the other campers. At least she did not have to watch what she said with them, as much as she did with her mother.

'It's been a good holiday, I have to admit,' she told Richard on their last day away. 'I didn't like the idea at first, but I'm glad we came here rather than going to Helidon. Maybe Mum's glad we did too.'

But she missed her little corner on the veranda and her times alone there.

Once they were home again, she found she missed Emma too and the good conversations they often had. She had heard nothing, but she wondered if Len Gillespie had told Richard about Emma.

'How's Len Gillespie managing things?' she decided to ask, when Richard arrived home from his first parish council meeting for the year.

'He seems much the same,' he muttered. 'I hate to say it, but I wish he'd be more organised. Still, he tries his best.'

She was unsure if he was keeping something from her, but

could see he was in no mood for any further questions about Len Gillespie—or St John's in general. He rarely talked about parish matters with her.

'Such things are none of your concern, Meg,' he had told her once, when she had suggested shorter sermons each Sunday, for the children's sake, and easier hymns too. 'We men can sort all that out.'

The evening before school began, she had just started a new painting when the front doorbell rang. She heard the vague sound of voices, as Richard opened the door, then footsteps along the veranda. A moment later, there was Emma, her face wreathed in smiles.

'Hello, Meg—Richard told me you were out here and I wanted to surprise you. I didn't show him, but ... well ...'

She gasped as Emma held out her left hand, complete with a dainty, diamond engagement ring.

'There was no time to write in the end—I hope you'll forgive me. Anyway, I wanted to see your face when I told you. Everyone's so happy for us. Len's even been to see the Archbishop, as well as Mr Barker at the bookstore, so it's all decided.'

She held Emma close then and could feel her trembling.

'Oh, Emma, congratulations—that's such wonderful news! But ... when are you going to be married?'

'In the May school holidays—so that means we have only a few more months here. Len's talking about it all with Richard right now.'

'Well, in my opinion, Len's a very fortunate man, Emma. You must both be so excited. But you'll have some busy months ahead, planning the wedding and teaching and all.'

'Yes—although we aren't having a big wedding. Len's going to ask Richard to be best man and I'd love you to be matron of honour. Please say you will. My sister's expecting another baby around then, so we don't think they'll even make it up from Sydney. ... But Meg, thank you for praying about Len and me. I'm sure I've made the right decision—and I'm sure God will look after us both.'

The early months of 1925 seemed to fly by so fast. Each day, while the older children were at school, she helped in the shop or did housework, as well as care for Stevie. He was such a delightful little boy and growing up so fast—soon he would be eighteen months old. Most days, he was happy to sit playing with his trains or tin soldiers when she served in the shop. But sometimes he would decide to get up and run to greet each customer, winning over even the gruffest farmer with his sunny smile. Now and then, she would catch her breath as he looked up at her. His eyes were a lighter colour than Jimbo's, but something in the way he tilted his head and smiled reminded her so much of her little brother. *Please, Lord,* she would often pray, *watch over him and keep him safe. And please help me do my best to care for him—and for each of our children.*

The trip to Brisbane for the wedding at St Thomas's on 2nd May was exciting for them all. Emma looked beautiful, in her cream silk dress with a shorter hemline and her mother's long, embroidered veil, and Len Gillespie was the happiest and most relaxed she had ever seen him, in his smart, dark suit.

'Go well, dear friend,' she whispered to Emma, as the newlyweds said their final goodbyes.

She meant it with all her heart, yet she was well aware of the big gap Emma's departure would leave in her life—and in their family and community as a whole. All the children loved her. And Alice and Robbie played the piano so much better as a result of their lessons with her. As for St John's, once again they would be without an organist.

'Looks like we'll need you to fill in again, Meg,' Richard told her. 'On top of that, the Archbishop says there's no one available right now to replace Len. However, I'm hoping he can talk Bill Fisher into coming back for a while.'

'I hope so too,' she sighed. 'I'm not looking forward to playing the organ, but it'd be wonderful if Reverend Fisher could help us out again.'

To her delight, he agreed to come, but could not do so until July. As a result, she often needed to cover for Richard in the shop while he attended to church matters. But one afternoon towards the end of June, the shop door opened and Reverend Fisher walked in, along with Richard. She had been sitting at the counter, her chin cupped in her hands, wishing she could curl up and sleep like Stevie was on a pillow on the floor. But as soon as she saw their old minister's smiling face, she sprang to her feet.

'Oh, how wonderful—I didn't know you were coming today. Richard never told me,' she babbled, as she tried to hold back her tears. 'Welcome back to Harrisville, Reverend Fisher—it's so good to have you here again.'

'It's good to see you too, Meg. But don't you think it's time you called me Bill instead of Reverend Fisher? Richard does, so why not you? I'd be delighted if you would.'

'It … well, it sounds a little disrespectful to me, especially considering how much you've helped me in the past.'

'I know you'd never disrespect me, my dear. Anyway, how are you? You seemed tired when we walked in. But now that I'm here and can lift some of those church matters from your husband's shoulders, perhaps you can relax a bit more, eh?'

A warm feeling began to well up inside her as they chatted together. Bill Fisher was much more stooped now and thinner, but he still had that same bright sparkle in his eyes and the gentle, caring manner she remembered. In an instant too, he had noticed how she was feeling. Yes, she was indeed glad to see him back at St John's.

The following Sunday, she was aware of him standing nearby as she practised the organ before the service. She could hear him talking to the children but knew she needed to keep practising the anthem Richard had chosen, as well as the hymns. She did not want to let anyone down, especially since they were so used to Emma's expert playing. He did not disturb her then, but one morning a few weeks later, he called in to see her.

'My dear, I've noticed the last few Sundays how hard it is for you to play the organ and keep an eye on the children. I'm wondering if Alice might be able to help you out with the hymns at times. Then you'd only have the anthem to worry about—and we don't always have to have an anthem either. I'll speak to Richard about that. I've noticed how Alice watches you as much as she can when you're practising—and I've heard her playing the piano here too when I've called in. She's quite good for a girl her age. Now I'm back at St John's, I'll be choosing the hymns—and I'm sure I could find easier ones that Alice could manage. What do you say, Meg? Will you ask her or would you like me to?'

That very week, before she had time to think more about it, Bill Fisher had sorted the whole matter out. Alice was delighted, if a little nervous, to be asked to play for a 'real service'.

'I love playing the piano, Mum. And I've wanted to try playing the organ for a while—as long as you don't mind.'

'Not at all, Alice. I'd much rather spend my time painting than practising the piano—or the organ. And while we're on the subject, your father and I have wanted to talk to you about music lessons next year. We wondered if you'd like to learn from a good piano teacher in Brisbane and perhaps attend the high school near Aunty Betty's. Or you could do some other course instead, if you wanted to. Remember how I told Annie you might join her there? I'm sure Aunty Betty would love to have you stay as well.'

She held her breath. She did not want to upset Alice again or press her into anything. Yet she wanted to give her every opportunity to spread her wings, the same as she had been given. But this time, Alice did not seem upset at all.

'I hate to disappoint you or Dad, Mum, but I don't want to go to Brisbane next year. I've asked God to show me what He wants me to do—and I think I need to stay right here at home. I like helping around the house and looking after the others. And I could work in the shop—Dad could teach me more about that. Then the other day when I went to the post office for you, Mrs Matthews told me she might need an assistant around Christmastime. I'd like that—I really would.'

She looked into her daughter's pleading eyes and was touched by what she saw. Again, something in Alice's response had reminded her of Isobel. Was it her gentle humility and willingness to help wherever needed? She could feel the tears welling up, although she was unsure why.

'Well … of course I'd love to have you home here with us, dear, but I don't want you to miss out on the opportunity to do something else either. Look, let's not decide right now. I'll talk to your father more tonight and see what he says.'

That night, she still found herself in two minds about it all, as she brought the subject up with Richard again.

'I don't know—I'm not sure it's fair to let Alice stay home here next year. If Annie had the chance to go to Brisbane, surely we can do the same for our own daughter.'

'But Meg, you said she doesn't want to go anywhere. And I don't think we should force her to continue on at school or take some other course she's not interested in. We've said enough about all this already, haven't we?'

She knew Richard was tired and had other things on his mind, but she had told Alice she would talk about it with him and wanted to keep her word.

'Perhaps we have—but I can't help feeling guilty about letting her stay home with us. After all, my parents gave me the wonderful opportunity of learning from Godfrey Rivers, as well as having lessons with a good music teacher in Brisbane.'

She flinched a little at Richard's exasperated response.

'Look, Meg, all I can say is Alice isn't you. And I'm sure your father had more money to spare too than we have right now. To be honest, I think we should save up for Robert's education, if Alice doesn't want to go to Brisbane. She's a good girl. Everyone seems to like her and no doubt she'll get married before she's much older. After all, look what happened to you. Instead of going on with your art course, you married me—so it was all wasted anyway. The same goes for Emma. After working so hard to become a teacher, she's had to give it all away now that she's married.'

She could feel the anger inside her but tried to keep her voice calm.

'Richard, that's all so unfair. If you remember, I stopped doing my art course because of what happened to Jimbo—it was later on that I decided to marry you. Besides, I don't consider my art classes were wasted at all. I still love painting. It's something that feeds my spirit like nothing else does. I love being out in my corner on the veranda by myself, listening to God and painting pictures I hope will bless others in some way. And this year, I plan to exhibit my work a bit more, perhaps in Ipswich or even Brisbane. ... As for Emma, do you really think all the years she's been teaching up till now have been a waste of time? I know the children in her class here loved her and I'm sure her pupils in Brisbane did too. Anyway, she still plans to teach music at home. Even having a baby wouldn't stop her doing that altogether.'

But Richard had had enough.

'Okay, have it your own way, Meg. I don't want to argue—and maybe I was unfair saying those things about you and Emma. But if Alice wants to stay here with us, I say let her. And I'll tell her that tomorrow.'

She sat where she was for a while, trying to calm down. Richard was right—Alice *was* different from her. Yet whatever Richard believed, there was no guarantee Alice would end up marrying in a few years. Only God knew what lay ahead. Then she remembered how Alice had told her she sensed God wanted her to stay right there in Harrisville. Who was she then, after all, to talk Alice out of what God might want her to do? Yes, Alice was still young, but her faith was deep and real. *Oh Lord,* she prayed, *please give us wisdom—and please let us know if we're making the wrong decision.*

# Chapter Thirteen

As the end of the year drew closer, she could see how much Alice was looking forward to leaving school, which encouraged her to feel they had made the right decision. In fact, she felt more encouraged in general, with Bill Fisher back at St John's and a frequent guest at their dinner table. She tried her best to take in his sermons, which were as clear and thoughtful as ever. And on those Sundays when Alice played for the hymns, she found she could worship God from her heart throughout most of the service. But she still felt selfish, letting Alice stay home with them. In the end, she wrote to Hettie about it and soon received a warm reply, although Hettie's words were fewer now and her writing even more spidery.

*You know, Meg, sometimes I think God's kinder to us than we are to ourselves. I know how hard it is for you to put time aside to paint without feeling guilty—and I can understand how you might feel you're imposing on Alice by having her stay home to free you up more. But Alice has chosen to do what she feels God wants and what she herself loves to do. And I suspect God wants you to do the same, my dear—to create your beautiful scenes for Him and be with Him when you can, while still caring for your family. So be kind to yourself, Meg, in the same way God has been, and is, to you.*

After Christmas that year, they holidayed again at Cribb Island. This time, Stevie was old enough to join in everything better with the others, which enabled her to relax more. She could see he slowed them down and spoilt their games at times, but they all loved him and were mostly patient with him. Yet she could not help smiling one day, as she watched them all try to handle things when he fell over in the middle of a sand garden Elizabeth had spent hours creating.

'Oh, Elizabeth, I'm so sorry he's messed it up, but he didn't mean to,' Alice said, as she hugged a sobbing Elizabeth.

'But he *wrecked* it—and I was making it for the sand garden competition!'

'I know. Well, we'll help you build an even better one tomorrow.'

'Anyway,' Robbie chimed in, 'it wouldn't have won anything, so don't be a cry-baby.'

'I'm *not* a cry-baby! You didn't like it when Stevie spoilt your cricket match yesterday.'

'Well … that's different.'

'No, it's not.'

She was about to intervene when Jane took Elizabeth's hand.

'Don't cry, Lizzie. Look what I found—a real live soldier crab, here in my bucket. See his pretty blue back?'

Everyone was diverted and the moment passed. She watched then as Alice picked up Stevie and cuddled him, helping him see the crab too. And again, she thanked God for Alice—and for each one of them.

Once school started for the year, she was even more thankful for Alice when she saw how well she helped out at home and in the shop. Even the older men who preferred Richard to serve them were becoming used to his daughter instead. She was glad Richard had been able to work in his office when Alice first began serving, to be on hand to help. But as the weeks passed, it was wonderful to see her grow in confidence. She felt proud too when Mrs Matthews told her how delighted she had been with Alice's help during the Christmas rush.

'I don't know what I'd have done without her,' she beamed when she came into the shop one lunch hour. 'Please let her do some more work for me. We could try one afternoon a week first off.'

With Alice around to help, she had more time to paint—and also more time to meet with one or two women Bill Fisher sent her way.

'I don't want to keep you from your painting, Meg, but I'd appreciate it if you could talk and pray with both Gwen and Jean now and then. Above all, I think they need to know God's love and realise that God can give them the peace and security they long for. Life's been hard for them, as it has for you at times, but God's taught you so much through it all. I know you'd be a blessing to them.'

She did not even think of refusing him and, as the weeks passed, she was humbled at how fruitful her times with both women became. Little by little, she was seeing how God did not waste anything in her life, as Hettie had often maintained, but could use it to bless and encourage others.

In the May school holidays, she was a little taken aback when Richard decided to start building a treehouse in the big gumtree in the corner of their backyard.

'I know Alice and Robert have wanted one for years. They're probably too old for it now, but Robert says he and his friends would like a place of their own where they can be by themselves. The girls can play there at times too and make it look a bit prettier for their games.'

'Well, I hope there aren't too many fights over it. But what about Stevie? That branch where you plan to put it looks far too high up for him.'

Yet Richard would not be dissuaded, whatever she said.

'Don't worry, Meg. He won't be able to climb the ladder I'm going to build. The others wouldn't let him anyway. And it's a good project to tackle with Robert. He's just the right age to learn a few basic carpentry skills. We won't finish it these holidays, but at least we'll have started.'

To her surprise, Robbie seemed keen to help. Whenever she wanted him during the holidays, she would often find him on his bed with his nose in a book. Perhaps it was the idea of having a place where he and his friends could be far away from his sisters that won him over. Yet, whatever the reason, she was pleased to see father and son working hard together.

They managed to complete the floor of the treehouse before the holidays were over and the project had to be set aside.

'I'll take the ladder down, Meg,' Richard told her. 'I don't want anyone up there until we've built the walls and railings. I might get time to work on it some Saturday afternoons, but it depends how busy I am. Otherwise, Robert and I can finish it off in the August holidays.'

She sensed Robbie's disappointment, as Richard was often busy reporting at sports fixtures on Saturday afternoons or meeting with Bill Fisher about the Sunday services. She would not have blamed him if he had lost interest by the August holidays, but as soon as Richard mentioned the project again, his face lit up.

'I'd like that, Dad. My friends reckon we're never going to finish it, but I think we could get it done these holidays.'

They finished it in record time. She was proud of how well Robbie worked with his father and she was equally proud of him when he allowed Elizabeth and Jane to spend hours in the treehouse—or cubby, as they insisted on calling it. They loved decorating it with flowers and holding endless tea parties there. And she suspected even Alice had a soft spot for it, judging by how often she could be coerced into taking extra supplies of biscuits up to her sisters for their special parties, along with glasses of lemon cordial. As for Stevie, they all made it clear to him he was not allowed anywhere near it.

'You know it's not safe for you to try to climb up that ladder, dear,' she told him yet again, one Saturday morning in September when they were hanging out the washing together. 'When you're bigger, you can.'

'But I big now, Mummy—I *three*.'

'I know you are. You're growing up so fast. Soon you'll be at school.'

She tried to divert his thoughts as he looked with longing towards the cubby, but doubted she had succeeded. Still, food would often entice him—and now, even out in the yard, she could smell the aroma of Alice's freshly-baked Anzac biscuits.

'Ooh, can you smell something nice, dear? What do you think Alice is baking in the kitchen?'

She laughed as he screwed up his button nose, then let out a cry of joy.

'Bickies! Yum—I love bickies.'

'Let's go and see if they're ready yet,' she told him, as she scooped him up and carried him inside.

Alice was just taking a batch out of the oven when they arrived.

'They'll need to cool down for a while, Stevie, but they'll be ready soon. Tell you what—how about you help me wash up so Mummy can go and paint?'

She smiled at Alice over Stevie's head. Alice was often insightful beyond her years and she was so grateful for her understanding. That was just what she wanted to do—try to finish a large painting for the upcoming art show in Ipswich.

'Well, if you don't mind, Alice, I'd like to do that. But let me know if you need any help.'

She was soon in her own world, as she added a touch of deeper green to the landscape she had begun earlier that month. Her mind wandered to the scene itself—a view across the nearby paddocks to the purple ranges in the distance. She loved the area where they lived. It was often so dry in summer, but most of the year there were pockets of green somewhere, especially along the creek banks. It was wonderful to feel so free, as she continued adding small splashes of colour here and there. And as she stood back and viewed her painting again, she found herself praying. *Dear God, may this scene bless others somehow. May they see Your handiwork in a fresh way through it.*

She had just put down her brush when she heard Alice scream out.

'Mum, Mum, come quick—something's happened to Stevie!'

She rushed out into the yard to see a small, crumpled form on the ground. Elizabeth was crying, as she knelt beside Stevie, and Jane was wailing in fright as she peered down from the cubby.

'I'm so sorry, Mum,' Alice sobbed. 'I left him washing up while I brought some biscuits out for Elizabeth and Jane. But I stayed to play a game—and he was just too quick for me. I told him to go back down, but …'

'Don't worry now, Alice. Run and tell your father what's happened and phone Doctor Waters. Then stay and mind the store for us.'

She leaned over Stevie, noticing as she did how his left leg was lying at a sickening angle. It was caked in mud and grass, but she could still see blood oozing out from below his knee—and a glimpse of something white. She had never been any good at first aid, but she knew should not move him.

'Elizabeth, go and get a blanket or rug. We need to keep Stevie warm. And Jane, please stop wailing like that. Stevie, Mummy's here—you'll be okay. Oh, Stevie … can you hear me?'

He was looking up at her now, pain and shock obvious in his eyes and his face as white as a sheet. He whimpered as she steeled herself to brush away some of the dirt and grass from his injured leg. She knew she should stop the blood flowing from his wound too and tried her best, with little result. *Dear God, please help Richard get here fast—and Doctor Waters too. And please let Stevie be all right.*

'Mummy, it hurts … Mummy, stop it hurting! I falled down,' he sobbed, his arms reaching out for her.

She stroked his forehead and tried to calm him.

'Hush, dear—try to keep still. Daddy will be here soon and so will Doctor Waters. You're going to be all right. I know it hurts a lot, but you're a big, brave boy, aren't you? Here, we'll put this blanket around you to keep you warm until the doctor comes.'

Richard arrived then and started barking orders left and right.

'Meg, get some water and clean cloths to wipe this dirt away. And Elizabeth, run and get some ice. We need to stop the leg from swelling up. Jane, come down here now and watch for Doctor Waters out the front. Tell him we're round the back. Stephen, were you trying to climb up to the cubby? Hmm. ... Good, that was quick, Meg. Now give me one of those cloths. I'm going to press here to try to stop this bleeding.'

She held onto Stevie's hand, unable to watch. He screamed, then went limp, his little hand dropping out of hers like a stone.

'It's okay, Meg, he's only fainted,' Richard told her. 'Now, let's try to clean away some of this dirt, so Doctor Waters can see what's happened. There ... that's a bit better.'

Stevie regained consciousness soon after and she tried to make him as comfortable as possible while they waited. The ice seemed to help with some of his pain at least, although he could not bear them to touch his leg anywhere.

She was relieved beyond words when Doctor Waters arrived at last.

'What have you been up to, young man? Hmm—you've made a pretty good job of breaking that leg of yours, by the looks. Let's see what we can do.'

Doctor Waters was mercifully quick and as gentle as he could be.

'Do you have anything we could use as splints? Even some rolled up newspapers would do. I can tear up these rags to secure them on his leg for now. Then we'll move him onto the back seat of my car. You can ride with me, Mrs McPherson—well take him straight to the hospital and I'll do my best to fix him up there. We'll keep an eye on him overnight, but he should be able to come home after that. I'm sure he'll be fine in no time. Children most often are, you know.'

She sensed he was trying to make her feel more confident and was grateful. But she was determined to stay with Stevie for as long as she could and told him so.

'That's fine, Mrs McPherson,' the doctor responded. 'He'll be calmer with you there anyway.'

'Are you sure you need to go too, Meg?' Richard frowned. 'I have to report on some sporting events at Warrill View this afternoon—I can't stay here with the children.'

'Alice will be fine looking after Elizabeth and Jane, Richard. And Robbie told me he'd be home from his friend's place by lunchtime, so he'll help too. I need to be with Stevie until he settles at least. He might be scared otherwise.'

She could not sleep much after coming home that night, as she thought of Stevie lying there so still in the hospital, and was glad when the doctor discharged him late the next day. She was touched at how all the children tried their best to make him comfortable, but had to stop Alice from constantly hovering around him.

'It's all my fault, Mum,' she sobbed. 'He wanted my Anzac biscuits and I left some in the kitchen for him, but he must've thought I'd taken them all out to the cubby. If I hadn't been so long, he wouldn't have climbed up.'

Her heart went out to Alice. She remembered how guilty she had felt over what happened to Jimbo and how much she needed her mother to forgive her. How could she deny her own daughter what she herself longed for so much?

She put her arm around Alice's shoulder and drew her out of the room.

'Alice, listen to me. It was an accident—that's all. Besides, I'm just as much to blame as you. I should have been watching him instead of painting. And Dad blames himself too—he says he should have made a better ladder up to the cubby with more steps, so Stevie couldn't have slipped through. Anyway, even if you were to blame, dear, I forgive you. I know how hard it is to feel responsible for things like that.'

She decided not to fill Alice in any further at that point. Perhaps she would one day—but not yet.

At first, Stevie seemed to improve, but by the end of that first week, she was worried. Despite all their efforts, he was nowhere near his old self. He was pale and lethargic and difficult to rouse, even when they made him his favourite food. He felt cold too and his breathing seemed laboured.

'He'll bounce back, Meg,' Richard told her when she pointed out her concerns. 'Don't fuss over him. Children are tough—remember what Doctor Waters said.'

But when Doctor Waters called in to check on his young patient again, he was concerned too.

'I suspect he might have a slight infection, Mrs McPherson. See, his leg's quite swollen and it looks a bit red. I think it might be wise to have the ambulance come from Ipswich and take him back to the hospital there. They're much better equipped to deal with complications like this—and they can check for other injuries too.'

She watched in agony as the ambulance drove away that afternoon. She wanted to go with Stevie with all her heart, but that was impossible. In a haze of pain, she headed to her corner on the veranda and fell on her knees. *Oh Lord, he's so little—please comfort him and keep him safe. And please give the doctors wisdom.* She stayed there for some time until Alice came to get her.

'Mum, Reverend Fisher's here and wants to see you.'

She almost ran into his arms. For a few moments, he held her close and patted her on the back.

'There, there, my dear. It must be so hard, seeing little Stevie suffer like this. I happened to come into the shop and Richard told me the news. Look, I hope I'm not interfering, but I knew you'd want to be close by, so I contacted my colleague at St Paul's as soon as I heard. He and his wife would be happy to have you stay, Meg— and you can walk to the hospital from the rectory. I'll get one of the women from church to look after the children this afternoon. That way, Alice can mind the shop and Richard can drive you to Ipswich.'

Somehow, Bill Fisher took it all in hand, even managing to convince Richard this was the best course of action.

'Meg needs to be with Stevie,' he told him in a voice of quiet authority that she had not heard him use often, 'and I'm sure your mind would be more at ease too, if she's with him. Leave it with me—we'll sort out today first and go from there. I'll call in again after you get back, Richard, and we can talk more then.'

But it was his final words that comforted her most and stayed with her throughout the following days.

'Meg, be strong—keep your eyes on the Lord. He is mighty to save. And Stevie's so precious to him.'

She could tell Richard did not want to talk much on the drive into Ipswich and neither did she. But she could not help worrying. How would Richard cope without her at home? She was sure Bill Fisher would find someone to care for the children for a day at least, but many of the women at church lived on farms and already led such busy lives. In the end, she could not help blurting out her fears.

'Richard, I … I don't know who to suggest to help out while I'm with Stevie. I hope it won't be for too long …'

'I think we need to ask your mother to come this time, Meg. That's the best solution, as far as I can see.'

'But I hate the thought of asking her. You know that, Richard. Anyway, I suspect she'd say she couldn't come at such short notice.'

'Well, we'll see. But don't worry—Bill and I will sort something out. You have enough on your mind with Stevie.'

'I'm so thankful I can be with him, Richard. I feel so responsible …'

'Meg, we've been over this before. It was much more my fault—I should never have built that ladder the way I did. In fact, maybe I should have listened to you in the beginning when you said that spot in the tree was too high up. But all we can do is hope and pray Stevie will soon be better.'

She did not say anything more then. Instead, she prayed for Stevie the rest of the way to the hospital.

In the days that followed, she tried not to worry about how Richard was coping at home—all she could do was hand the situation over to God. Each morning, she would walk to the hospital and sit beside Stevie's bed, speaking softly to him and praying. His cast had been removed and the wound cleansed again, but his leg was still swollen and painful. Sometimes he did not recognise her, yet even when he did, he had little energy to talk. When he fell asleep, she would walk back to the rectory to rest or sometimes down to the nearby Bremer River. It was muddy and swollen from the recent heavy rains, but somehow it suited her sombre mood. Many times, as she sat there praying for Stevie, the words of Psalm 23 would come to mind.

*The Lord is my shepherd; I shall not want.*

*He maketh me to lie down in green pastures: he leadeth me beside the still waters.*

*He restoreth my soul: he leadeth me in the paths of righteousness for his name's sake.*

*Yea, though I walk through the valley of the shadow of death, I will fear no evil: for thou art with me; thy rod and thy staff they comfort me.*

Right now, the waters in the river below and in their lives were anything but still, but she prayed they would soon be peaceful again. She prayed too for God's help to overcome her fears and for strength to keep on trusting, yet at times, she felt she was indeed entering that valley of the shadow of death the psalmist mentioned. But then she would stop and force herself to focus on the Lord, as Bill Fisher had urged her to do. In her mind's eye, she would picture Jesus, standing strong and tall beside her like a mighty warrior. And at times, she would even sense His hand warm on her shoulder, reassuring her and giving her the strength to go on.

She was particularly thankful He was present with her whenever the brown, turbulent waters of the river reminded her of Lockyer Creek on the day they had lost Jimbo—and of how her mother had blamed her. Then one afternoon, as if out of nowhere, it came to her how much more she now understood her mother's deep grief. In an instant, she realised God was teaching her something through Stevie and would somehow bring good out of the whole, awful experience. The realisation was so clear and strong it almost took her breath away—it was like an arrow piercing her heart. And in that moment, she also sensed God calling her to do something she had pushed aside for years. She had tried so many times to forgive her mother for blaming her. But now, in the midst of her own pain, she was sure God was challenging her to forgive her once and for all.

The struggle was intense. As she sat there, she felt the weight of her mother's pain and sorrow and her own pain and concern for Stevie too. But then she straightened and prayed out loud with all her heart. *Lord, I know You want me to forgive Mum for her attitude towards me. I understand more now … and I freely forgive her in Your strength. Because of the forgiveness You have shown me, I forgive her, Lord. And I bless her now in Your mighty name. Amen.*

Straight away, she felt a heavy weight lift off her shoulders. Then it was as if this weight rolled down the nearby embankment like a huge rock, gathering momentum as it went, before plunging into the brown waters below.

She sat still, sensing God's comforting presence all around her. *Lord,* she prayed, *I know You're teaching me things through all this that I could not have learnt any other way. Thank you for giving me the strength to forgive Mum. Now, Lord, please heal and restore Stevie— please don't let him die too!*

She found herself praying this same prayer with even more urgency a few night later, when she saw how concerned the doctor was. He kept checking Stevie's pulse and did not say no when she refused to leave the hospital. The matron came by at regular intervals too, but offered little encouragement.

'I'm afraid we must let the infection take its course now, Mrs McPherson. There's nothing more we can do,' she told her in a firm voice that sent chills down her spine.

She was thankful Stevie was in a room of his own because, after the matron left, she stood by his bed, determined to pray for him as she never had before. His eyes were open, although he did not seem to see her. Instead, he appeared to be looking somewhere beyond her. She watched as he struggled to sit up and reached out his arms.

… What was he dreaming about? … What could he see? … What was happening?

She felt a cold fear in the pit of her stomach but refused to give into it. Instead, she began praying out loud, as she pressed Stevie back onto his pillows. *No, Lord—it's not time for him to go yet. We need him and You have things for him to do. Let him stay here, Lord! You are powerful and mighty—You are the great Healer. You overcame death and rose again to give us life. Please let Stevie live, Lord!*

She was unaware how loudly she had prayed until the matron came to the door, her face red.

'What's the matter? What's happening?'

They both looked at Stevie. His eyes were still open, but now he was gazing directly at her. A beautiful smile spread across his face then and he reached out and took her hand.

'Hello, Mummy … I love you.'

Trembling, she reached over and hugged him close. And as she did, she could feel the warmth returning to his body. Then his arms slackened and his eyes closed, but his breathing was easier now and his skin seemed less pale and clammy too.

She glanced at the matron, who raised her eyebrows and smiled.

'Well, I'd say this little man just turned a corner. That's a miracle, if ever I saw one—I thought it might be touch and go with him tonight. Sit down, Mrs McPherson, then go and get some rest. He'll be fine now.'

The next morning, it was wonderful to talk to Richard on the phone for a few moments from the rectory.

'He's going to make it, Richard—he looks so much better,' she kept on saying. 'Even the matron said it was a miracle.'

'I know, Meg—I've phoned the hospital each morning, but I decided to call them last night instead, for some reason. Bill was here, so we all prayed. And even …'

'You mean, even the children? But …'

'Look, I don't have time to explain right now, Meg—I'll tell you more when I see you. The main thing is Stephen's on the mend. And we're managing fine, so don't worry about us.'

Two weeks later, Richard came to pick them both up—and it was not long before she discovered why they had managed so well at home without her.

'Is Alice by herself in the shop, Richard? I hope we'll be back before the children get home from school.'

'Don't worry, Meg—your mother's there.'

'Richard! You mean ... you mean she's been with you all this time?'

'Almost. Bill and I both felt we needed to contact her and she came the day after you left. She's managed well, Meg—she seems a bit more relaxed to me. And I think the children have liked having her there.'

She was silent for some time—she could not believe what she was hearing.

'Well, I'm glad it's all worked out, but I'm so amazed she was willing to come. That was good of her—I'll tell her that as soon as I see her.'

There was more she had to tell her mother too—she knew she had to try at least to share about her experience beside the river in Ipswich. But whatever her mother said in response, she was determined to stick by her decision to forgive her.

It was wonderful to be home again. The children raced out as soon as the car drove up and her mother was not far behind them.

'Thank you so much for coming, Mum,' she managed to get out, after she extricated herself from the children's hugs. 'I didn't know anything about it—you must be so tired.'

Her mother's smile was a little tentative, but her greeting was warm.

'I'm fine, Margaret—I'm glad I could come this time at least. But ... well, let's talk later, shall we? The children want to claim you now—and Stephen, of course. And they've made a special welcome home cake for after dinner too.'

It was not until the younger children were in bed that night and Richard was working in the office that she had a moment to be alone with her mother.

'Do you have enough energy to talk now, Mum? There are some things I'd like to tell you—but only if you're not too tired.'

'I have some things to tell you too, Margaret—and no, I'm fine.'

'Let's go out to the veranda. Alice and Robbie won't interrupt us there.'

It seemed surreal to be sitting across from her mother in her own special corner where she had talked so often with Annie and Emma. She prayed a quick prayer, asking God for strength to say what she knew she had to say. But before she could begin, her mother started speaking.

'Margaret, I hope it's all right if I go first. There are some things I've wanted to say to you for some time now, but just couldn't bring myself to. However, when I came here to help out, Reverend Fisher called in one day to see how I was managing and … well, we chatted a couple more times after that. He encouraged me to talk to you about what was on my mind, so here I am.'

Her hands were clammy, but she could also sense God's reassuring presence with her, as she waited for her mother to go on.

'Back when Caroline became engaged to Tom Davies, we began to have more to do with his parents, since we had to arrange the wedding together. May Davies was very kind and helpful and … well, she invited me to go with her to some women's meetings at the Methodist Church. After that, we had quite a few conversations about God and … well, to cut a long story short, I began to see how difficult I had made things for you after James died. Yes, it was a terrible time for us all—and I found it so hard to forgive you for the part I thought you had played in it. I felt I had to blame *someone*—and that was you. But I know you didn't leave that gate open. I know you would never have hurt James in a million years. It wasn't your fault—I know that now. And I'm … I'm sorry I blamed you, Margaret. Please forgive me.'

She could see how much her mother's admission had cost her—her face was pale and drawn and there were tears in her eyes. Without thinking, she reached out and grasped her hands.

'I forgive you, Mum—and I do understand,' she whispered. 'Thank you so much for everything you said just now. To tell you the truth, I had already forgiven you, but … well, it's so good to hear you say you don't blame me …'

She was almost overcome at that point, but knew she needed to go on.

'I've had quite a journey with everything too. Back when I had my miscarriage, I began to understand more of what it must feel like to lose a precious child. Reverend Fisher would often come and talk to me—he helped me recover and encouraged me to take up my art again. But he also talked a lot about God's love and grace and forgiveness—and God's continued to teach me so much more since that time. Then one day when Stevie was so sick in hospital and I was afraid he would die, I realised God was helping me understand through it all how terrible it must have been for you to lose Jimbo. I forgave you that day, Mum—and it was like a weight lifted off my shoulders. … God's been so gracious to us both, helping us learn to forgive, don't you think?'

Her mother had listened with her head bowed, but now looked her full in the face.

'Yes I do, Margaret. I still have a lot more to learn, of course, and no doubt that will take time, but I'm glad God's brought so much healing into your life, after all that's happened. … I must admit I wish your Reverend Fisher was our minister. Then I could talk with him more. But May Davies is a good friend now and I know she'll continue to help me.'

They hugged then, holding each other for some time. It was a fresh start for them both. But as they turned to go, her mother noticed a half-finished painting on her easel.

'Margaret, I want you to know too I'm proud of you—and of your wonderful, artistic ability. Keep painting, whatever you do.'

That night she lay awake for hours, trying to come to terms with all her mother had said. She would tell Richard one day soon, but she needed to think about it more herself first. It had been so healing to hear her mother admit Jimbo's death was not her fault and ask for her forgiveness. Yet it had also been wonderful to hear how proud she was of her. She had waited a long time, but the moment had come at last. And all she could do was praise God, who alone understood the depths of her heart and knew what she needed to hear.

Her mother stayed on for another week to help look after Stevie, for which she was thankful. He was still weak from his ordeal and not yet back to his old self, but he loved all the attention everyone gave him and ate as many of Alice's cakes and biscuits as he was allowed. And when Doctor Waters called in to check on him, he seemed happy enough with his progress.

'Well, my young man, soon we'll be able to take that cast off, if you keep improving like this. But no climbing up to that cubby again, do you hear?'

'Let's drive your mother back to Helidon, Meg,' Richard suggested that night. 'I don't have anything on Saturday afternoon and I can get old Tom to look after the shop in the morning. As for church, Bill Fisher will be fine with everything—and they can sing without music for once. We'd be even more squashed in the car than normal, but it'd be a nice change.'

She was glad the children were excited when they discovered they would all be sleeping on stretchers on their grandparents' veranda— even Alice and Robbie, who liked to pretend they were beyond such things.

'It'll be just like camping on Cribb Island,' Robbie said when she told them. 'We'll have lots of fun, won't we, Stevie?'

The trip was fun too in the end. They all sang as they drove along and even her mother joined in at times. That afternoon, while her father entertained Stevie and her mother rested, she joined Richard and the others down at the creek. As she watched them, memories of the many times she had played there with Will came flooding back. They had loved jumping off the high tree branches into the water, just as Alice and Robbie were doing right then. She sighed—it all seemed so long ago.

'Richard, I'd like to stay down here for a while by myself, if that's all right,' she decided to tell him, when it was time to go back. 'Mum will understand—we've talked quite a bit this week.'

He looked at her with one eyebrow raised but, to her relief, refrained from asking any questions.

'Let's go then, everyone—Mum will come in a little while.'

After they left, she wandered further along the creek to the spot where Jimbo had found her the day the flood swept them away. Yes, this spot still held great sadness for her, yet she remembered too the many pleasant hours she had spent painting there. God had known about her even then and had drawn her closer, little by little, through her art and through those who had ministered to her in different ways over the years. She thought of them all, one by one. Dear Isobel, so loving and faithful. Bill Fisher, who had taught her so much about God's grace and challenged her to forgive. Hettie, who had believed in her and prayed for her. And Emma, now with a child of her own to care for. She was grateful for each one—yet even more grateful to God for reaching out to her and showering such love and grace on her through them all.

She bowed her head then, sensing the Lord, her Shepherd and Protector, right there beside her once again, standing strong and tall. And as she gazed into the still waters below, she knew with great certainty that He would always be with her, restoring her soul, providing those green pastures she needed and leading her on further each day into all He had for her to do.

*Thank you, Lord,* she breathed. *Thank you, Lord—for everything. Amen.*

# Acknowledgements

This novel has been some years in the making, with many interruptions along the way. So, first and foremost, I am grateful to God for enabling me to keep picking up the threads and persevere in weaving them into a story I love.

Thank you so much to my manuscript readers, appraisers and editors at various times in the evolution of this novel—Ruth Allan, Marion Andrews, Lionel Berthelsen, Karen Brown, Rochelle Manners and Lorene Noble. I have appreciated all your honest advice, helpful suggestions and careful work on my behalf.

Thank you to the team at Impressum (impressum.com.au) for your professional approach throughout the design and layout of my novel.

Thank you once again to my faithful email prayer team who have tracked with me, not only in my speaking journey but also in the ups and downs of novel writing—Joan, Ruth A, Ruth S, Kerry, Marjan, Rhondda, Michelle and Judy. God bless you all.